WHEEL

IN THE

SKY

Asura Press books by Paul B. Spence

Darkness Rising
The Sorcerer
The High Priestess
The Tower (January 2025)
The Judgement (Forthcoming)
The Hanged Man (Forthcoming)

The Awakening Series
The Remnant
The Fallen
The Madness Engine
The Sleeping and the Dead
The Dark Plaza

The Endless Realms
Project Brimstone
Riders on the Storm
Doorways of Light (Forthcoming)

The Hand of Providence
I Won't Cry for Yesterday
The Instruments of Faith
Wheel in the Sky

WHEEL
IN THE
SKY

Paul B. Spence

Asura Press

WHEEL IN THE SKY

An Asura Press Book

PRINTING HISTORY
Paperback Edition / 2024

Cover Art by: Paul B. Spence

ISBN: 978-1-929928-53-8

www.paulbspence.com
author@paulbspence.com

To the sound of her wings.

CHAPTER ONE

I've always been fascinated by absurdity.

Being able to laugh at the absurd is vitally important if you wish to keep your sanity. The French philosopher Camus defined absurdity as a search for meaning in a universe *without* meaning. I suppose in some ways, my own life mirrors this. I am a woman who has seen the elephant, as they say. I have witnessed many of the horrors that people visit upon one another, and I have devoted most of my life to helping victims of violent crime. It isn't an easy thing, to find justice for those people. What could possibly be more absurd than seeking that most elusive of things, justice?

Yes, I *am* taking a stab at the American Justice System here.

I'm not sorry about it, either.

I don't say this because I don't believe in justice. Quite the contrary. I most certainly do believe in it. I just don't have much faith that our American judiciary system can deliver *actual* justice. All you have to do to understand that is read about all the mistakes made. I mean, how many innocent people have to spend life in prison for everyone to realize the system is broken? How many have to die on death row?

Now, someone could take that to mean I'm in favor of anarchy or vigilante justice. I have been known to partake of both at times in my life. My history of violence is mostly shrouded from me; I can't really remember everything I've done.

What I do know is that when I was at university, I killed a serial killer who was about to murder my friend. If I'd waited for the police, she'd be dead, and the asshole might have gotten away to kill more people. He might even have killed me.

After surviving that eye-opening experience, I took criminal justice classes at university. I learned about the laws, but more importantly, I learned about the failures in the system. Broken Windows is just the tip of the iceberg. Our prison system is essentially a private industry *designed* to create repeat offenders. More people incarcerated means more money for the people who run the understaffed and overcrowded prisons. It makes a perfect sense, if all you care about is money. Personally, I hate living in a world where that's most important to many people.

You see, money is the other real problem with our justice system.

It's really difficult to put someone behind bars if they have any real money. It's also really hard to convict someone of murder without a confession. People who care only about money aren't likely to confess. Not only that, but any halfway decent lawyer can easily plant the seeds of doubt in the minds of a jury. Reasonable or not, juries don't like to convict people.

I get it. I mean, I've served on juries. It's hard to know if you're making the right decision, when you weren't there to see the crime happen. Even with witnesses and overwhelming evidence, a killer may still walk free, if they just play it cool.

Witnesses can be a funny thing, too.

Lawyers will try to vilify witnesses, make them seem to not be credible. Jurors listen to witnesses. It's the closest thing they have to a real person being at the scene of the crime. The problem, of course, is that memory is fickle. A witness can easily be tripped up. I don't think they mean to lie on the stand; I think most people who agree to testify want to tell the truth. They just might not know what the truth actually is.

There's another kind of witness: the *expert witness*. This is someone who testifies, usually for the prosecution, and is an expert in a particular field. Doctors, forensic scientists, and college professors get called to testify, if a lawyer thinks their testimony might sway the case. An expert witness doesn't have a stake in the problem, the way a regular witness does.

Trust me, I know what I'm talking about. I've been there. The last thing I'd ever wanted to do was be an expert witness, but prosecutors like me. *I* don't like to sit on the stand and get picked apart by a defense lawyer because, make no mistake, those lawyers are sharks and will go for the kill if they sense any weakness in a statement.

Being a forensic specialist, I get called to testify a lot. Not just in my own cases, either. Prosecutors know that having someone who's an expert on a subject testify on the stand is a good way to sway a jury. People like to listen to experts. It helps that I'm above-average in looks, too. It shouldn't, but it does. I look good, and I speak well, and that has a perceptible influence.

After everything that happened in Eastern Kentucky over the holidays, I just wanted to get away from reality for a while. I wanted a damn vacation. However, because of the high-profile nature of the river murders, and the corresponding media coverage, the government had expedited the trial. So I was stuck in town until it was over.

Mr. Forester, one of the depraved perverts behind the river murders, was on trial, and I was a key witness. After all, I had been the one to find the kidnapped boy in the man's house. I had spent months investigating, and then discovered the murderers only because the sickos had gotten a disturbing thrill out of inviting me into their home.

It wouldn't surprise me if I were to learn they'd had plans for me, as well. I did fit one of the profiles of their victims: I'm a single woman with dark hair. They'd also liked young boys, which I most definitely do not look like. At the very least, I think they intended to frame me for the murders.

That was actually one of the things that made the River Murders case so difficult. Usually, a serial killer has a very specific type of victim. That made it difficult, because there wasn't a pattern at first. Mr. Forester was smart and hadn't left me much to work with.

Who knows what makes murderers do what they do?

A murderer might like young women who look a certain way; maybe the women remind them of a jilted lover. Or they might like young boys who remind them of a bully in school. There are volumes of case studies on serial killers.

I didn't study criminal psychology. I don't know, and don't *want* to know, how these sick bastards think. I just need to understand enough about them to help catch them. I did read the profiles the FBI psychologists put together. They had hit the nail on the head with Mr. Forester; he fit the profile almost perfectly.

I say *almost* because they had him pegged as an incel loner.

An incel might go after women who looked like a woman who'd rejected him. Maybe Mr. Forester had been an incel at one time, but he'd been married, and he and his wife worked together to murder at least three different kinds of victims. For all I knew, the Foresters had just taken people they thought would be fun to rape and torture.

The wide variety of victims made it difficult even to assign all the murders to the same serial killer. If it wasn't for the smoking gun, so to speak, of finding a kidnapped child in the Foresters' house... Well, we probably wouldn't have caught them for years.

As much as I hated being an expert witness at a trial, I was glad to be here today. This trial was only for Mr. Forester, who I think was the mastermind of the whole thing. Ms. Forester hadn't stuck me as being strong-willed enough to be behind the murders. Not that it mattered now, since Ms. Forester had killed herself in prison.

At least, that was the official story.

Given what usually happens to child molesters and child murderers in prison, she'd probably been killed by the other inmates. I didn't really care either way, or maybe I should say that it didn't bother me. Call me a monster if you wish, but I'm not shedding any tears over that bitch being dead. I'll save my tears for the kids she hurt and killed.

I was glad she was dead.

She was probably glad that she was dead, too, if she'd begun to think about what she'd done. I just wish the other prisoners had also gotten the husband. So, yeah, I wished that someone would kill him, too. Vigilante justice doesn't bother me, if it's actual justice.

CHAPTER TWO

I really hadn't wanted to spend a good part of spring in a courtroom. The Forester trial had been dragged out for weeks by the defense questioning every little detail of evidence. I was somewhat surprised that Mr. Forester hadn't taken a plea deal. It would have been easy to plead guilty but say his wife was responsible for it all.

Maybe he just hadn't thought of it.

Forester was as egotistical as they come. Maybe he still thought he could get away with what he'd done. It's hard to say. I'd never been able to get a read on the prick. He was way too good at hiding his emotions, if he actually had any.

I had testified early in the trial and technically didn't have to be here any longer. I had something of a vested interest in the case, however. I really wanted to see that scumbag sentenced to life in prison. For someone like Forester, that would be worse than just sentencing him to death. Normally I'm not vindictive, but Forester wasn't insane: he was a monster, and he needed to be punished for his crimes.

The final day of the trial finally arrived.

I tried not to be nervous as I sat down in the courtroom. I can't help it, though; the combination of psychic abilities I have means that I pick up on strong emotions from objects. *Everything* in a courtroom is smothered in layers of emotions, and most of those emotions are negative. I mean, have you ever thought about how many molesters, murderers, and just general scumbags are tried every single day?

My boyfriend, Michael Delling, was here in the courtroom with me. He didn't have anything to do with the case, but his presence helped keep me sane. Well, as sane as I ever am.

Boyfriend doesn't seem like the right word; it sounds so juvenile. We're lovers, Michael and I. We also have sex and like it. Deal with it.

As the person who'd discovered the kidnapped boy at the Foresters' residence, I'd already given my testimony. I'd described what I had seen and stated what I considered to be damning facts. The jury had seen the photographs and the other evidence. All that was left was for the defense lawyer to attempt to drag me through the mud and discredit me. I'd been expecting it from the start and was a little surprised the man had waited. He hadn't cross-examined me at the start of the trial, which was odd. I sat here through the trial every day anyway, because I wanted to see justice served.

Ironic, right?

We stood for the judge and then settled down into the daily grind. I was seated just behind the prosecutor, Mr. Gorman. I'd spoken to him frequently during the trial but couldn't get a good read on him. The deputy district attorney was friendlier. I think she was happy to get any help at all in putting away scumbags like Forester.

"The prosecution rests, Your Honor."

The judge nodded. "Do you have anything to add for the defense, Mr. Whittaker?"

The defense lawyer stood up. "Just one more thing, Your Honor. The defense would like to call Ms. Fredericks to the stand as a witness."

Michael gripped my arm.

I smiled at him and stood up. "It's *Dr.* Fredericks," I said, "if you please."

"Of course," the defense lawyer said smoothly. "We'll get to that in a moment."

He was a slimy-looking man in a shiny polyester suit, with slicked-back hair as oily as his voice. He also looked like a caricature of a bad lawyer. The Foresters had been reasonably wealthy, but most lawyers find it distasteful to defend child molesters. Still, I'd have thought Mr. Forester could afford a better lawyer than Whittaker.

"Objection, Your Honor. Dr. Fredericks was already called as a witness weeks ago, " said the deputy D.A. "The defense had the opportunity to cross-examine her then and didn't."

The judge looked irritated. "Mr. Whittaker, can you explain yourself? I am inclined to side with the district attorney on this matter."

"We would like to call Ms. Fredericks to the stand as a witness for the defense, Your Honor. I have no objection to the prosecution cross-examining after we've heard her testimony."

The deputy D.A. leaned back to speak with me. "You don't have to do this."

"I don't mind doing it, if going up will help," I said. I did, but I also wanted to see Forester put away in prison. I couldn't imagine that putting me on the stand again was going to help Forester in any way.

"Your Honor, we'll withdraw our objections, given the opportunity to cross-examine Dr. Fredericks after the defense has finished."

"Very well. It's unusual, but I'll allow it, given the nature of the charges. Do you consider Dr. Fredericks to be a hostile witness?"

"We do not, Your Honor."

I was relieved to hear that. A hostile witness was one whose testimony was averse to the position of the legal team that called on them to testify. I was originally called as a witness for the prosecution. If I was found to be a hostile witness, there was the possibility of my entire testimony being stricken from the record. I could see the defense wanting that.

"Dr. Fredericks, if you please?" the judge said.

I sat in the witness chair and was sworn in by the bailiff.

"Could you please state your full name for the court?" asked Whittaker.

"My name is Rhiannon Michelle Fredericks."

"And you call yourself a doctor?"

I smiled. This wasn't my first time on the stand. "I have a Ph.D. in forensic anthropology; *doctor* is the usual honorific for such. I've never claimed to be a *medical* doctor, if that's what you're implying."

"But isn't it true that you hire yourself out as a psychic detective?"

The lawyer put a lot of scorn into that question, as well as turning toward the jury for a shared chuckle. The jury, after weeks of seeing horrific pictures and testimony, didn't seem inclined to laugh along. He'd have done better to attack my credentials at the beginning of the trial, before they'd seen all of that.

"To the best of my knowledge, I have never worked for anyone using that rather peculiar job description," I replied. "I am a consultant."

"But you do work for the CRI, right? How would you describe that work?"

"I am a consultant with the Criminological Research Institute," I agreed. "As to the nature of my work, I am a specialist in occult crime. I think my record speaks for itself. I believe I have an impressive close record for my work on cases."

"Close record?"

"Yes: the rate at which cases I consult on are brought to a successful conclusion. That means a criminal trial, much like this one."

"Can you be more specific about exactly how you do work?" the lawyer said with a sneer. "Isn't most of that work actually as a psychic detective?"

"No. As I said, my work is as a specialist in occult crime."

"Isn't that the same thing?" he insisted. "You say *occult*, and I say *psychic*?"

"Not at all. I study crimes by people who believe in the occult, supernatural, or mystical phenomena. Unfortunately, there are cults, and individuals or groups, who use mystical trappings to commit very real murders."

"And what are your beliefs, *doctor*? Do you believe in such things?"

"Objection, Your Honor," the prosecutor said. "Relevancy?"

"I am trying to establish that this so-called *doctor* is delusional," Whittaker said, "if not actually a criminal herself.

CHAPTER THREE

I bristled at both the implication that I wasn't a doctor and that I had somehow falsified or planted evidence. I'm a professional, and I'm going to be paying off my student loans for most of my life. I didn't need some scumbag, third-rate lawyer telling me I hadn't earned my degree.

As for my beliefs, it wasn't any of their damn business. I may believe in some weird shit, but I have good reason to. How many of *them* have been stalked by a demon? I knew I couldn't truthfully answer that question, though; the jury wouldn't consider me credible.

"*Objection*, Your Honor," said the prosecutor.

The judge sighed. "Your objections are sustained, Mr. Gorman. Dr. Fredericks' credentials have been established to the satisfaction of this court. Her beliefs are not relevant. Mr. Whittaker, do try to remember that the witness is not on trial."

"Understood. My apologies. So, *doctor*, you claim to actually catch killers?"

"I believe that's why I'm on the stand today."

Someone in the jury laughed.

I couldn't help but smile at the stupidity of this lawyer. How did he think I was going to answer that question? I imagine he simply hadn't thought about it, which just showed how incompetent he was.

The lawyer sat down and conferred with his client for a moment. Mr. Forester smiled and kept eye contact with me. The bastard creeped me out, which I'm sure was his intention. I smiled back, and he looked away.

There hadn't been a lot of physical evidence tying Mr. Forester to the murders. I'd expected the lawyer to try to pin the blame on the conveniently dead Ms. Forester. That the child had been found abused in the house, there was no doubt. Whether one – and which one – or both of the Foresters had hurt the child was in question. I didn't doubt it was Mr. Forester. That made it all the more surprising that the lawyer had tried this angle. The child in question hadn't testified in the trial; he was barely able to speak.

That deep core of rage in me wanted to come out. I found Michael's eyes, where he was seated behind the prosecutors. He gave me a thumbs up, which helped calm me. A lot. I needed to keep my cool, but I really wanted to leap across the courtroom and kill that smug bastard, Forester. I found myself wishing I'd shot him at the scene of the crime. I'd been in shock, though, and the boy had needed immediate help.

"Dr. Fredericks, you gave testimony earlier in this trial that you had found a child inside the home of the Foresters. Could you explain what you were doing in the house of Mr. Forester?"

"Certainly. The Foresters had contracted with CRI to have *me,* specifically, investigate their house. It seemed an odd request at the time. She also mentioned poltergeists and unknown occult activity in the house."

"And you still claim not to be a psychic detective?" The defense lawyer gave the jury a knowing look.

"I believe at the time I suggested that Ms. Forester seek psychiatric help," I replied. "Evidently, she needed it, since she killed herself."

Forester lost his smile.

"Objection!" the defense lawyer shouted.

"You did ask a leading question, Mr. Whittaker," the judge replied. "However, Dr. Fredericks, please stay within the bounds of the questioning. Mr. Forrester is on trial, not his late wife."

"Yes, of course, Your Honor."

"So you were in the house to find a ghost?" the lawyer asked.

"No, I was contracted to determine the nature of the odd symbols Ms. Forrester claimed were appearing in her house. When I arrived, the Foresters suggested I enter the house and gave me a key. There were no signs on the outside of the house that anything was amiss. The interior was a mess, with books and furniture in disarray. Nevertheless, I entered and investigated, looking for the symbols the Foresters said were present. I didn't see many signs of the occult, but I did see that something was very wrong in that house."

"Something wrong?" the lawyer sneered. "That was your *professional* opinion, as a *doctor*?"

"Yes," I replied. "I could see by the size of the house that there was a hidden room. It isn't uncommon in cases involving murderers."

"I have no further questions at this time, Your Honor," the defense lawyer said suddenly.

I smiled at Forester. I think he'd expected me to crack under questioning. He certainly hadn't expected his lawyer to fumble the ball so badly.

The prosecutor, Gorman, stood up. "With your permission, Your Honor, I'll ask a few questions to clarify the testimony."

"Objection! The prosecution has already rested."

The judge sighed. "Mr. Whittaker, the cross-examination of the witness was a condition of allowing you to have Dr. Fredericks take the stand. Your objection is declined. Mr. Gorman, you may ask your questions."

"Thank you, Your Honor." The prosecutor stood and smiled at Whittaker. "Dr. Fredericks, your credentials have been called into question. Can you give the jury a summary of your degrees and work experience?"

"Yes. I have a Ph.D. in forensic anthropology, which is the study of human behaviors defined as criminal. My specialty is occult crime. I study patterns in crimes that appear to have an unexplained or non-ordinary component. I'm sorry to say that often murderers and serial killers follow certain patterns of behavior. Pseudo-religious trappings are not uncommon. So I have worked on many cases," I said. "I cannot tell you exactly how many, as some of those cases are classified or sealed, but I can tell you that in addition to working for several local police departments, I have also worked for the FBI and Homeland Security. Not to mention working with the Federal Marshal Service to track a fugitive last fall."

Michael smiled.

"Objection! Relevance?" Whittaker sounded tired and defeated.

"I think it is eminently relevant, Your Honor," said Gorman. "Her work history shows that Dr. Fredericks has had her credentials verified by our highest institutions of justice."

"You may continue your line of inquiry," the judge said.

"Dr. Fredericks, you mentioned in your testimony that you felt something was wrong with the house. Something about a hidden room. Can you please clarify that?"

"The house was too small on the inside. In my experience with investigating cults, I have often found that practitioners have secret rooms within their homes. As I testified before, I found a room hidden behind a bookcase where a teenage boy was being held in a cage. He… had been abused terribly."

"No more questions, You Honor."

The defense, unsurprisingly, didn't want to ask me anything else.

I sighed, stood up, and felt a little dizzy.

Something was wrong in the courtroom.

Something had changed.

I met Michael's eyes. He nodded; he'd noticed whatever it was, too. He looked around but couldn't find the source of the bad feeling. In hindsight, I should have seen what was coming, but I didn't. I was just relieved to be off the witness stand.

Mr. Forester stood as I passed through the gate to the seats. He moved quickly, but everything felt as if it was in slow motion. He shattered his drinking glass against the table and came after me.

Blood was dripping from his hand. Out of the corner of my eye, I could see the bailiff drawing his pistol, but it all seemed painfully slow. Unless I did something, the court officer wouldn't be able to shoot Forester before the man slit my throat.

Michael was moving, but he wouldn't get here in time.

The prosecutor was shouting something as he stood up, pointing.

I wasn't paying attention; I had eyes only for that jagged shard of bloody glass. My hands closed on the prosecutor's chair, and without thinking, I brought the chair around into Forester's head. I didn't hold back, and the results were rather spectacular, and suddenly time caught up with me.

Forester's head caved in with a spray of blood just an instant before the bailiff shot him. Both rounds hit Forester in the chest, but he was already dead. The impact of the chair sent the man flying into the people seated behind the lawyers.

Someone screamed, and people were stumbling back from the body and the spray of blood.

My ears were ringing from the gunshots, and to be honest, I was a bit in shock from what just happened. I didn't hear the bailiff shouting at me. When the officer grabbed me, I would have hit him with the broken chair if Michael hadn't grabbed my other arm to stop me.

"Put down the chair, Dr. Fredericks," the officer said. "You're okay."

"It's okay, Michelle. It's over," said Michael.

I dropped the broken back of the chair.

The courtroom was in shambles. People were running for the exit. Police were trying to force their way past them to enter the courtroom. The jury was quickly ushered out the side door.

Forester was *very* dead.

I had to admit, justice didn't feel so bad, after all.

It certainly felt good compared to the alternative.

CHAPTER FOUR

I had to go before a judge and explain my actions, but Forester's death was clearly self-defense. The judge seemed to be under the impression that it was the bailiff's bullets that had killed Forester. I wasn't going to disabuse her of the notion.

It helped that the district attorney was loath to press charges. Even if the DA had tried to charge me, I can't imagine any jury in the land convicting me of anything. To most people, I would have just looked like a normal woman being attacked by a maniac. A jury would think I'd been very lucky to fight the man off with the chair long enough for the bailiff to shoot him.

Yeah, normal little me.

Hopefully no one would look too closely at the coroner's report. I'd squashed that bastard like a bug. He was definitely dead before he was shot. I don't feel bad about it in the least, either.

I did hear that the leaked video from the courtroom became popular on YouTube. I never looked it up. I don't ever want to look at Forester again, even just to watch him die.

A few reporters wanted to talk to me as I left the courtroom. I brushed past them with Michael's help. The River Murders had been fairly high-profile, and the end of the trial got some national attention. That wasn't the kind of attention I wanted. I didn't want anyone asking awkward questions about how strong I was or where I'd learned to fight.

I wanted to get away from the trial and the murders and all the feelings that went with them.

Fortunately, it wasn't worth it to the reporters to follow me home. The story wasn't that big a deal.

"Are you doing okay, Michelle?" Michael asked as we pulled into the garage.

"Define *okay*," I said.

Michael sighed. "Is it the trial? Or how it ended? You aren't still bothered because you had to kill that scumbag, are you?"

"I never was bothered about killing him. I think maybe that's part of the problem."

"You're worried that because you don't regret defending yourself, and incidentally killing a sick, perverted, serial killer, that you're somehow like Julia?"

My turn to sigh.

Michael shut off the engine, and we got out of his truck.

Jean's car was gone; she was probably at school. Lawrence's sister had enrolled at Northern Kentucky University for the spring semester and was really enjoying it. Jean was still staying with me until she could get her own place. I didn't mind, and it was handy having her available to watch the house when I had to travel for work.

"Looks like we have the house to ourselves," I said.

Michael cocked an eyebrow at me and smiled.

We showered together and made love slowly and vigorously. I think I may have scared my cat, Samson. Ever since Jean moved in, I'd had to be quiet when Michael and I made love. I didn't want to hold it in any longer. Michael seemed to feel much the same way, as he was quite energetic.

Afterward, we lay in bed together. I enjoyed just relaxing in his arms. I hadn't had a lot of opportunities to relax in the last few months. Ever since Julia showed up, and I got onto Homeland Security's radar, my life had been complicated.

"You're tensing back up," Michael said. "Do I have to make you relax again?"

"What kind of incentive is that to not be tense?"

"Still thinking about the trial?"

"No, not so much. Not just that, anyway. I was thinking that we hadn't had much time to relax since we met last year."

"Since we were *reunited* last year," he said.

"You know what I mean."

Michael and I had met as children, in the project that made us what we are. Before last year, I had last seen him as a teenager. It had been quite a shock when we met and realized who we had been to each other. Back in the eighties, the government had tried real hard to make us forget all about that.

"What's really bothering you, Michelle?"

"I want to take a vacation," I said. "Maybe a month or two."

"You've certainly earned it. We have more than enough money."

"You'll go with me?"

"It would be kind of weird if I didn't. Where are you thinking? Mexico? The beach or something?"

I snorted back a laugh. "Yeah, can you see me around tourists?"

"So what did you have in mind?"

"I've been wanting to go out West."

I felt Michael tense.

"You've mentioned wanting to see the Grand Canyon," he suggested.

"Michael," I said, "we should go see her."

Michael knew I wanted him to try to reconcile with his sister. He talked about her to me last Christmas, and I wanted to meet her. I felt as if we owed her an explanation, if not an actual apology.

You see, Marie Delling had been a part of the same project as the rest of us. The memory blocks hadn't worked on her, though, and she'd gone insane from what had been done to us. It hadn't helped that the blocks *had* worked on her twin brother, Michael.

He'd come home after those long summers at the project and acted as if nothing had happened. Naturally enough, Marie didn't take that very well. They hadn't spoken since Michael went into the military, years ago.

I felt it was time to do something about that.

"I'd really rather not," Michael said.

"I think you're lying to yourself."

Michael got out of bed and started dressing.

"Is this a genuine desire to meet my sister, or do you just want more information about that damned project?"

"I think that's a little unfair." He wasn't wrong, though. "Marie deserves to know what we know, and I really would like to meet her. You don't have any other living family."

"You seem confident that she'll even want to see me."

"I would, were I her."

"I didn't believe her, Michelle. How could I?" Michael sat on the edge of the bed. "I remember her, there at the end, when I left home. She wasn't sane."

"That was a long time ago," I replied. "You told me she's an artist in New Mexico. You've obviously kept tabs on her. I think you've wanted to go see her for a long time, but you couldn't bring yourself to do it alone. Now you don't have to."

Michael nodded. He didn't look happy.

"Samson will be in good hands with Jean."

"Your boss isn't going to like it."

"I'm a contractor," I said. "If Tony doesn't like it, he can kiss my ass."

"I feel as if I should object," Michael replied. "On principle, if nothing else."

"To vacation?"

"No, to Tony kissing your ass. The man is a little sleazy."

"Yuck. More than a little. So are you okay with going out West to see your sister?"

"Do I have a choice?"

"Not really."

INTERLUDE

Forester lunges from his chair, and I kill him. Again.

I'm stuck in a loop, dreaming about that damn trial over and over.

Forester's head crumples under my savage blow; his blood slaps across my face.

I feel many different emotions as the memory plays out in my mind. None of them are remorse.

I wanted to kill the bastard that day. He gave me the perfect excuse.

The bailiff's bullets strike Forester in the chest as he stumbles back from my blow. He is already dead; chemistry just hasn't caught up with the fact. My perception of time slows. Pieces of the chair are still in the air. Forester's eyes bore into me. He hates me. Me, specifically. It isn't just because I caught him and his wife, either. What he feels for me could fill a dozen people with rage. He wants me dead, and not an easy death.

His lips are moving as he falls.

What the hell is he trying to say?

I try to focus on hearing the words, but the screams in the courtroom and the ringing of the bailiff's gunshots are too loud. I can't make it out, and I have a chill of premonition. It's important to me somehow.

I feel him die.

Someone is watching me.

I blink, in the dream. I am stepping down from the witness stand again. I see Forester move, but it doesn't register that he's going to attack me. His emotions are all locked down.

I hear the glass shatter again.

Blood drips from Forester's hand. He doesn't care about the pain. He just wants to kill me.

He knows he is going to die, I realize suddenly.

He wants to die.

Why?

It isn't remorse.

Monsters like Forester don't feel guilt for what they've done. Forester may be unhappy about having been caught, but he doesn't care about what he's done. He enjoyed hurting and killing those people.

Those women and children.

The prosecutor is pointing and warning me to watch out.

Yeah, thanks for the help.

Forester doesn't scare me.

Oh, I'm as afraid of getting hurt as any other person. Well, not really afraid. I don't want to get cut. It would hurt, and I'd have to get stitches. No, I'm not afraid because I know, more surely than Forester does, that I'm going to kill the bastard in the next few seconds.

The edges of the top of the wooden chair dig into my palms and fingers as I lift it.

Forester sees the chair. He knows what's going to happen. He can't stop what's coming, though. There just isn't time. He begins to say something. I'm moving far faster than a normal human, and Forester knows that, too.

He expects it.

What the actual fuck?

Forester's head caves in, and the blood sprays. Shattered wood from the chair flies away. The bailiff's bullets strike his chest with wet, hollow thuds. More blood. Forester is still trying to say something as he falls, and the blood gushes out of his mouth.

Something about his eyes makes me look away.

I don't want to know what his last thoughts are.

People are beginning to run from the courtroom.

Michael is gripping my arm.

The bailiff is coming up on my other side.

I am still gripping the ruined chair.

Not everyone is running.

Five people, scattered around the courtroom, are watching me intensely.

I caught only a glimpse of them, and there are limits to human perception and memory. I hadn't been looking at those people; I couldn't tell you anything specific about them, except that they were a mix of races, genders, and ages. All I could say for certain is that they had expected what happened and were watching me.

Forester and his wife hadn't been murdering alone.

CHAPTER FIVE

It took me until after breakfast to tell Michael about my dream. I don't think he believed the dream had anything to do with reality, and that hurt. He was supposed to believe me. I'd have believed him. Not that he ever told me about any of his dreams.

"I just don't see it," Michael said.

"Why?" I snapped. "Because murder cults are so rare?"

"No, because there's nothing else that even suggests there were other people involved in the murders."

"There wasn't much to tie the Foresters to the murders, either."

"You did find a traumatized young boy locked in their home."

"Yeah, I do remember. I'm not that far gone."

"Michelle, you're feeling guilt over having killed Forester, that's all."

"Actually, I'm not. The bastard deserved to die."

"Yes, but not by your hand."

"You think I shouldn't have killed him?" I asked. "He didn't give me much choice."

"I didn't say that. I just wish you hadn't had to."

"Me, too."

We were packing for the trip out West.

My cat, Samson, was watching me reproachfully from the dresser. He knew I was leaving again. The last time, he had to stay with Mark and Jen, which had been a nightmare for all involved. Mark didn't like cats; Jen was neat freak. Samson had picked up on that and barfed, shit, and pissed on anything that looked valuable.

So, typical cat behavior.

At least this time Samson could stay home. Jean was going to look after the little bastard while I was away. The two of them got along almost better than Samson and I did ourselves. I'd called him a traitor more than once in the last few months. He'd chosen to sit in her lap rather than mine.

Cats are fickle.

Jean had already left for school, but I wasn't really in the mood to take advantage of having Michael alone in the house. It wasn't Michael's fault. He hadn't seen what I had at the trial, nor had he just dreamed it over and over, all night long.

I sighed and rubbed my eyes.

I hadn't slept well the night before. I must have looped Forester's death a hundred times in my nightmares. No matter how many times the dream repeated, I couldn't figure out what he'd been saying. *If* Forester had actually been saying anything at all.

That was the trouble with dreams. I could never be certain whether or not what I dreamed was real. Had Forester actually been trying to tell me something? Or was my brain trying to flesh out information that I'd gotten through some other means?

Psychometry isn't exactly a science.

I often dream about the past. My dreams are usually about that damned government project that Michael and I survived as children. To dream of something else was a relief, to tell the truth. Of course, there could be a connection between the Foresters and the project that I'm not aware of. My dreams do that sometimes, too. They show me connections I didn't know existed.

Forester's blood had splashed onto me, bringing his twisted thoughts and some of who he had been along with it. Blood can be very powerful; I often get flashes of a murder from spilled blood at a crime scene. The overwhelming emotion I got from Forester was hatred. The man had hated me.

Why did Forester hate me so badly?

"Probably just because you're a strong woman," said Michael.

"I'm sorry, was I talking out loud?"

Michael smiled. "You often do, when you're working out a problem."

"So you think Forester hated me just because he was a chauvinistic pig?"

"That, and the fact that you caught him. You thwarted his plans, Michelle. His wife committed suicide."

I made a noise at that.

"Okay, she died in prison, and you had some hand in that. At least by putting her there," Michael said. "I'm sure that had something to do with his feelings. You took something that belonged to him, and you caused him pain."

I shivered.

I could remember those people watching me.

That wasn't just a dream.

"You didn't see anything out of the ordinary?" I asked.

"I was a little focused on trying to get to you and Forester."

"I think that was the point."

Michael frowned. "There was something odd going on just before Forester attacked you. I remember looking around, trying to figure out where the threat was coming from. I should have been more focused on Forester."

I nodded. "Something changed in the courtroom. We both felt it. It wasn't Forester, either."

"You think someone drove him to attack you?" Michael asked. "If he knew anything about you at all, he'd know it was suicide."

"I think that was the point."

"Well, you did give him an easier death than he faced in the prison system."

"I don't mean that," I said. "Forester died so someone could see what I was capable of."

"That is a bit of a stretch, don't you think?"

"Do you think so?" I asked. "Think about it: The River Murders were a part of what set off my memories of the project. Two murderers is just a couple of crazies. What if this really was a cult?"

"There isn't much evidence of that, is there?"

"It took so long to catch the Foresters because they did everything right to remove psychic emanations from the bodies. They dumped the bodies in the river for a reason."

"Which happens to be a really good way to destroy regular evidence, as well," Michael said. "Don't you think that maybe you're giving the Foresters more credit than they deserve?"

"Why did they hire me?" I asked. "Why invite me into their house?"

"Because the Foresters were crazy? Serial killers often taunt the police."

"I'm not police."

"You were the force behind the investigation."

"Yes, but how did they know that?"

Michael frowned. "I did wonder that but forgot it with all that happened."

"Exactly. Someone knew enough to tip the Foresters off about me. Then they invited me to their damn house. Why? To taunt me? Or to see if I could still detect something even though they cleaned the house. Hell, it was because the house was *so* clean that I got suspicious. There was nothing there. No psychic traces at all."

"You think this alleged cult sacrificed the Foresters so they could learn more about your abilities?"

"I think the Foresters may have been used from the beginning. Maybe they were just pawns in this cult's game. What do you think?"

"I think you need a vacation," said Michael.

I growled in frustration.

Michael held up his hands. "I'll mention this idea to some people I know. Have you mentioned your theory to the FBI?"

"I haven't said anything to anyone but you."

"You could tell Taylor, let her mention it to people."

I nodded. "Okay, yeah. That could work. I don't want to just drop this. I think there may still be murderers out there."

"I get that," Michael said, "but it isn't really your problem. Mention it to Taylor, then let the FBI do their job."

"You're right," I said. "Don't let it go to your head, though."

"I wouldn't dream of it."

Cute.

CHAPTER SIX

We made it to New Mexico in three days.

If I had been alone, I probably would have driven straight though in one day. It was only twenty hours, but Michael insisted on stopping and getting a room each night, not to mention stopping for regular meals and an occasional rest area or park.

It was a delaying tactic because he didn't want to face his sister.

I didn't mind spending the time with him; it was sort of the other reason for the trip. I wanted some time with him, alone. We didn't talk about ourselves as much as I thought we would.

We stayed at a hotel on the state line in Garcia, Colorado and left the hotel as the sun was rising on the morning of the third day. The snowcapped mountains glinted as we drove down the highway. I was glad we'd stopped the night before. I wouldn't have been able to see the mountains if we'd come into Taos at night. It was late spring, and the hills and slopes were covered in green forest.

"The mountains are pretty," I said.

"They're the Sangre de Cristo Mountains," said Michael.

"That's kind of morbid."

"Do you think so? The Spanish missionaries named them. The mountains have a lot of very red stone, and all the mountains out here are named after something red. Just to the south are the Sandia and

Manzano Mountains."

"A *manzano* is an apple?" I asked. My Spanish was a little rusty.

"Yes, and a *sandia* is a watermelon."

"Sure they didn't have something else on their minds. Like with the Tetons?"

"Hmm."

Damn, I couldn't even get him to laugh at breast jokes.

Michael had been distracted and quiet for most of the trip. I knew he really didn't want to be doing this. Hell, he could have tracked down his sister at any time. He'd known right where she was, after all. That he was willing to, when I asked him, meant a lot to me.

Marie was a fairly successful artist. She'd been living in Taos for twenty years, ever since she was released from the asylum. We hadn't called, since we both figured she'd be less likely to refuse to talk to Michael if he was there in person.

At least, I hoped Marie wouldn't refuse to talk to him.

The town of Taos was much smaller than I imagined. Barely six thousand people lived here, not including tourists. The town had been popular with artists for the last hundred years, but it had been occupied for long before that. Taos was a Pueblo settlement. Coronado had stopped here on his conquest of the West in 1500s.

I pulled in at the hotel.

"You're joking right? This place?" asked Michael.

"What's wrong with it?"

"It's a little kitsch, isn't it?"

"I think it's charming," I said. "Feels very *Southwest.*"

Michael sighed.

He stayed in the Jeep while I checked us in. I was a little worried about him. He wasn't normally broody by nature. I knew he was dreading a meeting with his sister. I don't know that I would have felt much different, if the situation had been reversed.

I tapped on the glass of the passenger window.

"Our room is around the other side. Do you want to go and rest up, or—?"

"I'd prefer to get this over with," Michael said.

"Do you know where Marie's gallery is?"

"It's on the corner of Kit Carson and Jaramillo. You know that as well as I do, Michelle."

I walked around and got behind the wheel. "You're acting as if we're going to your execution."

"You don't know my sister."

"Neither do you."

"Can we please just get it over with?"

We didn't say anything else as we drove the couple of miles to the gallery. We passed many interesting shops, and I hoped we'd be staying in Taos long enough to take a look around. I wanted to see those mountains, maybe get out and hike a bit. I knew if it went poorly with Marie, though, we'd be heading back home.

The gallery was a tasteful little shop with a few cars outside. I could see some couples inside looking at the paintings. I didn't see anyone else.

"You ready?" I asked.

"Would it matter if I said no?"

"No. Come on."

I got out of the Jeep and held the door of the gallery for him.

Michael reluctantly entered, and I followed him.

I recognized the style of a couple of the pieces in the front. I couldn't be certain, but one looked like a Thomas Cole. Two of the artworks were authentic Burt Harwoods, or looked really damn close to me. The other work in the gallery was unfamiliar, the subject matter disturbing. The paintings looked a little like Georgia O'Keeffe's work, if O'Keeffe had painted demons instead of flower vaginas.

At the back of the gallery, a tall woman with white hair was straightening pamphlets on a table. She stiffened and then turned suddenly. She had intense green eyes, much like Michael's. Her white hair was a shock, framing her youthful-looking face.

She stared at me as we approached, and then she shifted her gaze to Michael, who flinched.

"Now do you believe me?" Marie asked.

Awkward didn't begin to cover how I felt.

"It was never so simple a thing as belief," Michael said.

"No? Because I distinctly remember you saying that you didn't *believe* me. That was right before you left and I was locked up for ten years."

"I can't change the past," Michael said. "Surely you've figured out by this point that I truly didn't remember what happened."

"You seem to have remembered now," Marie said, glancing at me. "Don't say you being here with her is just coincidence."

"I'm Michelle Fredericks," I said then, holding out my hand.

"I know who you are," Marie snapped. "Shouldn't you be off toppling third-world countries or something?"

I sighed. "I'm more of a solving murders kind of woman. Julia was the one recruited by the CIA."

"Really? I thought you would have been better suited to it. How is dear Julia these days?"

Ouch.

"I haven't seen her in a while," I replied. "Not since she tried to kill me last fall."

"Looks like you've been having a reunion without me."

"Listen, Marie, we drove here from Cincinnati to talk with you," said Michael. "Please don't send me away. At least come and have lunch with us. I really need to talk to you."

Marie shook her head. "Consuela? Can you watch the gallery for a bit?"

A portly Hispanic woman in her fifties came out of the back of the gallery. "Sure, boss."

"Thanks. I'll try to make it back to cover your lunch. If not, just take off at four."

"No worries. I have some enchiladas with me. We're usually pretty quiet at lunchtime."

Marie tucked her keys in her pocket and gestured out the front. Like me, she evidently didn't bother with a purse most of the time. I wondered which of the cars was hers. I didn't get to find out, as she turned and walked down the highway toward a Mexican restaurant about a quarter-mile away.

I glanced at Michael. He just shrugged and followed her.

CHAPTER SEVEN

The restaurant didn't look like much, with rickety old tables and chairs scattered haphazardly inside, but it smelled amazing. The people eating looked like locals, not tourists. We sat down at a table in a corner. A young waitress brought paper menus along with fresh, warm tortillas and salsa. I ordered three beef enchiladas with red sauce, beans, and rice.

Marie and Michael didn't talk much.

The salsa was really hot.

My phone rang.

I ignored it, but it started ringing again. I glanced at the caller ID: Tony, the director of the CRI. I didn't want to answer my phone, but I knew the bastard would just keep calling me if I didn't.

"I'm sorry, I have to take this," I said, standing up. "Work."

"We'll be fine," Michael said.

"I promise he'll still be breathing when you get back," said Marie.

I sighed. Getting these two to reconcile wasn't going to be easy.

I stepped outside. "This had better be good," I answered. "I'm on vacation."

"Would I call you if it wasn't important, Michelle?"

"You'd call me if some fat-cat client wanted my services."

"You're half right," Tony said. "Remember that guy from the

Department of Homeland Security?"

"Henderson?"

"Yeah, he called here and asked that we assign you to a case."

"Dammit, Tony, I'm on vacation! I'm in New Mexico, for god's sake!"

"Yeah, that DHS guy somehow knew that, too. Said you're in Taos. What are you doing in Taos? Please don't tell me you've joined some spiritualist retreat. I know you don't ski."

"It's none of your business what I'm doing here."

"Right, right, right. Listen, kiddo. This Henderson guy, he didn't make it sound like we had much choice. Also, he's offering three times your normal commission."

"I'm not flying back to Cincinnati for you." Tony's cut of my commission was high enough to have him salivating at the prospect.

"This job he's got, it's in Taos. You *are* in New Mexico, right? Just think about it."

"Tony, do you know the meaning of the word *vacation*?"

"Sure, and it ain't something you do in Taos, New Mexico."

Damn Henderson. The man wasn't going to stop interfering in my life. He'd been a royal pain in the ass during the problems last fall. He'd been responsible for pointing me to the case in Eastern Kentucky, as well. I didn't know what Henderson's angle was, but he knew about the project. If he asked for me, there was probably a good reason.

"What's the case?" I hated myself for asking.

"The FBI has some weird-ass serial killer shit going on there. Half a dozen bodies in the last couple of months. They're trying to keep it out of the news, but it's only a matter of time before it blows up on them. The agent in charge will know more. Should I give them your number? Have them sign the papers?"

"Woah, slow down, Tony. I didn't say I'd do it. I'm curious as to why they would reach out to us."

"Like I said, weird shit. Probably occult. They wouldn't say much more to me. Said I didn't have clearance. As if you do. Say, you don't have a security clearance, do you?"

"If you don't know, then you don't have clearance to know. Tell the FBI I'll meet the local agent in charge. I'm not agreeing to take the case, but I will look at what they have going on. This probably won't be something I'll be interested in."

"I'll let them know. Michelle, you're a lifesaver."

"Oh, and Tony?"

"Yeah?"

"Call me *kiddo* again, and I'll feed you your balls."

"Message received," he said very seriously.

I hung up. Michael wasn't going to like this. I'd begged him to take a vacation with me, and now here I was, signing up for a new job. I'd told Tony I'd only consider the job, but I knew myself well enough to know I wouldn't refuse. Anything weird enough to send the FBI to the CRI was definitely my kind of job. Not to mention Henderson's penchant for meddling.

The waitress was just setting down our plates when I sat back down. The food smelled amazing, and my stomach growled in anticipation. Glass bottles of soda were already on the table, glistening with sweat.

"What did I miss?" I asked.

"Well, so far my sister has called me both an asshole and a coward," said Michael.

"So you've just covered the obvious."

Marie laughed. "Okay, you're not so bad. You didn't used to have much of a sense of humor. What are you doing with this jobless loser?"

"Believe it or not, I love him."

"I believe it. I just don't understand it."

"I think you do," I said. "You wouldn't still be angry at him if you didn't love him. I know it had to be difficult for you. I only just started remembering everything about the project last year, and it almost did me in."

Marie violently stabbed her burrito with her fork. "I'd really prefer not to talk about that."

"Okay, but it has to be tied to why you're angry. You're going to have to talk about it sometime, and at least we're safe to talk to."

Michael gave me a look that said he'd tried that angle, too.

I sighed and dug into my enchiladas. They tasted every bit as good as they smelled. We sat and ate in silence until the waitress brought sopapillas and honey to the table. The sopapillas looked fantastic, but I didn't think I had room. I tore a corner off one, doused it in honey, and sighed in contented pleasure as it melted in my mouth. It was divine.

"So, Michelle, what did Tony want?" asked Michael.

"The FBI wants me to consult on a local case. I don't know the details yet."

"How did they –? Ah, Henderson?"

"Right in one."

"Who's Henderson?" Marie asked. "And the FBI? You really do solve murders?"

"Henderson is a Homeland Security agent, or at least pretends to be. We're not sure who he really works for. He knows a lot about the project. He was tasked with cleanup last fall. You see, Julia had gone on a murder spree, and Henderson conspired to put Michael and me on the case together. I think Henderson wanted to see what would happen."

"Julie went on a murder spree?"

"Julia started hunting down and killing doctors from the project."

"Good," Marie said. "I hope she made them fucking suffer."

"Well, she certainly wasn't easy on them."

I wasn't quite sure how to feel about Marie's raw emotional response. On the one hand, I was appalled by her rage. On the other hand, I kind of agreed with her. That was part of what had made things difficult with Julia, as well. I'd never thought of her as evil, just out of control.

"So this Henderson guy pointed the FBI to you here?" Marie looked thoughtful. "It must have something to do with the aliens."

I exchanged a glance with Michael. "Excuse me?"

"The aliens. You know. Surely you're heard about the cattle mutilations. I heard recently that a couple of bodies had been found out in the desert. No one officially knew anything about the bodies, except they weren't local. The wife of one of the deputy sheriffs, who sometimes buys my art, told me the bodies had the same marks as the cattle. Her husband was pretty shaken up about it."

"Okay." I shook my head. "I know don't any details yet. Somehow, I don't think it's going to be about aliens."

Marie shrugged and smiled smugly.

She looked much like Michael just then.

CHAPTER EIGHT

"I'm going to be here for a while, however, if I take the case. So are you two good?" I asked.

"I think we are for now," Michael said with a glance at Marie, who nodded. "This isn't easy, and we still have a lot to talk about. Yeah, I think we're good."

"So you won't be angry if I take the case?" I asked. "They're offering me a hell of a lot of money."

"They must be kind of desperate, then," Michael said. "Marie, do you have any idea who the two people were that they found in the desert?"

Marie shook her head. "I don't pay much attention to the tourists. We get all kinds here, from the art collectors and the snow bunnies to the yuppie Indigenous Spiritualists and the alien abduction hopefuls."

"*Alien abduction hopefuls?*" I asked. "What the hell is that?"

"People who either claim to have been abducted by aliens or just really want to be. They hang out in the desert, hoping for another chance. I don't really mix with that crowd. They usually don't have any money for art that doesn't have a flying saucer in it. I'm not quite that desperate an artist to go that route."

"Aren't most alien abduction stories scary? I mean, I read a few accounts, seen a few shows on the subject. An abduction doesn't look like something I'd want to have happen."

"Is our own story so different?" asked Michael. "What would we have thought happened if we had remembered?"

"Maybe it isn't so different," I said, "but I'm not going to hang around outside the Pentagon hoping it will happen again."

"I did remember what happened," Marie said. "I never thought it was aliens."

"I'm sorry," Michael said. "Please be angry at the people who suppressed my memory and not at me."

Marie sighed. "I'm sorry. I have a lifetime of resentment to work through. It may take me a while to process everything. I'm glad you came out to see me, both of you. I can't say that I'm going to want to talk about what happened when we were children, but we still have a lot of catching up to do."

The waitress brought the check, and Michael settled up with her while Marie went to the restroom. I decided I probably should go, as well. Women are cursed with small bladders; too much other crap in our abdomens pressing down.

The bathroom was very clean. Marie was washing her hands as I came in. She nodded to me and left without a word. I was having trouble getting any kind of read on the woman. She seemed to have very tight control of her emotions. I suppose if I had been through what she had, I would be afraid to express my emotions, too.

Michael and Marie were waiting outside.

"You said Henderson was involved in this?" said Michael.

"That's what Tony told me."

Michael nodded. "I think one of his DHS agents is here. A woman was paying a little too much attention to us during lunch. She's still inside."

"What did she look like?" I was surprised I'd missed it but not surprised Michael hadn't.

"Average height for a Hispanic woman, so short. She's mature, but I couldn't guess her age: maybe thirty-five. Black hair and eyes. Wearing blue jeans, boots, a black tee-shirt, and a black leather biker jacket."

"You're sure she's DHS?" I asked.

Michael shrugged. "She was watching us, and I got a strange vibe off her. Nothing bad, just weird. She followed us from outside Marie's gallery. I can't say with any confidence what agency she's with, but she isn't just some bystander."

"I think maybe I'll go inside and have a chat with her," I said.

"Be careful. She might be working for someone else."

"I won't give anything away," I said. "I'd like to know who she is and why she was following and watching us."

"Want us to wait?"

"No, go on back to the gallery."

I went back into the restaurant. The woman was sitting at a window seat not far from where we'd been, wearing a Death Cab for Cutie tee-shirt and working methodically through a plate of tamales. A shiny black rock, maybe obsidian, hung on a cord around her neck. I waited for a moment, but she was pretending not to notice me, so I sat down across from her.

"Why were you watching us?" I asked.

She finished eating before saying anything.

"Took you long enough to come talk to me," she said. "Which one of you noticed me? It was the guy, wasn't it?"

"Who do you work for?" I asked. "DHS? CIA? FBI?"

"Ugh, too many acronyms. What makes you think I didn't just think you were hot and was hoping you'd stop and talk to me? You're new in town."

"So you're just a hard-up local?"

The woman smiled lopsidedly. "I wouldn't say that. No, I'd never claim to be a local."

"Then who do you work for?" I asked.

"Let's just say that I'm an interested third party. I don't work for anyone."

I stood up. "Just leave us alone, okay? Whatever you're after, or selling or buying or whatever, we aren't interested."

"Suit yourself," the woman said. "Although I think we're in town for the same reason. That means we'll probably end up working together anyway."

"You're investigating the murders?" I asked. "Are you FBI? If so, why not just say so?"

"Murders?" The woman genuinely seemed surprised. "No, I'm not here about any murders. Maybe... No, all three of you are tied to all of this somehow. I know it."

"Who the hell are you?" I demanded.

"You can call me Erin," she replied. She stood up. She was average height, maybe five-foot-four or so, half a head shorter than me. She didn't look very dangerous, but then, neither do I.

"What's your real name?" I asked.

She lost her smile. "Erin is the only name I've ever been given. That I can remember, anyway. It'll have to do."

"Really, who are you?"

"Not FBI. As I said, an interested third party. If you want to know more, ask your handsome friend about Projects Brimstone and Wormwood."

Anytime someone mentioned a project, I get a bit worried. I still wasn't completely comfortable even thinking about the government project that had... *changed* the kids who'd been part of it, those of us who'd been tortured for some unknown scientific goal. Michael suspected the project had been to make super-soldiers, but then, he was one, so he would think that.

"Projects Brimstone and Wormwood?" I asked.

"He'll know what I mean. The two projects are connected to the three of you, and this place, even if you don't know it yet."

"Connected how?"

"By Providence."

The waitress bumped into me just then. "Pardon me," she said.

I was distracted only for a moment, but Erin had disappeared. No one had left by the front door – it had a bell – and she wasn't in the restroom, either. It was if she'd never been here. That was more than a little disconcerting, especially considering her last words.

I had a lot to think about as I walked back to the gallery.

CHAPTER NINE

Michael was inside Marie's gallery, looking at the paintings and chatting with an older couple in matching Minnesota sweatshirts. They were asking him about Marie's inspirations. Michael, for his part, was doing a good job with the bullshit explanations.

He excused himself and came over to me when the bell by the door rang. He looked relieved to have gotten away from the couple, and I could tell from his body language that he was both agitated and amused. I probably would have felt about the same.

"Thank god, Michelle," he said. "I was about to commit murder."

"How did you get stuck talking to the snowbirds?" I asked.

"Marie, of course. They jumped her when we came in, asking about where she got her ideas, how she was able to put them on canvas. She pretended to have a call and left me to talk to them, for which I will pay her back later. How did your conversation go? You seem... *disturbed.*"

"Yeah, you could say that." I shook my head. "I don't even know where to begin. I think maybe we should wait to talk about it until we can be sure we won't be overheard."

"Okay, but Marie asked me about spending some time with us. I'd hate to disappoint her now that she's starting to open to me."

"I'd be fine talking about this in front of her." I said. "I think it concerns Marie, as well."

"That woman really has you spooked."

Marie closed up the gallery as soon as the couple from Minnesota left. It wasn't quite five o'clock yet, but she didn't seem concerned about the potential loss of revenue. Marie appeared to be in a better mood. I hoped what I had to say about Erin didn't ruin that.

All the cars were gone from the lot except my Jeep.

"Where's your car?" asked Michael.

"I don't have one. I walk here," Marie replied. "It's only a couple of blocks. You're welcome to come to my house to talk. Where are you staying?"

"We have a hotel room up the road."

Marie made a face. "That tourist trap?"

I sighed. "I like the place. Anyway, we'd love to come to your house and talk more. Hop in the back of the Jeep."

We didn't talk much as she guided us to her home, a modest little adobe house near the edge of town. Not that Taos is all that large a place. The house was very blocky but pretty; it looked exactly like what I thought a house in the Southwest should look like.

"Nice place," I said.

"I just rent it," Marie replied. "I've lived in this one for about ten years."

"Well, I like it."

"I kind of do, too. Come on inside. I hope you're not allergic to cats."

"I have a cat," I said as I stepped inside.

Marie had more than just one cat. The house smelled faintly of old wood and cat urine. Three cats were visible in the room, and I suspected there were more elsewhere. A variety of cat trees, scratchers, and toy mice were scattered around the living room.

"Yes, I'm a crazy cat lady. Can I get you two something to drink? Tea, water, soda, beer?"

"I'm good," I said.

I sat down on the couch. A small tabby cat immediately came over and sat in my lap. She was pretty, with pale green eyes. I petted her, and she stretched out, purring. Michael sat down next to me after also politely refusing a drink. I think he was nervous.

Marie got herself a Corona beer and sat in the easy chair nearby. "So where do you want to start?" she asked.

"Well, I thought you'd be a redhead," I said. "Like Michael."

"My hair turned white when I was thirteen," Marie said. "It never recovered."

"And how about you?" Michael asked. "Have you recovered?"

Marie sighed. "I gave up worrying about the project years ago. I admit that seeing you two today was a bit of a shock. I hadn't realized the old anger was there until I saw you. I'm good now."

"I can imagine you'd be angry," I said. "Sorry. It was my idea to ambush you."

"No, it was the right thing to do. I think I would have told Michael go fuck himself if he'd called. I don't know why you waited so long, though."

"I just started remembering things a few years ago," said Michael.

"That doesn't explain why you never reached out."

"No, it doesn't excuse my actions, but fear of rejection can be a powerful inhibitor. I checked up on you, found out you were a successful artist here in Taos. I didn't want to bother you."

Marie snorted. "You were always an ass. I tried to find you but never could."

"I was in the military for years, then a deputy federal marshal. I was never in one place for very long. I didn't even remember Michelle well enough to really recognize her when we met last year. I wasn't sure if she was the one I remembered, or Julia."

"Julia had black hair, you idiot," Marie said. "She looked nothing like Michelle, other than height."

"Well, you weren't sure about me, either, when we first arrived," I said. That comment about toppling third-world countries had been sharp, it had cut deep, and I wasn't even the person it had been aimed at.

"Hair can be dyed. Okay, yeah, you did have lighter hair when you were younger. I guess the two of you looked much the same, now that I think about it. She was more Nordic, but your cheekbones and eyes are similar."

"Sometimes I wish I could remember everything," I said. "But then, what I can remember isn't very pleasant."

"Take your amnesia as a mercy," Marie said. "Only thing merciful those bastards ever did for anyone."

"They didn't do it to be merciful," said Michael.

"I know."

The silence between us wasn't just uncomfortable; it hurt.

"So are you going to tell us about the woman in the restaurant?' Marie asked. "I don't think she's DHS or FBI."

"I don't think so, either," I said. "She said she's an *interested third party*."

"That sounds ominous," said Michael. "Interested in what?"

"She mentioned Providence."

"What's that?" Marie asked.

Michael looked surprised. "The name of the project we were in," he said.

"Oh. I never knew the name."

I shook my head. "She also mentioned a couple of other special projects, Brimstone and Wormwood. She said to ask you about it, Michael."

Michael stiffened next to me. "Do you mind if I have that beer now?" he asked.

"The kitchen is through there," Marie said. She waited for Michael to get up and leave the room. "I think that struck a nerve."

"I do, too."

I had felt Michael's response: something like fear. It may have been the first time I ever felt him have that emotion. Michael was usually unflappable. Whatever those two projects were, they were close to Michael's heart.

CHAPTER TEN

Michael came back into the living room and sat down.

He'd brought two beers for himself and one each for Marie and me. Something about the way he methodically downed the first beer told me he was hurting inside. He didn't want to talk about those special projects.

"Are you going to tell us or not?" Marie prompted.

Michael took a deep breath and sighed. "Okay. It's hard to know where to begin. I suppose I'll just start with things in the order that I learned about them. Michelle, you may remember that I was going to visit with some friends last Christmas but instead came to Lawrence's father's funeral in Pikeville."

I nodded. I'd known he had plans; I hadn't known what they were.

"I was going to meet some military buddies of mine. Old comrades I'd served with in Special Operations. I was lucky not go to Brownsville, Indiana, as it turns out. There was an outbreak of a vicious flu-like contagion there over Christmas. It never made the news, or rather the news reported a tragic toxic chemical spill. The reality was far worse. It was a deliberate release."

Michael stopped and drank down half of his second bottle of beer.

"All of this is classified. Not that I really give a shit about that anymore." Michael sighed. "There were only a few survivors of the outbreak. One of them was my old buddy, Harrison."

"I remember you mentioning him before," I said. "Who was responsible for the outbreak, and why did they do it? Also, why Brownsville, of all places?"

"I only heard about it secondhand, so I don't have all the details. Brownsville has a large strategic oil reserve. From the reports, it sounded as if some of our troops were there but not as friendlies."

"A coup?"

Michael shook his head. "I don't know. Harrison said a few things… No, that wasn't it."

"Then what?"

"Harrison said they were stealing the oil."

"Domestic terrorists, maybe," I said. "This can't be real."

"I spoke to Harrison about it directly."

"And you said *I* was crazy," said Marie. "Welcome to the club."

"Wait. So the incident in Ashland a couple of months ago… That wasn't just a fire, was it?" I said. "It was the same domestic terrorists?"

Michael nodded. "I almost rejoined the service after those attacks. I was *asked* to return. The Ashland, Kentucky raid was another attack by the same people, except they released smallpox there instead of the flu. I don't know how many others there have been. Harrison knew only of the two, but he was in the hospital. We didn't talk about it when I spoke to him later."

"So what the hell are we doing about it?" I demanded.

"By *we*, I assume you mean the US military. Harrison is leading an assault team against them."

"What does any of that have to do with these two projects, Brimstone and Wormwood?" Marie asked. "Not to stray too far from the original topic."

"Project Brimstone is a current special project, using abandoned technology from an older one. Back in the 1960s, there was a lot of interest in figuring out new ways to get troops around the world faster. The ever-increasing conflicts meant US troops needed to deploy as quickly as possible. Someone had the idea of developing spacetime displacement."

"You mean a teleporter?" said Marie. "Philadelphia Experiment shit?"

"I don't know. What I heard was that Project Wormwood had been about making a device that could open a portal to another place. The project was shelved, very suddenly, in the late sixties. There'd been some kind of accident. I do know that some of the scientists with Wormwood went to work on Providence."

I shook my head. "What was the connection?"

Michael shrugged.

I drank my beer and thought about what he'd said. The beer was good, with a sweet and tart taste. Michael must have found some lime juice in the fridge. I wasn't really surprised he hadn't told me about Harrison and Project Brimstone; I'd known he'd been a little distracted. With something that secret, the only real surprise was that he'd chosen to tell us at all.

"That woman, Erin, said we were connected to both Project Brimstone and Project Wormwood," I said. "She also said the projects connected to *this* place."

"You mean Taos?" asked Marie.

"That's what she said."

"Now I wish I'd spoken to her," said Michael. "She has access to some *very* classified information. I'd like to know how."

"She seemed surprised that I didn't know what she was talking about. I didn't tell her why we're here. I lied and told her it was because of the murder investigation. She didn't know what I meant."

"Or acted like it," said Marie.

"She believed what she was saying. She really was surprised; I felt it."

Marie smiled. "I forget that I'm talking to another person with abilities. I've had to hide mine for years. 'Believe in ESP? You're crazy!'"

I nodded. "I'm primarily a psychometrist, but I have some skill as an empath."

"That must suck, in your line of work."

"It isn't fun, but it does give me unique insights into a crime scene."

"Back on topic," said Michael, "who do you think this woman really works for?"

"At best guess, I'd say she works for Henderson." At Marie's look, I added, "The guy from Homeland Security who seems to know so much about our project. He's always sticking his nose into things. This seems like exactly his style."

"I don't know," said Michael. "Henderson didn't seem like a guy who played well with others."

"I've managed to keep uninvolved in all of this for thirty-five years," Marie said. "Then you show up, and I'm neck-deep in it all over again. Thanks a lot."

"I'm sorry if it's disconcerting," Michael said. "I'm also sorry that I didn't come find you sooner."

"It wouldn't have worked out until you remembered what happened."

"I only remember a few of the less savory details. I don't even remember as much as Michelle."

"Good enough for you to accept it as real."

"Julia knew more," I said. "I wish I could ask her about this."

"Didn't you say she tried to kill you?"

"Well, yes, but she's had a rough life. She never left the project."

Marie shuddered. "You mean they just kept her there and kept…?"

I nodded. "She went from the project straight into the CIA. They used her for wet work, assassinations, and things like that. She was pretty crazy when I met her."

"I can only imagine."

"She was consumed by revenge," Michael said. "But she's dead. I shot her. Unless you know something I don't?"

I sighed. "Remember Reggie the Snake?"

"I *thought* you were holding out on me. You got something on that rooftop, didn't you?"

"Julia shot him."

"Dammit, Michelle, why didn't you tell me? She was probably still in Pikeville. We could have gotten her!"

"And then what?" I asked. "You arrest her, and she goes back to federal prison to be tortured some more? She was only a problem when she came after me, and that was only because I killed her brother!"

"You killed Victor?" said Marie. "Wow, good job."

"He had it coming," I said.

"Oh, you have no idea." Marie cocked her head and looked at me oddly. "Or maybe you do."

"I'll tell you about it someday."

"In any case, Julia is long gone," said Michael.

"I wouldn't be so sure," Marie said. "You two showing up here like this. All of these projects woven together. I have a feeling Julia may come and join us."

CHAPTER ELEVEN

Michael tried to call his friend Harrison but couldn't get ahold of him.

I wasn't surprised. If Harrison was involved in a secret project, he wasn't in a position to be receiving phone calls. I thought about what Michael had told us. It felt as if he was leaving something out.

I had no idea what, though. Michael was too hard to read. We didn't actually talk much about what he'd done in the military. I suppose that was natural. Not only was most of his service classified, it was also a decade in the past. From what little he did say, I'd gotten the impression that he'd had to do some pretty awful things.

War is like that, or so I understand.

Nobody comes out of it without scars.

I heard Michael talking to a colonel somebody. He stepped outside just as he started talking. I figured he was asking about Harrison.

"So how did you get into working with the FBI?" asked Marie.

"Well, I don't always work with the FBI. I'm an independent contractor working with a think-tank in Columbus, Ohio. The Criminological Research Institute studies crime statistics, mostly. I'm signed on as a consultant in occult crime. I specialize in serial killers."

"I think it's interesting, but I'd never want to do that," Marie said. "Why do you?"

"I had a run-in with a serial killer in college."

"A run-in? With a serial killer? How does *that* happen?"

"A psycho targeted my group of friends. I ended up tracking down the killer and, well, killing him. After that, I switched majors and studied forensic anthropology. Given my extra skill set, I studied the occult. It's a niche specialty, but it's in higher demand than you might think."

"By *extra skill set*, you mean your psychic abilities?"

"Yes, the psychometry, in particular."

"You didn't wonder how you had an ability like that?"

I shrugged. "Sometimes people have abilities. The group of friends from college I mentioned had gotten together to talk about stuff like that. Some had seen ghosts; others had more unusual talents."

"I was locked away because I said I believed in stuff like that."

"I think there was more to it than that," I said.

Marie looked away, out the window. "I remembered everything," she said. "I hated myself. I just wanted to die. I tried to… kill myself, several times. No one would believe me about what had been done to me."

"I'm sorry, Marie. I don't know what they did to us, to make us forget about what they'd done, but it worked really well. I think I always had the emotions. I felt this rage inside; I just didn't know why. Last year, when the memory block broke, and I remembered some of what they did to us… Yeah, I didn't feel real good about myself, either."

"I used to get so angry," said Marie. "I blamed Michael, but I knew it wasn't his fault. I could tell he really didn't remember anything. It made me question my sanity."

"I certainly questioned mine."

"Why *was* Julia trying to kill you? Other than you killing her brother, I mean."

"Oh, that's complicated. I'm not sure she really wanted me dead. I mean, she was angry at Michael and me, because we'd gotten out of the project and she hadn't. I don't think that was the whole story, though. She had plenty of opportunities to kill me. I think, maybe, she just wanted someone to talk to. I don't harbor her any ill will at this point. I covered for her in Eastern Kentucky. I didn't want Michael to go after her. I guess I just wish things could have gone differently."

"You think she could be redeemed?"

"I don't know that she's actually bad," I said. "She did some awful stuff, but we all know that the people she killed deserved it. I just wouldn't have done it the way she did."

"What the hell did she do?" Marie asked.

"She tortured them to death, in a fashion similar to the torments they subjected us children to."

"Sounds like it was quite the moral quandary. They deserved death, and more, but what does it do to a person, to do that to someone else? What did Julia lose by doing it?"

Michael came back at that point, and I knew something was wrong. His shoulders were hunched, and he looked a little pale. He came over and sat down on the couch.

"I take it your call didn't go well," said Marie.

"That depends upon your definition of *well*, I suppose," Michael replied. "I spoke to my former commander. He was quite concerned about this Erin woman."

"That isn't what has you shaken," I guessed.

"No. My friend Harrison is missing in action, presumed dead."

My hand closed over his. "I'm sorry, Michael."

"I am, too." He shook his head. "Harrison is a tough son of a bitch. He'll make it back home, if anyone could."

"Want to talk about it?"

"No, not really. I can't do anything for him. So let's focus on our current problem."

"What to eat later? I don't really have much for dinner," Marie said, "so if you want something other than salad, you'll need to go out."

Michael smiled. "I meant the problem with Erin, and the project."

"I know this is all fascinating, new, and interesting to the two of you," Marie said, standing up, "but I think I've talked enough about that shit for one day."

Marie's shift in mood was sudden but not unexpected.

I squeezed Michael's hand. "It's been a long day," I said. "We were up early, traveling. Maybe we could have lunch again tomorrow?"

Marie nodded. "As long as we don't talk about the project, lunch would be great."

"It has been good to see you again," Michael said. "I'd like to have lunch and catch up tomorrow."

We said our goodbyes and walked out to the Jeep. They didn't hug.

"Did you want to stop for dinner?" I asked.

Michael shook his head. "I'm not hungry. I'll go with you, if you want to eat."

"I'm still pretty full from lunch."

I actually was a little hungry, but I decided I'd skip dinner, since Michael wasn't eating. I don't like to eat when the other person isn't. Michael didn't say anything else on the way to the hotel. Whatever else he'd learned was bothering him a lot, and I didn't think it was just his friend being MIA.

I took a shower and changed into pajamas. Michael didn't join me but took a shower right afterward. I think he hadn't noticed I was taking a shower, which told me a lot about how distracted he was.

I checked my email on my phone. I'd a missed call. The local FBI agent left a message, wanting to meet in the morning.

I texted Agent Oliver that I'd be happy to meet in the morning.

I wasn't actually all that thrilled about the prospect, but the sooner I learned what the FBI wanted, the sooner I could decide if I wanted to take the job. At this point, I was still lying to myself about having a doubt. I knew in my heart I was already committed to the case. They were offering me a lot of money, but it was more because of Henderson. If he thought I should take the case, it was probably important.

This Erin intrigued me, too.

Michael finished his shower and came out with just a towel around his waist. I found myself distracted by his near nudity. I wanted to make love with him, but I knew he was too caught up in whatever was bothering him.

I thought about hopping on my laptop and playing a game, or even just going to sleep. I knew Michael well enough to know when something was eating at him, though. He wouldn't initiate the conversation, but I knew he wanted to talk.

"Want to talk about it?" I asked.

"No. Yes. Sorry. Yeah, I do. After Brownsville, Harrison and I were the last survivors from our squad. Brownville was a shock, but losing Harrison... I don't know. I never thought I'd be the last one."

"You said you thought he'd make it back from wherever he is. You think he's been captured?"

"Nothing so simple, I'm afraid."

"You can't talk about it?"

"Not right now."

I sighed. "Did you learn anything else?" Sometimes getting Michael to open up was difficult.

"I did, actually. Colonel Jackson, my old commander, told me what he knew."

"Isn't all that classified?" I asked.

"I think we're a bit past worrying about that, don't you?"

"So what did he say?"

"Jackson told me that he didn't know anything about Project Providence, although he'd heard of it. He'd seen it mentioned in the older classified records about the project. Operation Aquarian Frequency was restructured into Project Brimstone about two months ago. My friend Harrison was the key operative for Aquarian Frequency. You see, Harrison was sent to stop the enemy from attacking us. With a nuke. He must have succeeded, because the attacks stopped, but he didn't come back from the mission."

"I think someone setting off a nuke would have made the news," I said. "They couldn't have covered that up."

"He didn't set off the nuke on our world."

CHAPTER TWELVE

Michael and I have talked about some weird shit, but he caught me off guard with that one.

"I'm sorry, *what?*"

"Maybe I should start at the beginning," he said. "I didn't want to say anything in front of Marie. The attacks at Brownsville, Ashland, and other places were raids to steal strategic energy reserves. Oil and gas, mostly, but also nuclear material."

"Holy shit." I rubbed the sleep away from my eyes and sat up. "Who's behind this?"

"That's where it gets complicated. I talked to Colonel Jackson, and to Harrison a couple of times before – ah, fuck it. I don't know why I'm worried about you believing me... Imagine two United States, in two universes. They're very similar, but then something happens, and they go in two very different directions in development."

"You're talking about alternate universes."

Michael nodded. "From what I was told, the other universe was very similar to ours until recently, but then the United States next door fell to fascists. After that, things got even worse for them, as they were invaded by other factions of universe travelers."

"You're pulling my leg, right?"

I knew he was telling the truth, but it was so far-fetched that I could barely believe it.

"I wish I were," Michael said. "Harrison met his doppelganger from that universe during the raid on Brownsville. The other side had a nasty nuclear and biological war. That's why they're stealing resources from us."

"Oh, my god. I thought life couldn't get any stranger, but this…"

"It gets even weirder. Operation Aquarian Frequency was about stopping the attacks here, on our soil. Project Brimstone was about taking the fight to the enemy. Harrison traveled to the other universe, more than once. The last time, he took a nuke with him and detonated it in their base to destroy their portal device. He was supposed to have used the device to return home before the nuke detonated, but something must have gone wrong."

"But you don't think he's dead."

"Harrison is very resourceful. He would have found a way to survive. Colonel Jackson thinks the portal device must have been damaged in the fight, and Harrison went someplace other than our world. Jackson's team has some sort of detectors. They recorded the device being used in that universe, but it didn't open a portal here. If I know Harrison, he'll find his way home, no matter what."

I won't lie: my head hurt, trying to understand everything Michael was telling me. If it had been *anyone* other than him, I would have slapped them for lying. Michael wouldn't have done that, though. He might keep information to himself, but he wouldn't lie about it.

"Was this Project Brimstone out here in New Mexico?" I asked.

"No, Project Brimstone is under Jellico Mountain, on the border between Kentucky and Tennessee."

"So what's the connection with Taos?" I asked. "There has to be one."

"Project Wormwood developed the portal technology. Colonel Jackson didn't have much information on it; I think he'd have told me if he did. That project was based out of the Angel Fire Air Station, which is now closed. There's a small civilian airfield there, although I suspect most of the military installation was underground."

"Angel Fire?"

"It's a town to the east, on the slopes of Agua Fria Mountain," he said. "The military isn't always very original with project names."

"Hey, at least that mountain isn't named after boobs or something red."

Michael smiled. "All Jackson knew about Wormwood was that it was shut down abruptly in the late sixties."

"You think the project opened a portal to someplace they didn't like?"

"I don't know. Jackson didn't think the project ever got the portal working, although the machine worked fine when they used it at Jellico. I think there's a lot more to that story that we just don't have enough information about."

"I could ask Lawrence to try to dig up some information on the dark web," I suggested.

"If anyone could find anything about the project, it would be Lawrence."

"I think we need something, because I still don't get the connection to Providence."

"I don't, either," said Michael. "I don't see how a project about portal technology could be connected to what was done to us. Surviving personnel from Wormwood went on to join Project Absolution, which became Project Providence."

"*Surviving personnel?* That's an interesting way to put it."

"Those were the exact words in the brief Jackson read. I asked him about that specifically."

"Project names change too much. Absolution? Providence? It might help if we actually knew what the purposes of the projects were," I said. "We know Project Providence enhanced those of us who survived, but we don't know how or why. The machine we both remember seemed to be made to force us out of our bodies. I always assumed that we were part of some kind of fucked-up remote viewing project."

"Maybe, but that wouldn't explain the enhancements or the combat training," Michael said. "I know we don't really talk about the project, and Marie doesn't want to talk to us about it, but I think we should talk about it with her. She might know more that we've forgotten."

"I think we should go slowly with that," I said. "Marie might push you away if you press her about it. She needs some time to deal with how she feels, and she needs to know you're here for more than just information about the project."

"Well, maybe we can drive over to Angel Fire and ask around. Who knows what we might uncover?"

"That sounds – Crap. I almost forgot. I'm supposed to meet with an Agent Oliver from the FBI in the morning, to talk about the murders."

"Do you want me to go with you?"

"Not this time. I just want to get a feel for what they want from me. It isn't like the FBI to offer more money for a job, and with Henderson involved… It probably has something to do with that Erin woman. I plan to ask Agent Oliver about her in the morning. Maybe I'll be able to make some trouble for Henderson."

"He's got it coming," Michael agreed. "Well, in that case, I'll just bum around town until you're finished."

"I'm sorry, Michael. I know this wasn't what we had planned."

"Actually, it's okay. Meeting Marie again went better than I expected. You working out here means that I can spend more time with my sister, just the two of us. I think she was a little inhibited with you there."

"I think so, too," I said. "I liked her, though."

"I hope we can work out all of our problems. She's the only family I have. I want her back in my life."

"Just go easy," I said. "She has legitimate concerns. Listen to her."

"I will, and you should be careful with Agent Oliver. Who knows if he's really what he appears to be?"

"I've worked with the FBI for years, Michael. I'll be fine."

INTERLUDE

I'm back in the courtroom.

I never wanted to see that fucker Forester again, and now I couldn't stop dreaming about him.

Well, dreaming about killing him, anyway.

My eyes focus on the blood dripping from Forester's cut hand. He'd broken his glass against the table. Someone hadn't been doing their job very well; he should've never had actual glass.

Without taking my eyes off Forester, I reach out to the nearby chair. The edges of its top dig into my palms and fingers as I lift it. Just as every other time I've had this damn dream.

Forester sees the chair. He begins to say something. I'm moving too quickly for him to react.

I swing the chair, except it isn't Forester there anymore, and I'm not in a courtroom.

My body is younger, and I'm wearing a hospital gown.

A man in military fatigues looks surprised as the school desk in my hand catches him across the side of his head. The impact jars my arms, and the instructor is flung across the room like a ragdoll, spraying blood.

All around, the other children leap up and begin to fight.

It's pandemonium.

A guard charges me with a raised baton, yelling something, and I swing the desk again.

Forester's head caves in, and the blood sprays across my face.

This isn't right.

Forester didn't have anything to do with the project.

Bullets strike Forester's chest with wet, hollow thuds; more blood fountains.

"I know what you are," the guard says, just before my desk crushes his skull.

Forester is still trying to say something as he falls, and the blood pours out of his mouth.

I need to know what he's saying.

"I know what you are."

No, that's the guard, back in the Providence Project.

The guards have beaten us and handcuffed our hands behind our backs. Several of the other children aren't moving. They might have gotten lucky and been killed. Doctors and orderlies are working on them, trying to save them – not out of the kindness of their hearts. We are property, and they must have invested a lot in us, to make us what we are.

Dr. Green, the monster who runs this place, is shouting at one of the instructors. The soldier points at me, and they both look over. Dr. Green doesn't appear happy, and that usually means he has some especially horrible punishment planned for me.

Something about his eyes makes me look away.

Forester isn't dead yet, despite the crushed skull and gunshot wounds.

People are hard to kill.

Sometimes humans don't perish easily, like in the movies. We don't pass gently into the night. Sometimes we linger, and death comes hard, after long suffering.

The people in the courtroom are watching me, as if I'm something alien to them. It's the same way the doctors used to watch me, when they tortured me and the other children. I hate being looked at like that. It isn't my fault, I want to scream. I didn't choose to be this way. For that matter, I didn't choose to kill Forester. He didn't give me any choice.

I resent having had to kill Forester. He shouldn't have come at me with the broken glass.

His lips are moving, even as the pulsing blood slows from his wounds. There's a pattern to the movements. He's repeating the same thing each time. I catch bits and pieces of the words and put them together.

I know what you are, he mouths. Monster.

CHAPTER THIRTEEN

Michael ironed my suit for me while I was in the shower the next morning.

I kissed him as I got dressed, and wished I had time for more. He seemed to be feeling better, which meant he was thinking about the same thing I was. I sighed and pushed him away, then finished dressing.

He had that smug look he gets when he knows I'm turned on.

"You're sure you don't want me to come with you?" he asked.

"I'll be fine." I slipped my pistol into my shoulder holster under my jacket.

Michael had gotten me a Sig Sauer P229 Legion for Christmas. I hated to admit it, but he'd been right. After using the Sig, I couldn't imagine using another handgun. Mine was loaded with .40 caliber jacketed hollow-points. It was beautiful and compact. I loved it.

"Don't look at porn on my laptop."

"Why would I need porn? I just watched you shower. Besides, I have my own laptop."

I rolled my eyes. "Promise me you'll eat something."

"I promise." Michael stood up. "I think they have free breakfast here."

I kissed him again and left the hotel room. Agent Oliver wanted to meet at the Guadalajara Grill, which was just up the road from the hotel. Traffic was light. I parked next to the black Ford SUV with government tags and went inside.

I was just thinking I should have gotten a description of the agent when a small, dark-skinned man in a suit walked over to me. He was a few inches shorter than me.

"You must be, Dr. Michelle Fredericks," he said, holding out his hand. "Agent John Oliver."

I shook his hand. He had a strong grip. "Nice to meet you," I said. "With a name like that, I figured you'd have an English accent."

"Alas, I do not. I hope you like Mexican food," he said. "I tried this place when I was first assigned to this case. Now I find I can't stay away. My husband is going to kick my ass when I finally get back home."

"You're not from here?" I asked.

"The closest FBI field office is in Albuquerque. Well, Colorado Springs might be slightly closer, but we like to stay in-state if possible."

He led me over to the line where we ordered food. I got the beef tip menudo soup with a side of grilled potatoes and a carnitas taco. I'd never tried horchata but had always wanted to, so I got that, as well. My stomach was growling as we waited for our food.

Oliver paid for the meal.

"The weather is nice, if you'd like to sit in the patio area," he said.

We took our food and sat out in the sun. A cool breeze blew from off the mountains. The view was amazing. I could understand why Marie had chosen to live in Taos. I love Kentucky – it's a beautiful state – but this was breathtaking.

We ate in companionable silence.

I thought about how many times I'd had meals like this, with strangers. I'd worked with a lot of FBI agents, as well as police departments. The police never bought me food; the FBI always did. The police had better coffee, though, at least most of the time.

"I understand that you haven't agreed to consult on the case yet," Oliver said when he finished eating.

"All I know is that there *is* a case," I said. I'd finished eating before him, and had been looking at the distant mountains and sipping my horchata. "I don't know anything about it."

Oliver nodded. "We've been trying to keep it quiet, but we think we've got a serial killer."

"I assume there's something unusual about the murders. I don't usually get asked to consult on normal cases."

"You could say that. You came highly recommended, both from our own Special Agent Taylor and from Homeland Security, which is a bit more unusual. I'll have to trust you not to talk about this. You see, all the evidence points to alien abductions."

"Excuse me?"

Oliver grinned. "Believe me, I'm not saying it really *is* aliens. I just think we have some sicko who wants to make it looks like that."

"I was told there were just two bodies," I said. "That normally isn't enough for the FBI to be involved, is it?"

"Yes and no. You see, there have been more than just the two bodies. Most of the bodies were found on federal land, at least one on tribal land."

"How many?"

"Five so far, not including the dead cows with the same marks."

"Same marks?" I asked. "What's the cause of death?"

"That's difficult to say. The coroner wasn't sure. It's a toss-up between exsanguination and shock from the trauma."

"It might help if I knew what the trauma was."

"I'll need you to commit to working with us before I can tell you that."

I sighed. "I understand DHS Agent Henderson recommended me. He knows the types of cases I work. I suppose I'll have to just go with it."

"If I may ask," Oliver said, "what brought you to Taos?"

"My boyfriend's sister lives here. We came out to visit her."

"Would that be Deputy Marshal Michael Delling?"

"You did your homework," I said. "So you're almost right. Michael quit the Marshal Service."

"Oh, I didn't realize," Oliver said. "Is he freelance now? We might be able to offer him work with you."

"I'm not sure what he'd want to do, but I'll ask him. I work for CRI as a consultant, so you can have your office send the paperwork to my office. Now, can we talk about whatever it is that has the FBI freaked out?"

"I wouldn't say we're freaked out," Oliver said. "Just a little out of our depth."

"The FBI has some very good occult specialists. I've worked with them. Whatever this is, you decided to go out-of-house on it. That suggests it's big and weird."

"One of the two most recent bodies is the daughter of a senator."

"Politics," I said disgustedly.

"I couldn't agree with your feeling more," Oliver replied. "However, it did allow us to procure extraordinary funds to expedite this case. That's also how Agent Henderson got involved. May I ask how you know the agent?"

"Henderson oversaw a case I worked on last fall. It was hate at first sight, and mutual."

"He recommended you highly," Oliver said. He seemed surprised.

"Doesn't mean he doesn't hate me. He's been involved in a couple of my cases now. I really don't know what his angle is."

"Hmm. Well, anyway, let call my office and have them send over the paperwork to the CRI."

"I'll give them a call and let them know to expect it."

I got into my Jeep and called Tony. The annoyingly cheerful receptionist Jamie answered the phone on the first ring. I told her to connect me to Tony, and I didn't care if he was available.

"Michelle! You meet with the FBI yet?" Tony asked.

"I took the job. They're sending the paperwork."

"That's great news. I knew you'd come through for u—"

I hung up on him.

He needed me working for him more than I needed to work for him. There had been quite a few times when I thought about going completely freelance. Hell, Michael and I could go into business for ourselves.

With our credentials and reputations, we'd have plenty of work.

CHAPTER FOURTEEN

Oliver knocked on the glass of the passenger-side door, and I unlocked the door and let him into the Jeep. He had several thick folders with him. He kept them in his lap as he settled into the seat, then shuffled the folders.

"I take it you called the CRI," he said.

"I did. You should have the signed paperwork back soon."

"Good enough for me. These are the case files," he said, handing me the folders. "Since the first bodies were found on federal land, we've been involved since the beginning."

"How long has this been going on?" I asked.

"Since last summer. Two bodies in July, then one in December, and then the last two bodies just two weeks ago. Cows have been found in between the murders but aren't always reported."

"What are the chances that there are more bodies out there?"

"Who knows? Better than average, I'd say." Oliver shook his head. "This is some rough terrain around here. We only found these last two because of the vultures. Sometimes murder victims aren't found for years in the desert. Welcome to New Mexico, Land of Enchantment."

I opened the folders and flipped through the pictures.

It was difficult stuff to look at, and I've seen a lot of dead bodies. There was no blood around the corpses, despite the mutilation. The report said that all of the victims had been completely exsanguinated. That isn't easy to do. The coroner wasn't sure whether the bodies had been drained postmortem or during their impromptu surgery, or maybe something else. The dead cattle and humans had the same wounds: the eyes, ears, breasts, external sex organs, and anus and rectum had been cleanly cut from each of the corpses. Close-ups of the heads showed that the lips and tongues had been removed, as well. The autopsy reports indicated that the uterus and ovaries were missing from the females. The wounds looked cauterized. There was no sign of bruising around the injuries. The wounds were likely made postmortem; I could think of only a few other ways to avoid bruising.

"I don't know how you can look at that after eating," Oliver said. He was looking out the window.

I glanced at him. "I've seen worse." I shook my head. "Can you tell me anything else about the bodies?"

"They were all naked, as in the pictures. Their personal items have yet to be found. There were no tracks around any of the bodies. Nor any indication of impact: they weren't dropped from any significant height. We don't have any theories on how that works. For that matter, we don't really know how long the bodies were in the desert."

"So no time of death?" I asked.

"No clue."

"And this just started last summer?"

Oliver shrugged. "Cattle mutilations have been reported since the seventies. There was even a big investigation around 1980. Nothing ever came of it. The ranchers were convinced it was the government."

"Not UFOs?"

"Strangely enough, no. Nothing a rancher hates more than the government, I guess. Almost everything else out here gets blamed on flying saucers, but not this. The conspiracy theorists and UFO people have an uneasy alliance here nowadays."

"I heard there's some kind of abduction cult, or something like that."

"I'm not sure I'd call it a cult," Oliver said. "But yeah, we have those people, too."

"Is there any chance of me seeing the most recent bodies?"

"I'm afraid not. Given the family connections of the deceased, we had to release the bodies pretty quickly."

"Worth a shot." I glanced through the files. The GPS coordinates of the human bodies were on the paperwork. "Could I look at the crime scenes?"

"Any of them except the body found in December," Oliver replied. "That one was on tribal land. You'd need special permission to enter. I doubt they'd give it to you. The Indigenous peoples in the area don't want anyone disturbing the dead."

"I think I'll start with the most recent. There may be subtle signs left that your team may have missed – no offense."

"None taken. You're the expert. We reached out to you for a reason."

I nodded. I didn't want to step on Oliver's toes. I also didn't want to reveal that I have exceptional ways of finding clues.

"Can I hang onto these files for now?"

Oliver nodded. "You'll have to hand them back in at the end of the case. You know the drill."

"I do. Thanks."

"Okay, I'll let you do what you do, then. I suggest we meet for breakfast every morning and exchange notes. I'll be in town for the duration, in case you need me. If, god forbid, we find any more bodies, I'll get you to the scene ASAP."

"That sounds good," I said. "Oh, I almost forgot. I ran into someone odd yesterday. She asked me some strange questions and seemed to have a lot of information that she shouldn't. Said her name was Erin."

"Erin what?" Oliver asked.

"She wouldn't say. I thought she might be a DHS agent."

Oliver shook his head. "No one I know, but I wouldn't put it past that Henderson guy to have someone here. I can make some inquiries."

"If you don't mind asking. She's Hispanic, average height, athletic build. Maybe thirty-five or so – hard to say. Dark hair and eyes. Wearing street clothes."

"No one I know," Oliver said again. "I'd steer clear of her until we know more."

"I'd planned on it."

"Okay, see you tomorrow."

Oliver got out of the Jeep and waved as he settled into his SUV.

He seemed as if he was going to be easy to work with. That was good. I'd worked with some real assholes at the FBI. Oliver was friendly and competent. I doubted we'd develop much of a friendship past a working relationship, but that was fine. Not every agent could be like Taylor.

I drove back to the hotel and stopped by the lobby. They had a rack full of brochures advertising sightseeing tours, ski trips, helicopter rides, and UFO spotting expeditions. I took the UFO brochures and drove around to our room.

Michael wasn't there. I figured he'd gone out for breakfast. I'd hoped that we'd be able to spend a little time together this morning, but it didn't look like it.

I spread the case files out on the bed.

The most recent bodies were the most promising. The area around Taos doesn't get a lot of rain. Any evidence near the crime scene should still be here. I hoped the forensics team hadn't trampled the scene into oblivion.

A quick internet search turned up far more information on cattle mutilations than I ever wanted to see. It seemed that the phenomenon was global. Humans mutilated in a similar fashion were less common but still sometimes happened. The few pictures I could find were uncannily similar, both to each other and to the victims here.

Either this was a much bigger problem than I had realized, or there was a very skilled copycat killer in the area. Despite my brushes with the supernatural, I tend to assume that dead bodies are left by normal people with bad intentions. While I think it would be sheer hubris to believe humans are the only kind of people in the universe, I just don't think aliens are coming to Earth to steal organs from cows.

Humans are more than capable of being sick and twisted without any help.

CHAPTER FIFTEEN

Michael came back around eleven in the morning.

He had a twelve-pack of soda and a few bags of beef jerky from the Albertsons up the road. I would have driven him there, but it was typical Michael to just not say anything and walk. He sat down on the other side of the bed and looked at the reports.

"That looks like fun," he said.

"Yeah, loads and loads. These murders started last summer," I said. "The FBI is sort of out of ideas, so they called me in."

"Hmm. I've seen this sort of thing before. I remember reading the reports when in Special Operations. The situation got so bad back in the eighties and nineties that the ranchers in Iowa and Wyoming would shoot at helicopters if they flew too close to their land. We were warned not to do any training exercises near their ranches."

"No one ever thought it was aliens?"

"Yes and no. Sometimes the carcasses would be found the day after lights were seen in the sky, but that doesn't rule out helicopters."

"What's your take on it?"

Michael shrugged. "My money has always been on the cattle mutilations being some weird government experiment. I wondered if they were testing for toxins or radiation poisoning or something. I don't know. I haven't heard of people being found in the same condition."

"Well, the alien conspiracy sites on the internet say it's fairly common," I said. "Some of the sites even have pictures. If you can trust that crap."

"Do the wounds in the pictures online match those of your victims?"

"They sure look like they do. Hard to tell without an actual medical examination. Most the photos were taken by amateurs."

"Do we have current bodies to look at?" Michael asked. "In person?"

" *We?*" I teased.

"I assumed you'd like my help. If you'd rather I stayed out of it…"

"Put away your bruised ego. Of course I'd like you to help. The FBI agent in charge even suggested that they would be willing to pay you."

"Really? Well, I was planning pro-bono."

"Mmm, *bone…*"

Michael sighed. "I don't think we have time for that before lunch."

"Raincheck, then." I put down the file I was reading for the third time. "I say take the money, if they'll pay you. And no, sadly, we don't have any current bodies to examine. The last ones, which normally would have been available… Well, there were political reasons to release them to the families."

"Too bad."

I gathered up my courage. "Michael, Agent Oliver seemed to think you were still a deputy federal marshal.

"Oh, well, technically I suppose I am. I had a lot of saved vacation and comp time. I'm officially still on paid leave."

"Thinking of going back?" I asked, carefully not looking at him.

"I always like to keep my options open," Michael replied. "I didn't know if I could find work after I retired. I didn't want to burn my bridges."

"I can understand that. I just wish you'd told me."

"There is no doubt in my mind about our relationship," he said, taking my hand. "I'm right where I want to be."

I leaned over and kissed him. He responded passionately. I pushed him away before it could go any further. We didn't have time to make

love before we were supposed to meet his sister. Michael likes to go slow
– so do I – and he has a lot of stamina. Damn, I wanted him badly right
now.

I sighed and stood up. "We should go."

"If that's what you want," Michael drawled.

"Oh, don't you dare."

He just laughed and stood up. I really wanted him. I could tell that
he wanted me, too.

"Marie is waiting for us," I said, trying to convince myself we should
go.

"We don't have to get there before noon. You only said lunch; you
didn't specify a time."

"Just get in the damn Jeep."

We drove over to the gallery, and I had to listen to Michael chuckle
the whole way. He loved teasing me. I supposed I loved to be teased, to
some extent. I was happy that Michael was in a good mood. It should
help with his sister.

Marie was waiting for us outside the gallery.

"Sorry we're a little late," I said as I got out of the Jeep. It was just
one minute past twelve, but I was teasing Michael.

"No worries. I just stepped out here," said Marie. "Where would
you like to eat?"

"You know this town better than we do," Michael said. "That
Mexican place was good."

"We ate at the Guadalajara Grill for breakfast," I said, "So I
wouldn't mind something else."

"There are quite a few good places to eat around town. Do you like
Italian?"

"I love Italian," I said, glancing at Michael. "And so do you."

"Yes."

Marie grinned as she climbed into the seat behind me. I drove us
across town to the restaurant. Tourist season was just beginning in
Taos, and we had inadvertently hit a sweet spot: the temperatures were
good, but there weren't throngs of tourists yet.

It helped us that the locals all knew Marie, although I thought I probably should have changed out of my suit. I looked a little out of place. Marie and Michael were both in jeans.

We ordered our food and wine. I ordered fettuccine alfredo with chicken, in case anyone cares. Michael – the heathen – ordered a beer with his. Michael also ordered fried calabro mozzarella sticks and cheesy garlic toast as appetizers.

Now you know why I love him.

"So, Michelle, did you meet with the FBI guy?" Marie asked.

"I did."

"What did he say?"

I gestured emphatically with my hands. "Aliens!"

"Seriously?"

I shook my head. "They don't have any ideas yet, although aliens did come up."

"Did you take the job?"

"I did. You're going to be stuck with us for a while."

"That doesn't seem so bad."

The waiter brought our drinks and appetizers. We were still eating those when the main meal showed up. It was a lot of food, but I was hungry, not having eaten the night before. Michael seemed to have his normal appetite back, as well.

I started to relax as the food worked its magic.

Having lunch with Michael and Marie seemed normal and right.

"Our friend is back," Michael said. He tilted his head to my right.

CHAPTER SIXTEEN

I glanced over to where he indicated.

Erin was sitting at a nearby table, eating fried zucchini chips. She smiled and waved when she saw me looking at her. She was dressed much the same as the day before, with a Beatles *Magical Mystery Tour* tee-shirt under her leather jacket. I decided she might be older than she looked – there was something about her eyes. She was probably closer to our age. I wondered suddenly if I knew her from the project and just didn't remember her.

There had been lots of kids in Project Providence. My memory of what happened was spotty at best. If Erin had been there, Marie would remember. It might have been a burden for Marie, but her memories were going to come in handy.

Erin stood up and walked over to our table. "Mind if I join you guys?" she asked. "I'll share my appetizer."

Michael shrugged. Marie was staring intently, probably trying to fit Erin's face to one of the kids she remembered. I sighed. So much for a relaxing lunch. At least it would be an interesting one. Erin certainly wasn't boring.

I met Erin's eyes. I realized that I liked Erin for some reason I couldn't define. I knew I shouldn't trust her, but I really wanted to. It felt strange. I'm not normally a trusting person, especially not with someone I don't know well.

"Sure," I said. "Why not?"

Erin settled into the empty seat between Michael and me, pushing the plate of fried zucchini chips onto the table. She called the waiter over and told him she was sitting with us, and would like another soda. She snatched a piece of our garlic toast, took a big bite out of it, and grinned as she chewed.

"Ready to come clean and tell us who you are?" asked Michael.

"Where would be the fun in that?" Erin responded.

"You have a strange aura," said Marie.

Erin looked startled. "Uh, thanks?"

I pointedly ate one of her zucchini chips. It was pretty good, actually. "I spoke to the FBI about you this morning," I said.

"Oh? Am I in trouble?" She didn't look concerned. She appeared to be concentrating on the piece of garlic bread she'd pilfered.

"Whether or not you're in trouble," Michael said, "depends on what you can tell us about what's going on, and what you want in return."

"I looked into those murders you mentioned, Michelle," Erin said, ignoring Michael. "You don't mind if I call you Michelle, do you?"

"It is my name," I replied. "I'm still not sure about yours."

"I *always* answer to Erin." She smiled wryly. "Anyway. I didn't have much luck finding out anything about the murders. As I said, I'm not here for that. I didn't even know about them until you mentioned them. I don't think they're connected. At least, I hope not. I really, really hope they aren't."

"Connected to what?" asked Michael.

Erin glanced at me. "You did ask him about what we talked about, didn't you? It's important."

"We discussed things," I said. "I don't think this is the right place or time to go into the details. Why don't you tell us what you want?"

"I want in," Erin said. "When you find Wormwood, I want to be there."

"What is it to you?" asked Michael.

"Let's just say that I have a vested interest. I think you'll find I'm very capable and useful to have around. I'm really cute, too." She batted her eyes. "Seriously, I think you'll need me there."

"If you're so interested, why not just find Wormwood yourself?" said Michael.

"I *have* tried. If I knew where to look, I'd be there now. I have *been* looking. It's been a pet project of mine for a few years now. I always look around when I'm in the area. Imagine my surprise when I found the three of you here."

"How did you know we were here?" I asked. "Were you looking for us?"

"I wasn't looking for you, but I'm glad I found you."

"You're going to have to earn our trust, if you want in on anything," said Michael. "You can start be telling us why you were surprised to see us here."

"Three of the kids from Providence here? Now?" Erin asked. "Why wouldn't I be surprised?"

"How do you know about that?" I asked. "Were you part of it? Are you one of the other kids?"

"No," said Marie.

Erin grinned. "What she said."

"Who do you work for?" Michael asked.

"I'm afraid that will have to be a conversation for another day," said Erin. "Trust goes both ways. I *think* I can trust you, but I need to be sure first. Besides, if I told you, it wouldn't make much sense, and you wouldn't believe me." She pulled out some crumpled bills from her pocket and dropped a twenty on the table.

Michael gripped her right forearm to keep her seated. "I think you need to answer some questions, now."

"Don't get handsy." Erin glared at him.

"Who do you work for?" Michael asked again, squeezing tighter.

Erin shook her head and then suddenly gripped Michael's wrist with her left hand. She removed his hand from her arm in one smooth motion. She made it look easy, but I could see Michael straining to keep her from moving his hand away. Michael gasped in pain before she released him.

"I wouldn't recommend doing that again," said Erin. She stood up.

"Wait," I said. "Please ignore him. He still thinks he's a marshal. Let's assume we're willing to work together. How do we find you again?"

"I'll be around. Don't go looking for Wormwood without me. It's important." She glared once more at Michael and then left the restaurant.

CHAPTER SEVENTEEN

I watched Erin leave and then turned back to the table.

Michael was rubbing his right wrist.

"Did she just overpower you?" I asked.

"She's a hell of a lot stronger than she looks," said Michael. "She has to be enhanced, and I mean *really* enhanced. I know you didn't think she was in the project with us, but I think she was part of the same project."

"I was just wondering that," I said. "She knows too much, and she *is* enhanced. She has to be."

"We can't keep away from it, can we?" said Marie. She didn't sound angry, as I'd expected, only sad. "I don't remember anyone there who looked like her, but there could have been multiple groups of kids. She might be younger than us. I can tell you that there's something very strange about her. She doesn't read like a normal person, in her aura."

"Do *we* read as normal people?" I asked.

Marie smiled. "No, we don't."

"I don't think she's actually DHS," said Michael. "What did she tell you? That she was an interested third party?"

"Yes. I'm inclined to believe her at this point," I said. "We now know she's enhanced. She also really seems to want to be a part of this investigation. She must know more."

"That was a pretty effective demonstration. She couldn't have faked that."

"Are you okay?"

"I'll probably have bruises, but yeah, I'm okay. I wouldn't want to get into a fist fight with her."

"She's that strong?"

"You saw," Michael said. "I was actively resisting. She moved my arm almost casually."

"Well, we all have different gifts," said Marie. "I wonder what else she can do."

"I'm not sure I want to find out," I said.

"I suppose you'd better tell me what you know about this Project Wormwood."

"We don't actually know much of anything," Michael said. "We think it may have been based out of the air station at Angel Fire."

"That's only about twenty minutes to the east," said Marie. "We could go take a look around."

"I'd love to," I said, "but I have some work to do. I did agree to work with the FBI, and they're paying me a lot of money to consult on this case. When that kind of money is thrown around, the FBI is going to expect results, and quickly."

"How much do they pay you?" Marie asked. "Out of curiosity."

"I'm normally paid fifty dollars an hour to consult," I said. "They offered me three times that for this case, which means they're desperate and will expect the impossible from me."

"Damn," said Marie. "I went into the wrong line of work."

"You seem to be doing well for yourself," I said. "Money isn't everything."

"Ah, the common platitude of those who have enough of it," Marie snapped. "Sorry, I didn't mean that. It's not your fault. Money has been tight most of my life. I've never known much comfort. Even now, the gallery mostly stays open because of donations and government grants."

"I'm sorry. I'm sure Michael would help. Hell, I can give you—"

"I'm not looking for a handout," she interrupted.

Michael looked uncomfortable. I didn't blame him.

"Then what are you looking for?" I asked.

"I love doing my art," said Marie. "I hate selling it, though. Making art for money just feels wrong somehow."

"We all have to pay the bills. I'd love to do something that didn't involve looking at dead bodies all the time."

"I understand, but talking to you, I keep thinking that I should be doing something else. I'm forty-three years old, and I don't have any retirement plans. I barely have any savings. When I heard about what you do, I thought I could do that, too."

"I have a Ph.D. in forensic anthropology," I said. "It took me years of study, a lot of student debt, and years of working in the field before I could work as a consultant. I had to prove myself before I could make this kind of salary."

"Well, it was just an idea."

"I've been meaning to bring this up for a while now," said Michael. "I've been thinking about going into business for myself. Why share the money with the CRI?"

"I've been thinking the same thing," I said. "We've got the credentials and experience to pull it off."

"I still don't have any of those things," said Marie. "Sorry. I don't mean to sound sorry for myself. I've got a decent enough life here. I just don't see doing it forever. The art market is hard."

"Well, I was going to ask you about that," I said. Michael smiled and nodded. "I don't know how long this case is going to take, but these things can take months. If we're going to make any progress, I'm going to need some local help."

"What do you mean?"

"I was wondering if you'd be interested in being a guide. To be honest, I wouldn't mind having your insights into the case. I've asked Michael to help, too."

"I'd be glad to help as much as I can. I have to be at the gallery most days, though."

"I was hoping I could make it worth your while to take some time off."

"I'm sure Consuela could cover for you," said Michael.

"So, to be clear, you're offering to pay me?" Marie asked. "You know I'd be willing to help without pay."

"I'm offering to pay, and I have the money. With the possibility of a partnership when we go into business for ourselves," I said. "It wouldn't be a huge amount. I'm offering you a standard consulting fee of fifty an hour, eight hours a day, every day, until this case is solved."

"No offense, but that seems like a lot of money to me," said Marie. "If this goes on for a couple of months, I'll make as much as I do at the gallery in a year."

"Paranormal investigators don't come cheap," Michael said.

"Are you suggesting *I'm* paranormal, or that I'll be investigating the paranormal?"

"Both," Michael and I said together.

The waiter chose just then to stop by the table and ask if we were ready for dessert. I thought the man was joking. I couldn't have eaten anything else if someone had been holding a gun to my head. We got to-go boxes while Michael settled the check, adding Erin's appetizer into our bill.

He added her twenty to the tip he left.

CHAPTER EIGHTEEN

Going out for lunch had been stranger and more interesting than I expected.

Erin was an unknown factor, but despite her overpowering Michael, I still trusted her. Hell, maybe I trusted her more *because* she was like us. I couldn't see someone enhanced working directly for Henderson at Homeland Security.

I was inclined to believe that Erin really was just an interested third party.

I'd have given a lot to know more about her, though.

"Where to now?" I asked as we settled into my Jeep.

"We could head back to my house," said Marie. "I'd like to talk some more about your offer."

"You don't need to get back to the gallery?" Michael asked.

I saw Marie shake her head, in the mirror. "Consuela knows I might not make it back today."

I drove us over to her house. There were four cats waiting for her inside, and I recognized only one of them. I could hear a cat in a litter box, somewhere else in the house.

"How many cats do you have?" Michael asked.

"Don't judge me," said Marie, smiling. "You said yesterday that you had a cat, Michelle?"

"I do – just the one. His name is Samson. He's a little ginger monster."

"What did you do with him when you came out here?" Marie asked. "You didn't kennel him, did you?"

"Gods, no. My friend Jean is watching him. She rents a room from me anyway while she's going to college. She gets along well with Samson, and then he only has to miss me and not his house."

"That's good. I don't trust kennels. Can I get you guys anything to drink?"

"Ugh, I'm too full to think about putting anything in my stomach."

Marie took the leftovers to the kitchen, and I settled onto the couch. A tabby cat came and sat on my leg. I petted the cat; I missed Samson.

Michael sat next to me and looked like he wanted to take a nap. I didn't blame him. I felt that way, too.

Marie came back and sat across from us. "So what's the deal with Erin?"

"I wish we knew," I said.

"You don't know anything?"

"No more than you do."

"And Project Wormwood?"

"It may have been based at Angel Fire and may have something to do with what was done to us."

"I moved all the way out here and still didn't get away from the project?" Marie shook her head in apparent disgust. "That isn't what you've been hired to investigate, is it?"

"No. The FBI is investigating the murders of the couple you mentioned yesterday. They were the fourth and fifth people found like that in the area, in the last year."

"Shit. Really?"

"The case files are back in our hotel room. The pictures are rather difficult to look at."

"I can imagine," said Marie. "What is it you need me for?"

"Michael is a federal marshal, and I'm a consultant for the FBI. Neither of us is from around here, and somehow I don't think people are going to want to talk to us."

"You understand small town mentalities well."

"The culture might be different from the one in Kentucky, but people are people."

"So you need me to talk to people and guide you around. That's a lot of money for something I'd do for free."

"That's is not a very good bargaining position," said Michael.

I'd thought he was asleep.

"You're one to talk, Michael," I said. "You were talking about taking the case pro bono."

"That was before you said they'd offered to pay."

"I think I'd feel bad taking you money," said Marie.

"Look, the FBI is giving me more money than I usually ask for. Not to mention that I could really use your help. I'll feel a lot better about using up all your time if you let me pay you."

"I don't know."

"Don't worry, you'll earn it. Working a case like this isn't easy. There could also be some danger."

"All right, yeah, I'll do it."

I was sincerely glad. Not just because I needed her as a guide, either. With her around more, I was sure she and Michael would start getting along better. I was also beginning to think of Marie as a friend. I don't have many of those.

It would be nice to have someone to talk to again.

We stayed for a while, talking about our interests and hobbies. Michael and Marie had been separated for a long time; they needed the time together to catch up and get to know each other again. I was glad to be a part of that.

As the afternoon wound down, I starting thinking about the hotel room. Lunch was sitting on me and pulling my eyelids down. I was ready to go back to my room and put the case away. I didn't even care about dinner. I just wanted to sleep.

I didn't get the chance.

CHAPTER NINETEEN

Agent Oliver called while I was still nodding off in Marie's living room. There'd been a new development in the case, and Oliver gave me GPS coordinates to meet him to the east of Taos. That could only mean that another body had been found. The photographs were bad enough; I wasn't looking forward to seeing a mutilated body in person.

I explained to Michael and Marie what was going on.

"Go," Michael said. "I'll stay here and catch up. If necessary, I can walk back to the hotel."

"Or you can crash here for the night," said Marie, "if you don't mind cats."

"Cats are fine. Thanks," Michael said. "I may take you up on it."

"I don't know how long I'll be," I said. "I'll try to call if I'm there too long."

Michael stood and kissed me.

I waved goodbye and went out to my Jeep. I didn't feel sleepy any longer. I wasn't excited by the prospect of another body, but I was feeling anticipation. I felt that what I would discover tonight could be important to the case.

The app on my phone said the GPS coordinates were to the southeast, past Angel Fire. The setting sun blazed on the peak of the mountain as I drove east. I could see why the mountain had made an impression on people: it was beautiful.

I turned off Highway 64 onto New Mexico 434, imaginatively named Mountain View Boulevard. The road took me past the Colfax County Angel Fire Airport, and I felt a chill sense of foreboding work its way down my spine. Project Wormwood had been based at the air station, whatever Project Wormwood had been.

The highway wound through the mountains. Signs by the road pointed to dozens of lodges and resorts. I could see the impact tourism had on the small town. How ever much people might loathe tourists, the influx of people drove the economy in Taos and Angel Fire.

Driving that lonely highway, I felt as if hours had gone by, but my phone said it was barely half an hour since I'd passed the airport. I turned onto NM 120 toward Ocate. Agent Oliver wanted me to meet him a few miles north of that small town, by the highway.

I wished it was daylight. What little I could see of the mountains looked very pretty. On the other hand, I hoped I wouldn't be out all night. These roads were as crooked as anything in Kentucky. I didn't want to drive them when exhausted.

Maybe forty-five minutes later, I came around a curve and saw the flashing lights ahead of me. There were a lot of them. More than I'd expected. Nothing really ever happens in small towns, and local police and sheriffs always show up in droves to crime scenes. I think it makes them feel useful.

I didn't have my FBI ID card yet. I hoped that wouldn't be a problem. The state police must have been given my name and a description, though, since they waved me through after checking my driver's license. Now I was glad I was still wearing my suit. I left my pistol in the glove box. I wouldn't need it, and I really didn't need to be harassed about it.

The state police must have radioed ahead, because Agent Oliver met me by my car. "As you probably guessed, we've got another body," said Oliver. "It's fresh – my guess is no more than a day old. I've kept the forensics team back. I wanted you to see the crime scene unaltered."

"I appreciate that," I said. I had to raise my voice so he'd hear me over the sound of the generators powering the floodlights.

I got my small forensics kit out of the back of the Jeep. Rubber gloves dry out my hands, but so does washing my hands a hundred times to get the feel of rotting flesh off my skin. I'd rather put up with the gloves.

"We're too high for rattlesnakes here," said Oliver, "so at least there's that."

"It gets too cold at night," I replied absently.

It was colder than I'd expected. I hadn't brought a jacket with me from Kentucky. I wished I had. I could see snow around us, in areas that were shadowed during the day.

I concentrated on the ground, where my gaze was being drawn. There was only one set of tracks – I assumed from whomever had discovered the body – but the ground *was* disturbed in the area. I stopped and squatted down for a better look.

"Do you have something?" asked Oliver.

"Not sure," I replied. "Is the wind strong here?"

Oliver shrugged. "Not that I know of. At least it hasn't been. What have you got?"

"I think there may have been tracks here, but they're obscured. The whole area is churned up."

"Well, someone had to dump the body. Maybe they swept their tracks."

"Maybe."

The victim was male. Age was difficult to guess, but probably in his twenties. He was heavyset, and bearing the same wounds as the other victims. He was on his back, laid straight, with his hands folded on his chest. There were no visible ligature marks. I got close enough to brush his head and flinched.

He'd been alive and awake as the wounds were inflicted. One theory had been that the wounds were postmortem. I now knew that to be incorrect. He must have been drugged.

"Any traces of drugs in the toxicology reports from the other victims?" I asked.

"I don't think labs were done, given how long the bodies been exposed to the elements and the fact that they'd been exsanguinated."

"Well, we should get toxicology run on this victim, if we can. Maybe a liver biopsy would reveal something."

"You think they were drugged?" said Oliver.

"There are no ligature marks, but the wounds show minor signs of bruising. The victim was unbound but tortured. He had to be drugged."

Oliver nodded. "Makes sense. Why didn't we see the bruising before?"

"The bodies were probably too old," I said. "What little blood was left in their bodies pooled at the bottom."

"Ugh. I hate cases like this. How long have you been doing this, Dr. Fredericks?"

"Too long," I said. "The wounds are definitely cauterized. I can smell that distinct burnt-pork smell of singed human flesh."

"Are you *trying* to make me sick?"

"Not at all." I stepped back from the body. There was something strange about it: it felt greasy, even through my gloves, but didn't leave any residue. "Any identification?"

"No, it's the same as the others. We'll have to wait for the dental records search to come through. That or the fingerprints."

"Who found him?"

"A Mr. Martinez. Lives in Ocate, just down the road. He saw some coyotes acting funny, walking around in circles, shaking their heads. Got out his binoculars and saw the body from the road. Said he came down to check it out, took one look, and ran back to the highway. Called the local sheriff from his car."

"That's strange," I said. "The body hasn't been scavenged. None of the other bodies had been, either."

"Yeah, you'd think if the coyotes were sniffing around, they'd have chewed on the body."

"You mentioned some of the other bodies being found because of vultures, but they didn't show signs of pecking."

I stepped a little farther back from the body. "I don't suppose you have a Geiger counter."

Oliver shook his head. "You're serious?"

"The body should have been chewed on, but it isn't. There's no smell of decay. The other bodies didn't look as if they'd rotted, just desiccated in the dry air. Trust me, I'm hoping I'm wrong."

"I don't have one, but I can ask around."

One of the deputy sheriffs was an amateur geologist; she had a Geiger counter at home. I backed a little farther away from the body while were waited for the sheriff's husband to bring her the Geiger counter. It took about an hour.

I was feeling a little queasy and trying to ignore it.

"I'm Deputy Garcia," the woman said as she walked over to us. "What do you need a Geiger counter for?"

"Just a hunch," I said. "I hope I'm wrong. Can you set it to detect a radiation source and strength?"

"That is what it's for," said Garcia. "You looking for background, or something stronger?"

"Stronger. Set it to detect gamma radiation."

Garcia shrugged and clicked a dial on the front of the device.

It started ticking rapidly.

Garcia frowned and tapped the side of the Geiger counter. "This can't be right."

"What does it say, deputy?" asked Oliver.

"I think it's broken. This thing is reading around a hundred."

That was high but not lethal. "Point it at the body," I said.

It started ticking even faster.

"One seventy, one ninety, two twenty, three—"

"Get back to the road," I ordered.

I hoped it wasn't too late.

CHAPTER TWENTY

I was definitely feeling nauseated, and I didn't think it was from stress.

"What's going on?" asked Oliver.

"The body is radioactive," I said. "You need a containment team here STAT."

"Oh, shit," said Garcia. She looked pale.

"You're sure?" said Oliver.

"I'm sure. We're going to need containment, and also a medical team. I'm feeling nauseated, and I suspect you are, too. Anyone who got within twenty feet of the victim should be checked out. We'll need to round up the guy who found the body. Radiation danger is cumulative, based on how long you're near the source. We weren't near it long enough. At least, I hope we weren't."

The closest radiation response team was at Los Alamos. They flew to our location in helicopters, with a military escort. The troops were in full NBC gear and looked very post-apocalyptic. Tents were set up, and the medical teams began testing us. A captain with a medical insignia gave me a potassium iodide tablet and some water. I wasn't sure it would stay down, but I took the small pill anyway.

I was told to strip and was then scrubbed and hosed down before being taken into a tent for a blood draw and physical exam. I didn't see any of the others as I waited for the doctor. The small space heater did little to warm the tent.

"You're Dr. Fredericks?" a woman said as she bustled into the room. "I'm Dr. Nhung. I understand you recognized the danger. What are you a doctor of? Medical, or something else?"

She was short. I couldn't see much of what she looked like, because she wore a hazmat suit with a bulky hood. Her accent sounded Texan. She had a chart with a lot of pages. She flipped through them too quickly to read, pausing sometimes, then flipping on.

"Nice to meet you," I said. "I'm a doctor of forensic anthropology." I felt a little less sick to my stomach. I hoped that was a good sign.

"I'll tell you right away that you didn't take a lethal dose, but it was close. If you hadn't noticed the signs, you probably would have. Are you ex-military?"

I shook my head; I get asked that a lot. "No."

"All right, let's get you checked out."

Dr. Nhung placed a pulse oximeter on my finger. She listened to my lungs and abdomen with a special stethoscope that plugged into her suit. She shined a light into my eyes, too, although I had no idea what she expected to see there.

"How old are you?" she asked.

"Forty-five – well, I will be in June."

"You're in good shape," she said. "Any health issues? A family history of cancer?"

"No, nothing like that."

"You've got a scar from a gunshot. When were you shot?"

"I've been shot a few times. I'm usually wearing body armor. That time, I wasn't."

I'd been shot in the back a couple of times last winter, but my ballistic Kevlar protected me. The scar was from when I was a teenager, when I was shot trying to escape from the Providence Project. I wondered idly what would happen if I told her that.

"You've had an interesting life, for a forensic anthropologist."

You have no idea, I thought.

"I specialize in occult crime," I said. "It can be difficult to know whether you've found all the cultists, and sometimes I get shot by someone I thought was safe."

Dr. Nhung shook her head. "I just thought most of your line of work was done in a lab."

"I'm more interested in the investigative side."

A tech came in, handed the doctor a printout, and left.

Dr. Nhung nodded, which looked odd in the hazmat suit. "Your lymphocyte count is depressed, which is expected. You blood counts look pretty good, all things considered. Red blood cell count is lower than I'd expect. You're not from around here?"

"I'm from Kentucky."

"The FBI brought you in from Kentucky?"

"No, I was visiting, and they hired me on as a consultant for these murders."

"Oh, that makes more sense. What's the elevation in Kentucky?"

"The part I live in is around a hundred meters above sea level."

"You haven't been here long?"

"No, why?" She was asking a lot of odd questions.

"Your red blood cell count is lower than in someone from this elevation. The body usually adjusts within a couple of weeks. You may feel a little lightheaded, if you exert yourself too much. The amount of available oxygen is much lower at this elevation than you're used to."

"So how bad is this?" I asked. "The radiation, I mean?"

"Well, getting dosed with radiation is never good."

A tech came in; I couldn't tell if it was the same one as before. She had a Geiger counter and checked me over with it. My fillings made it tick a little higher. Otherwise, the device didn't sound too bad. I say this as if I have any idea what's normal on one of the things.

Dr. Nhung removed her hood. She had some silver in her short, black hair. The tech helped her out of her hazmat suit. She was wearing military fatigues underneath, with colonel's insignia.

"I take it I'm not radiating," I said.

"We never thought you were. I'll give you a card of potassium iodide pills. You should take them every day, although if they cause you gastrointestinal distress, stop taking them."

"Aren't those just for radioactive iodine poisoning?"

"Better to be safe than sorry. We don't know the actual radioactive contaminate yet."

"Right. Okay. What was done with my things?" I asked.

"Your clothes are being destroyed," said Dr. Nhung. "Sorry. Your phone and keys will be returned if they're not radioactive. Neutron activation can make metallic objects radioactive. You weren't near the source for long, though. We *are* going to keep you for a couple of days for observation. Just to be safe."

"Will I need to remain nude the whole time?" I asked.

Dr. Nhung grinned. "We'll get you something to wear before we fly you back to Los Alamos."

"I'll need to make a call," I said. "Also, I should speak to Agent Oliver."

"He said much the same. Oliver will be in the room next to yours in the base hospital, so you can talk to him there. I'll see about getting you a phone. Surely someone around here has one."

"Thanks."

It was almost midnight before someone found me a phone. I called Michael and told him what had happened. He had my spare Jeep key, so he said he'd make arrangements to pick up my Jeep and drive it back to Taos.

I didn't tell him everything; I didn't have to. The fact that the body was radioactive changed everything. I just didn't know in what way. I'd discounted aliens, but radioactive material isn't easy to come by. I didn't know what to think of the radiation at that point, and I was too tired to really care.

This was definitely not the vacation I'd been expecting.

CHAPTER TWENTY-ONE

True to her word, Dr. Nhung put me in a room next to Agent Oliver. The next morning, I tightened up my hospital gown and walked to see him. For the record, I really hate hospital gowns. I know that they're designed to facilitate care of a patient, but that doesn't matter. I don't like wandering around with my ass hanging out.

Oliver was looking rough. They had him on IV fluids, and something else that was milky. He had a grey tinge to his skin and was sweating, despite the cold of the room. He managed a small smile when I knocked and came into his room.

"You look well," he said.

"I feel okay," I replied. I hadn't realized how bad the dose of radiation had been until just then. "You going to make it?"

Oliver laughed a little. "Yeah, I think so. I don't know how I got a worse dose than you, though."

You didn't. I'm a bioengineered super soldier, I thought. "Radiation effects people differently."

"Apparently."

I settled in the chair next to the bed and tried to adjust my gown so I didn't flash anyone – not that Oliver would care. Did I mention that I hate hospital gowns? Yeah. I hate hospitals, too, but that's because I can feel all the misery and sorrow permeating the walls of places like this.

"You up to talking about the case?" I asked.

"Let me check my social calendar," Oliver said. "Yes, looks like I'm clear for today."

I smiled at his attempted levity. "Radioactive material isn't easy to come by. We need to have the body examined to determine the source of the material."

"I'm still hoping it's aliens."

"Why?"

"Outside my jurisdiction."

"Aren't all crimes on American soil in your jurisdiction?"

"Oh, I suppose I could get them on illegal disposal of a corpse. They'll probably just claim diplomatic immunity, though."

"Probably. Doesn't that have to be issued by the State Department, though? I'm smelling a cover-up."

"I wouldn't put anything past the bureaucrats in D.C."

"Can an alien even commit homicide?"

Oliver thought about that one for a few minutes. "The DA would have to be real careful about bringing up charges. Maybe manslaughter?"

"That would probably work."

"I don't think it's aliens," Oliver said after a while.

"Okay, well, if it isn't aliens, what then?"

"Then we hit them with every law we can, from violations of EPA regulations to murder."

"That's better," I said.

"I asked Dr. Nhung to put a team on the investigation of the source. She'd already started looking into it. Right now, we don't even know *how* the body was radioactive, much less why."

"This could be how we catch the scumbag."

"Michelle, I'm scared," Oliver said suddenly. "Cancer runs in my family. It doesn't kill easy. I lost my father to it."

I was thinking about my friend Lawrence's father, who'd just died last Christmas of cancer. His hadn't been an easy death, either. I didn't know what to say, to make Oliver not worry so much. Everything I knew about the Big C wouldn't make Oliver feel any better.

"Dr. Nhung said it wasn't that big a dose," I said. "It was probably just like getting a bunch of x-rays at once. You weren't very close to the body, either. You'll be okay."

"It was a lot higher than that," Dr. Nhung said as she walked in without knocking. "You're correct that distance is a factor, but at heightened risk. You're both in the range of acute radiation sickness. Fredericks, you probably took around four hundred rads. I honestly don't know why you aren't presenting worse symptoms. Your bloodwork was almost normal. Oliver, you took about two hundred rads. Much less. You're outside the risk zone, so at most it only raised your cancer risk factors by about five percent. You'll want to have yearly exams, and have any lumps or spots checked, but you'll almost certainly be fine."

"How long does it take to recover from acute radiation sickness?" I asked. "You seem surprised I'm okay. I suppose four hundred rads is bad, then?"

"It depends on the individual. You both have excellent prognoses. Two hundred rads will make someone feel terrible but isn't really life-threatening."

"And four hundred?" I asked.

"Fifty percent of people dosed at your level die within sixty days," said Dr. Nhung. "However, we think there must have been other factors we don't know about. Despite your physical contact with the source, your symptoms are very mild. Just by bloodwork, I'd guess you got less than a hundred rads, absorbed dose."

"What about my keys and phone?"

"That's how we estimated four hundred rads. Your phone and keys are still hot. We may have to destroy them."

I nodded. "I'll miss my phone, but I can get another one. My boyfriend has copies of my keys. Do what you have to."

"So I should start feeling better soon?" asked Oliver.

"I would say so, yes," Dr. Nhung said. "Your bloodwork has

improved a little. You'll be out of here in less than a week."

"And me?" I asked.

"We want to keep you for a day or two, just to be sure. I've never heard of acute radiation poisoning presenting late, but you never know."

"What's the date today?"

"The fifteenth."

"As long as I'm out of here by the seventeenth," I said. "It's my boyfriend's birthday."

Dr. Nhung chuckled. "Well, I can't recommend you engage in any vigorous physical activity after you're discharged, but you should be good to leave by then."

"We came out here on vacation together to patch things up with his estranged twin sister. I really don't want to miss their birthday."

"You're doing almost miraculously well, under the circumstances. I'll try to have you out of here by tomorrow afternoon, okay?"

"Sounds good."

"What about me?" Oliver asked.

"You're improving. I'd like to keep an eye on you for at least another few days, and you're going to want to take a couple of weeks off work."

I felt a little guilty that I was being cleared so quickly. Oliver was a good man, and here he was, worried about his cancer risks. Here *I* was, taking twice the dose and walking away like nothing had happened.

I felt an absurd impulse to tell him everything and knew I couldn't.

I didn't sleep well that night. Bad dreams.

Dr. Nhung discharged me the next afternoon. I said goodbye to Oliver, promising to keep him informed of any developments, and left for Taos. Dr. Nhung had arranged for a car to take me back, as well as some fatigues and boots for me to wear. They fit me well enough.

My Jeep was outside the hotel room, so I knew Michael was waiting for me. I was glad. I really needed to talk to him. I had come to rely on having him around. I needed that emotional support.

CHAPTER TWENTY-TWO

Michael answered the door on the first knock.

A moment later, he'd drawn me inside, shut the door, and was embracing me tightly. It was almost painful: he's very strong. I didn't mind, though. I'd missed him terribly while I was stuck in the hospital. Since he came back last winter, Michael and I hadn't spent much time apart.

I felt so good just to stand there and be held.

After a few minutes, he pushed me out to arm's length but kept a hold on my shoulders. I knew he was looking at me with more than just his eyes; I could feel the pressure of his regard. Then he sighed and helped me sit down on the bed.

"Do you need anything?" he asked. "Can I get you anything?"

"I'm fine, Michael, really."

"How many rads?"

Michael wasn't the kind of guy who avoided tough questions. "I don't know, exactly. At least four hundred."

He looked concerned. "That's a lot of radiation. I'm surprised they released you from the hospital already. They *did* release you, right?"

"Well, I didn't walk here from Los Alamos."

"I wouldn't put it past you. What did the doctor say about your dose?"

"That I was lucky. The military kept my keys and phone, said they were still hot. From them, they estimated four hundred rads, but my bloodwork showed less than a hundred. Maybe I really did just get lucky."

"Or you have heightened radiation resistance to go with your usual rapid recovery." Michael shook his head. "You need to be more careful."

"And I was to expect the body to be radioactive *why?* None of the other bodies had been radioactive. Of course, they sat in the desert longer."

Michael nodded. "Okay, fair point. I guess you got lucky. How did you know the body was radioactive?"

"I didn't, really. I suspected it might be. None of the bodies had been eaten by scavengers. Also, I felt ill. There was something greasy feeling about the corpse that didn't have anything to do with decomposition. Someone had a Geiger counter, and we were off."

"Well, do more careful next time, please."

"State police and local law enforcement have been informed. The next time they find a body, it will be much different. Trust me."

"I hope you'll be more careful, too," Michael said.

I just glared at him.

"Okay! I'll drop the subject. What can I do for you?"

"I need a shower. After that, I'd like to get a new phone, and then some food. How is Marie doing?"

"She's well. We had lunch together the last two days. Dinner last night. I think things are going to be okay between us. She wanted to look over the files about the murders, but I wanted to wait for you before agreeing to let her see them."

"Gruesome stuff," I replied.

Michael shrugged.

I knew what he meant. We'd all seen worse, even Marie.

I felt much better after getting cleaned up and dressed in my own clothes. That hospital soap had left my hair and skin feeling dry. Michael was more than happy to help me with lotion after my shower.

I had to restrain myself from jumping him, although my brush with death had left me wanting him even more than usual. I was, however, feeling a little weak.

There was no Apple store in Taos, so I bought an iPhone at Walmart and used my laptop to set it up. Fortunately, I back up my phone often, so I didn't lose anything. I was mostly worried about my contact list. I can't remember more than a couple of phone numbers. I texted everyone to let them know my new number.

Marie gave me a hug when we picked her up for dinner.

"You're sure you're all right?" she asked.

"As sure as I can be," I said. "I was cleared by the military doctor at the hospital."

"It's just so crazy. Taos is usually a quiet little town without much crime."

We ordered drinks and appetizers. I dug into the chips and salsa while we waited. I was hungry. The hospital food hadn't been very good or particularly calorie-heavy. I eat more than a normal woman; I think it's the enhanced metabolism. I'd have starved if I'd been stuck in that hospital much longer. As it was, I'd lost enough weight for my clothes to feel loose.

"You guys figure anything out about Wormwood?" I asked. "No offense, but I'd rather talk about that instead of my time in the hospital or what put me there. I'm still processing it all."

"We didn't have a lot of time to look," said Michael, "and I was a bit distracted, worrying about you."

"Has the enigmatic Erin put in another appearance?"

"Fortunately, no."

Marie chuckled. "I kind of liked her."

"You would," said Michael. "I don't like that her story doesn't add up. She's enhanced, but from what project? Not Providence, I think. I'm strong, but she was beyond me. I still have bruises."

"I'm going to have a talk with her," I said. "No one gets to bruise you but me."

"All joking aside, could she be from our project?"

I glanced at Marie. I remembered she didn't like talking about it. "Maybe we should shelve the conversation until we know more."

"It's okay," Marie said. "Kind of funny, actually. I went years without even thinking about this stuff, and now here we are. The last few days, I have trouble *not* thinking about the project. You told me about Julia and Victor, but what about the other kids who survived?"

I shook my head. "We recovered a lot of documents from Julia, but they were encrypted. My friend Lawrence works on them sometimes, as a side project. I don't know if he ever got any names. We haven't talked about it in a while. He was kind of busy over the holidays."

"I was just wondering about Amy," said Marie. "She wasn't anything like her sister."

I glanced at Michael; he shook his head. "I don't remember an Amy. Whose sister?"

"Amy was Julia's twin sister," Marie replied. "Fraternal, I think. Her hair was lighter, almost white like mine is now, but she looked a lot like Julia. She was an empath, like me, and suffered in the project until she was rejected and sent home. I liked her."

"I'm sorry," Michael said. "There wasn't a mention of a sister in Julia's file with the Federal Marshals Service. Which is odd, because that's exactly where that kind of information should have been."

"Do you think she'd still live in Pikeville?" I asked. "Like Victor did?"

"I don't think so. It isn't a very big town, and if I'd seen someone who looked like Julia, I'd have reacted badly."

"Yeah, me, too."

My memories of the project aren't very clear. Most of what I remember is from dreams, which may or may not be completely accurate. It doesn't help that we were just kids – young teenagers – when all that happened.

I hadn't gotten any hint from Julia or Victor that Amy existed. Granted, both of them had been rather focused on killing me. If Amy was still alive, I don't think she'd had anything to do with her brother and sister for a long time.

I hoped she wasn't the revenge-seeking type.

CHAPTER TWENTY-THREE

I wasn't disappointed that we didn't talk about Julia any more at dinner. She wasn't my favorite topic of conversation. Not just because she had tried to kill me, but because she was an unknown factor, still out there somewhere. I also couldn't decide how I felt about her, and I had no idea how she felt about me now. She'd tried to kill me the last time I'd seen her, but she hadn't tried again, and she could have.

I didn't agree with Julia's actions, but I could sympathize with her anger.

I think that maybe if I could tell her that, it might help.

Instead of talking more about Julia, Marie told us about her own life. It hadn't been great. When she was younger, she had been in and out of the hospital, as money and insurance permitted. No one believed her about the project; doctors said she was delusional but not a threat to herself or others. The psychiatrists lost interest in her after that.

She tried medications. Nothing worked. It wasn't until she accepted as fact what had happened that she was able to move on with her life. I felt bad for her and what she'd been through. We'd all been tortured as children, but at least Michael and I couldn't remember much of it.

I've had nightmares almost all of my life from my suppressed memories of the project. I couldn't imagine having all that in my head all the time, though. It would have driven me even crazier than I already am. That isn't even counting the frustration of knowing that what happened in the project was real, and no one else believing it, not even her own twin brother.

I sighed and knocked back the rest of my drink.

"Are you really doing okay?" asked Marie.

I shrugged. "Somehow, I either didn't get as big a dose of radiation as the two people with me, or I'm more resistant to it. In any case, other than being poked and prodded by doctors, the whole thing wasn't all that bad. It was scary, but no, I'm fine."

"I suppose it makes a certain kind of sense. The project seemed to be about making super soldiers. We wouldn't be super without some radiation resistance."

"I don't know about all of that," said Michael. "Wormwood was run by the Air Force. Providence seemed to have something to do with remote viewing. That machine –"

"Yeah, we don't need to talk about that," I said. "You might not remember much of the stuff with the machine, but I do."

"What about that project your friend was a part of?" asked Marie.

"Brimstone?" Michael said. "It was focused on rapid transit, like Wormwood."

"I know you have reservations about trusting Erin," I said. "So do I, but I'm inclined to believe her. She said the projects were related. I'd really like to ask her more about what she knows."

Michael nodded. "She appears to know enough for me not to doubt her. Project Absolution is probably the key to all of this. Whatever that was."

"I don't think Providence was the original project," said Marie. "When we were little, different doctors were involved. There were tests, medical and otherwise, and I remember training with weapons and unarmed combat, but they didn't begin to get mean until we were teens. Before, we were in a barracks, sort of like camp. Later, we were in cages in a hospital."

"I remember that," I said. "I think you're right. Maybe we were part of Project Absolution, and later pawned off to Project Providence. I've read that projects often get passed around, following the funding."

Michael shrugged. "We could speculate all night."

I think it annoyed him that Marie and I could remember something he couldn't.

"The names bug me," said Marie. "Can we infer anything from those?"

"No," Michael said. "Project names are chosen to fulfil a generic requirement from the Pentagon having to do with the year and a letter of the alphabet. If you can figure out what the project was about from the name, it isn't a very good name."

"Okay, but why the biblical angle?" she asked.

"What do you mean?"

"Wormwood was a place in the Bible, or something, wasn't it?"

"Wormwood was a star that fell to Earth and poisoned the waters," I said. "From *Revelations*. I don't see how that can connect to a project about rapid transport of personnel."

"Still, Wormwood, Absolution, Brimstone, Providence: You don't see those as connected?" Marie insisted. "Providence, the all-seeing eye? A project about remote-viewing? Maybe I *am* crazy, but the names seem related."

"I've found that in some cases, a special project name makes sense if you know the context of the project, but you can't guess otherwise. Who would automatically think of a project about remote viewing? You know, it could just be that the person handing out names thought it would be funny," I said, "since Project Wormwood was at Angel Fire."

Marie shook her head. "I don't think so. In fact, it's another point in my favor."

After that, we talked about other stuff until the restaurant closed.

Michael paid the bill, and we dropped Marie off at her house on the way to the hotel.

She'd invited us in, but I was too tired to socialize. I may not have been suffering most of the effects of radiation sickness, but I had taken a large dose and didn't feel one hundred percent yet. I just wanted to sleep for a week.

Michael had other ideas.

Sadly, not the kind that involved making the bed squeak.

"Have you thought about what you're going to do?" he said.

"About what?"

"Are you going to stay on the case?"

I sighed. "Yeah. If nothing else, because I want to get the bastard who tried to kill me."

"I'd like to get ahold of him, too," Michael said. "How's your FBI friend?"

"Oliver? Hanging in there. He took the dose harder than I did."

"Well, he's only human."

I chuckled.

"I think I need to stay on the case," I said. "I'm scared, because someone crazy enough to cover a body with radioactive material is going to be unpredictable."

"I assume you've ruled out aliens?"

"Yeah, I think we can safely rule out little green men. Unless you know something I don't?"

Michael shook his head. "I've heard rumors, of course. A place in Utah where they keep alien detainees, crashed spaceships, monsters, the usual crap. If I had anything like actual information, I'd tell you."

"Well, I guess in a way, we do know about some aliens," I said.

"What do you mean?"

"You told me your friend Harrison said Brimstone was about stopping an invasion from another universe. That sounds like aliens."

"The other people were human."

"As far as we know."

INTERLUDE

I sometimes think we're being tested to destruction.

Maybe to the doctors, we're just rats to be experimented on. I'm not even certain where I learned of the concept. I just know many of us children have died. Not just from the vigorous military training or the injections, either. Many of us have died from the tests given.

The medical examinations are constant.

They take blood and tissue samples. They record how long it takes for us to recover from injuries. If we're not injured enough in training, they break us. It is surgical, precise, and done without any emotion.

These doctors are different from previous summers. They seem excited to get their hands on us. It disgusts me to be touched by them. Not because they want anything gross from me, like some of the old guards did, no, but because they want to hurt me and watch to see what happens.

A man comes into the classroom. He wears a silver suit that covers him completely. We learned about those suits; they're for protection from radiation. The dark glass of his helmet shows little, but I can tell he's excited.

He has a large, heavy box.

I try to leave but am beaten. Not enough to send me to the infirmary, but enough to make me decide not to try again. I don't want to know why he's wearing that suit, but I suspect it won't be long before I find out.

The man makes a great production of opening the box.

Nothing happens.

At least at first.

The man in the silver suit sits and takes notes. He glances at a badge on his suit that is slowly changing colors. I know it's a dosimeter. We learned about those during our classes on sabotaging enemy nuclear power plants.

My pulse quickens.

I feel panicked. I don't want to be here. Not that I have any choice. I never want to be in this place, but they bring me back every year anyway.

I start to feel lightheaded and queasy.

Across the classroom, someone else is noisily sick.

I understand what this is. I remember learning about it. I just don't understand why they're doing this to us. I never understand any of what they do, though.

My desk feels greasy.

I stand and stumble away from the man and the box.

Someone yells at me over the room intercom.

I ignore them. They aren't going to come into the room and make me sit back down. They aren't going to risk themself. I wonder absently why the man in the suit does it. What does he hope to get out of it? Maybe he's terminal anyway, so he doesn't care about the radiation. Maybe they didn't tell him that the suits aren't perfect.

I try to move toward the man, to put a stop to this.

I can't. I'm weak. My legs give out, and I fall. My guts feel watery, and it's all I can do to hold it in. From the sounds and the smell, others around the room have been unable to hold back. I think the radiation is killing off our gut fauna. We learned about that, too.

The tall, red-haired boy Michael stands up.

He sways and looks as bad as I feel. He begins walking, leaning forward, as if there's a strong wind. There's a lot of shouting over the intercom. Michael doesn't care about that. He's focused on the man in the silvery suit.

The man doesn't look scared until Michael lunges forward and grabs him. They struggle. Michael pulls the helmet from the man and forces his head down into the box. The man is screaming, but no one is going to come save him. I can see the glass in his dosimeter. We've all taken a lethal dose.

Michael shoves the limp man away and closes the box. His hands are shaking. Neurological effects are stage two. Michael must have taken a stronger dose, that near to the box. He collapses. Our eyes meet.

At least we'll die together.

I wish I could hold his hand, but I can't move.

I know it'll be at least forty-eight hours before the radiation fades from the room. Surely we'll be dead by then. I hope so, anyway. I don't want to do this anymore.

CHAPTER TWENTY-FOUR

My phone woke me up way too early the next morning.

I heard Michael in the shower and wished I was in there with him. I was in the mood but still didn't feel all that great. I think some part of me was hoping that if we made love, I'd feel better. That part of me wasn't what hurt, though.

How was it that I was okay? I didn't know. Yeah, I felt a little weak. What I was feeling had little to do with the radiation. I was tired of all the death. Bad thing to feel in my profession, I know.

The phone started a new cycle of buzzing.

I grabbed it before it could vibrate off the night stand. "This is Fredericks. What do you want?"

"My, aren't you testy. Someone hasn't had any coffee yet."

"Taylor?"

"Still sharp as ever, I see. What are you doing?"

"Right now? Lying in bed. I had been sleeping. I'd like to go back to that."

Michael chose that moment to come out of the bathroom with only a towel around his hips, and I really didn't want to get out of bed, and not to sleep. In fact, I was suddenly thinking about anything other than the person on the phone. Michael grinned and began dressing. It was extremely distracting.

Taylor cleared her throat. "Wake up, Fredericks."

"I am awake."

"Well, then, get your ass out of bed and come pick me up."

"Taylor, I'm in New Mexico."

"Yeah, no shit. That's why I'm here, too."

"What? Where?"

"I just caught a puddle-jumper from Albuquerque to the airfield at Angel Fire. Figured I'd wait to call you until I arrived. You're bad enough at eight. I'd hate to think what you'd be like earlier in the morning."

"What are you doing here?"

"Trying to keep your sorry ass alive," said Taylor. "Are you going to come pick me up or not?"

"You don't have a car?"

"They're driving me one up from the field office. Sometime this week. There isn't a car rental at this poor excuse for an airport, either."

"I'm in Taos," I said. "About an hour away."

"Fucking hell," Taylor muttered. "I guess I'll try to find some coffee here, then. You coming?"

"Okay, I'll be there ASAP." I ended the call and lay back down.

"What's going on?" asked Michael. "Not another body?"

I shook my head. "No. Taylor just flew into Angel Fire airport."

"Special Agent Taylor?"

"How many Taylors do you think I know?" I said. "Sorry. I'm going to pick her up."

"I planned to meet with Marie this morning. Unless you need me to come along."

"I'll be fine. It's a short trip, and I can catch up a bit with Taylor."

"Are you going to tell her about the projects?"

"I might as well. She already knows about Providence. Want me to drop you off at the gallery?"

"No, I'll walk. The weather here is great."

"It's a little dry for my taste."

"Well, at least it's sunny," Michael said. He kissed me and left.

I took a quick shower and dressed. I was going to have to buy more clothes if I'd be staying in Taos for a while. I brought only enough for a week, and the clothes I'd worn to the crime scene had been confiscated and destroyed. Not that I wanted them back after having been irradiated.

There was very little traffic as I left Taos, and none of it headed to Angel Fire.

Michael was right: the weather was great. The morning was sunny and the temperature mild. The last time I'd driven to Angel Fire, the mountains had been bathed in the sanguine light of the setting sun. It looked different in morning light. Gone were the bloody hues and ominous lighting. I sort of missed the red, but the mountains were still beautiful. The landscape, not the resort town. The town was built for tourists, and signs and billboards everywhere advertised the resorts and lodges.

It wasn't my kind of place.

At first, I didn't psychically feel much of anything as I approached the airport. The constant exchange of tourists overwhelmed any subtle traces that might have remained from something decades before. As I closed in on the town, I could sense there was something odd about Angel Fire. A strange tension was building, combined with a sense that I was going to discover more in that town than I wanted to know.

It also felt as if something was waiting. For what, I couldn't say, but it fueled that tension in the air. The world felt *thin*. Maybe it was just the altitude.

I didn't really believe that, though.

I've felt places where the world was thin, places where spirits and demons lurked, usually places where something horrible had happened. Why a place like Angel Fire would feel that way, I couldn't say. My discomfort grew, the closer I got to the airport. Something was wrong with the world here. It sounded crazy, even to me, but I didn't want to get any closer to that airport.

I usually trust my feelings and intuitions, but in spite of that, I gritted my teeth and turned in to the airport. The Colfax County Angel

Fire Airport wasn't much to look at. Fences surrounded the two long landing strips. There was just one major building: a hanger. Taylor waited under the awning at the front of the building with a couple of bags.

She looked tired and more than a little irritated.

Taylor waved and dropped her bags in the back seat before getting in.

"Thanks for coming and picking me up," she said. "Typical bureaucratic mix-up and delay. The local FBI office claimed they hadn't known I was flying out. That's bullshit."

"It's good to see you, Taylor, and I don't mind giving you a lift. I wanted to see this place anyway."

"This airport?" Taylor asked critically.

"There's something strange here."

"Yeah, not a concession stand in sight. No place to even get coffee. It should be illegal."

"Not that. I… I don't know."

"All right, cut the bullshit. I know you too well. What's interesting about this place? And don't say the damn scenery."

I sighed. "There's something weird going on out here, Taylor."

"You mean other than impossibly mutilated, radioactive bodies?"

"Yeah, other than that. I don't know if it's connected to the bodies."

"You going to tell me about it?"

"Working up to it. Let's get a little distance from the airport, though. I don't like how this place feels."

"You are so damn strange," said Taylor. "If you weren't so damn good at your job, I'd think you were crazy."

I laughed. "I *am* crazy, Taylor. You know that."

"Yeah, okay. So talk."

I told her about Erin, and about the projects.

Taylor kept rubbing her eyes and face as we talked. I don't think she'd gotten much sleep. Jet lag is a killer. It's one reason I drove out to New Mexico instead of flying. Not to mention that the secret fears of a plane-full of people tend to be overwhelming on flights.

Being psychic isn't much fun most of the time.

CHAPTER TWENTY-FIVE

Taylor and I stopped at the edge of town for breakfast at a little greasy-spoon diner. It reminded me of the Windmill Café in Pikeville. Taylor and I had often breakfasted there, during the case with the occult murders over the winter. We had become friends over those meals.

"Okay," Taylor said after she sipped her coffee, "I feel a little more human now. Tell me about this Erin person."

"Not sure what to tell you about her. I don't know much. She's a little taller than you, and lightly built. Hispanic, I think. She has shoulder-length, black hair, dark brown eyes, and an oval face. She's attractive, but not so much as to turn many heads."

"Accent?"

"Nothing I could identify."

"Hmm. Any *other* observations?" Taylor asked.

"What do you mean?"

"You didn't try your psychic whammy on her?"

I laughed. "No, it doesn't really work like that."

"It worked on that preacher last winter."

"Yeah, but I touched him, and his guard was down. The circumstances were different. I don't think I'd get anything from Erin, and I'm not sure I'd be able to handle it if I did."

"Sounds like she has you spooked."

"She isn't normal, Taylor."

"You're not so normal, yourself."

"Maybe, but Michael tried to hold her at the table, the last time she showed up. She overpowered him. Think about that."

"I am, and I'm trying not to giggle."

"I'm serious."

"When am I not serious? Okay, so she's strong. So are you. A lot stronger than you look. I've seen you pick up a man bigger than you."

"Michael is strong, too," I said. "He's much stronger than me. Erin didn't look like it took any effort."

"She seem angry? Drugged? PCP, maybe?"

"No, nothing like that."

"I don't know, then. I don't know as much about these project things as you and Michael anyway. They're classified way above my pay grade. So high I'm not even supposed to know they exist, much less any of the details."

"That was the weird thing for me: Erin's knowledge of the projects. She knows stuff about them that we didn't. At least she's hinted as much. Given what she did tell me, I'm inclined to believe her."

"Her knowledge was the weird part? You mean you didn't think her super strength was weird?"

"No, there are probably a lot of different super soldier projects. She could just be from one of those, or even a later version of the one I was part of."

"Now, *that's* a scary thought."

The waitress brought our huevos rancheros, and we didn't say much for a while. The food was really good, as all of it had been in town. I'd be tempted to move to New Mexico just for the food. At least the food in Taos. I don't think I could have eaten in Angel Fire.

"So you were getting twitchy at the airport because you think this Project Wormwood was based out of there?"

"Not exactly," I said. "It's hard to explain. I just didn't like the feeling of the place, mainly."

"You're just full of useful insight."

I sighed. "Look, I don't know how to explain it. The area around the airport felt just *wrong* to me."

"Well, I guess we'll just go with that for my report. They'll love that in Washington."

Taylor has a rather dry sense of humor.

"Not that I mind seeing you again, but what are you doing out here, Taylor?"

"I heard about what happened."

"Keeping tabs on me?"

"Believe it or not, one of our agents getting dosed with radiation while on a murder investigation is not a common thing. It was talked about around the office. Your name came up. Since I'm a special agent, I get to choose the cases I take – to some degree, at least. I reached out to the local field office, and they accepted my offer of assistance. I don't think any of them were looking forward to stepping up to the plate after Agent Oliver got irradiated. Not to mention the scrutiny this case is getting from Washington."

"Do you know Agent Oliver?"

"No, why would I?"

"Just curious. We hadn't worked together long, but we got along okay. He's a good person. I think we could be friends."

"Now you're just trying to make me jealous," said Taylor.

"Taylor, you know I'm glad you're here."

Taylor yawned and nodded. "I'm not sure I am. Damn, I'm jetlagged. Okay, so why are *you* out here? You didn't come out here just for this job."

"Michael's sister lives here."

"Okay. You just decided to take a job out here while on vacation?"

"The FBI made me a very good offer: three times my normal fee."

"I really am in the wrong line of work," said Taylor. "You'll make more on this one job than I do in a year."

"So hang out a shingle and go into business for yourself. The private sector is where the money is. You know that."

"I don't have the same skillset as you. Besides, I like the idea of a government pension. The benefits are good, too."

"Yeah, I don't have any benefits with my job."

"I hope you have health insurance, at least."

"I have to buy my own."

"That sucks."

"Where are you staying?" I asked.

"Haven't gotten a place yet. Where are you staying?"

"Just up the road. It isn't too expensive."

"I imagine the FBI would spring for it even if it was. This case is really high-profile. Other than almost dying, have you made any progress? Have any leads?"

"I'm not sure almost dying counts as progress," I said. "I have a few tentative leads. Have you seen the case files?"

"Just a bad fax."

"My copies of the files are back at the hotel."

"Okay, let's go and get me a room. Let me take a shower and get some more coffee, and I'll have a look at the files." Taylor yawned again.

"Are you okay?" I asked.

"I'm damn tired."

"Cincinnati is only two hours' difference in time zone."

"I've been traveling for hours," Taylor said. "Last-minute flight, so two transfers, with two layovers. I've been on the road for nine hours. No sleep last night at all."

"You didn't sleep on the plane?"

"I don't like to fly."

"Fair enough."

It wasn't peak tourist season yet, so the hotel still had plenty of rooms vacant. Taylor got a room close enough to mine to visit easily, but not so close that Michael and I would have to worry about being quiet when I was feeling better.

Taylor is considerate that way.

CHAPTER TWENTY-SIX

Taylor knocked on my door about forty-five minutes after I dropped her off at her room.

She looked considerably refreshed. Her black hair was still damp, and she was holding a large, steaming paper cup of coffee. I could still see lines of a fatigue around her eyes, though.

"What have we got, Fredericks?"

We sat at the small table, and I dug the files out of the drawer. Taylor spent some time reading over the case notes and studying the pictures, jotting notes on a small pad. I couldn't decipher her handwriting without staring, so I didn't try. She'd talk when she was ready.

"Gruesome stuff," Taylor said finally.

"I've seen worse."

"I'm sure. By the way, I passed on the tip about possible cult activity related to the River Murders case."

"Thanks. Forester was trying to say something to me, that last day in the courtroom. There were also several people watching us and acting weird."

"Did you really kill the prick right there in a court room?" she asked, chuckling.

I sighed. "He attacked me. I didn't have much choice."

Taylor shook her head. "Kill anyone here yet?"

"Hey! I thought you were on my side."

"I am, and you haven't answered my question."

"No, Taylor, I haven't killed anyone here. Haven't even felt the urge. Now, of course, if I get my hands on the murderer who tried to poison me with radiation…"

"I think everyone is gunning for that bastard," Taylor said. "Assuming there is one."

"What do you mean?"

"You're not the slightest bit tempted to think about aliens?"

I recalled what Michael had told me about the invasion from another universe. It seemed too unreal, and yet I didn't doubt it happened. I wasn't sure soldiers from another universe counted as aliens, though. Nor did I think they had anything to do with these murders.

"You still with me, Fredericks?"

"Sorry. Lost in thought there for a moment. No, I don't think it's aliens."

"The evidence is compelling."

"Oh, come on. You don't believe that. I know you too well. I've seen a lot of weird shit, Taylor, but I haven't seen anything to suggest aliens are coming trillions of miles to steal sex organs from cows and humans. I've also seen enough to know that we, as a species, are more than capable of sick shit like this."

"Amen to that. I think the alien angle is worth looking into, though."

"Say again?"

Taylor smiled. "I haven't lost my faculties for reasoning. Someone went to a lot of trouble to make these murders look like aliens did it. Why?"

I shook my head. "I've been asking myself that since I signed on."

"That's what you have me for. Whenever I get a case like this, I think about who would do such a thing and why. Serial killers are motivated by the need to hunt. There's often a sexual component. This doesn't look like the work of a serial killer, despite the number of bodies. These murders were planned and carefully orchestrated."

"So the victims almost certainly all knew the killer."

"Exactly. You have to ask yourself why the killer would go to such elaborate lengths."

"To hide the murders?"

"I think it's just the opposite," said Taylor. "Why hide them like *this*? The bodies were dumped in the desert but near roads. I think the killer wants the media exposure. That suggests they have some means of profiting from these murders."

I stood and retrieved the UFO tours pamphlets I'd found in the hotel lobby. I felt a little dizzy as I stood. I hate not being at one-hundred-percent healthy. That radiation dosing had taken some of my energy reserves away.

I showed the pamphlets to Taylor. "I wondered about that angle," I said, carefully sitting back down.

Taylor looked them over. "Not bad, Fredericks. I think these people are exactly who we should be talking to."

"That could be a problem," I said. "My experience with people who believe in fringe conspiracy theories is that they *really* don't trust the government. You sort of exude FBI agent vibes, even when you're not in a suit."

"You mean people who believe conspiracy theories like those concerning government experimentation on children?"

"Ouch."

"Okay." Taylor pushed the files away from her. "We'll deal with that later. Let's talk about this other problem."

"Other problem?"

"Erin. I want to know more about her. You said she knew about Project Providence and seemed to be an enhanced individual."

"She mentioned a special project that had been based in this area, a Project Wormwood that was somehow related to Project Providence."

"She make it up?"

"No, Michael had heard of it. The project was based out of the

Angel Fire Air Station, which is now the airport."

"Well, I guess that explains your discomfort when you picked me up."

"I don't know," I said. "There was something else. The area around the airport felt… wrong. I'm sorry I can't put it better than that,"

"I so I guess Erin is one of those things we put on a backburner for now. I doubt she's connected to these murders, and they have priority. I just don't like the coincidence of her being here."

I nodded. "Erin didn't seem to know about the murders, so there is that."

"I still think we should consider her as person of interest in this case," said Taylor. "If you encounter her again, I want to be involved."

"I'll try. She doesn't stick around for long, and as Michael found out, restraining her isn't a good idea."

"What's this?" Taylor asked. "You said something about him trying to keep her at a table, not restrain her."

"Michael grabbed her arm to make her stay and answer questions. She overpowered him."

"He's lucky she didn't press charges for assault," Taylor said. "What was he thinking?"

"I don't think he was. I think his deputy marshal instincts kicked in."

Taylor sighed. "Isn't he retired?"

"I thought so, but it turns out he's just on leave."

"Hmm. Is he having second thoughts?"

"I don't think so," I said. "He said his boss just wanted him to take his back vacation time before making a decision."

"Well, having him still as an official deputy federal marshal could come in handy. You two are still good, though, right?"

"Yeah, we are."

"Good, because I don't think I could kick his ass, but I'd try."

"Thanks."

I didn't doubt her sincerity.

Taylor was a good friend.

CHAPTER TWENTY-SEVEN

Taylor and I met with Michael and Marie for lunch.

It was a little strained at first; Marie is shy. She warmed up to Taylor by the time the food made it to the table, though. Taylor's good nature and humor won her over.

"You're actually going to take one of the tourist trap tours?" asked Marie.

"Someone wants everyone to believe the murders are alien abductions," I said. "If anyone would benefit, it's the people running the tours."

Marie nodded. "I'm not sure about your reasoning. Yes, the bodies look like classic examples of alien mutilations, but I have a bit of trouble seeing how that would make more people want to go on tours to see aliens. I'd think the murders would scare people off."

"You'd think," Taylor said. "But cultists often act contrary to reason."

"Calling them cultists is a bit extreme, don't you think?" said Michael.

Taylor shrugged. "If you know of a better word, I'd be happy to use it. My point is that people who have fringe beliefs will often look for any form of validation. There are some who'd probably welcome being abducted, just to prove to themselves they were right."

"People looking for validation might even commit murder themselves," I said. "Occult killers often use the murders they've committed as proof that they're doing what they're supposed to be doing. They see the murders as a sign that god, or the devil or whatever, is guiding them and giving them power. I can see people who strongly believe in UFOs as doing the same. They've replaced gods, goblins, and fairies with aliens, but the foundation is the same, as is the fanaticism."

"Most of the ones I've met have been nice people," said Marie.

"Certainly," I replied. "As are most people who believe in and practice the occult. I think predators such a serial killers join those groups because the people in them are somewhat isolated and ostracized by society. If a known occultist is killed, the police are likely to shrug and say they had it coming."

"Okay, yeah, I just didn't want you thinking that because they believe in UFOs, they're bad people," Marie said. She sounded a little defensive.

"I don't," I said. "I do think a predator is preying on a local group, though."

"I saw one once," said Michael.

"One what?" Taylor asked.

"A UFO," Michael said. "It was in Afghanistan. The airspace was restricted, a no-fly zone. We had two birds to the west of our position, F-22s on patrol. It was full dark, around 2200, when we saw the strangest damn thing. Something silent found our position. It had downward-pointed lights, like search lights, but no other navigational lights. We called it in but were told nothing was on radar over our position. I worried it was going to give us away to the enemy. The F-22s were diverted, but it took off and outran them. We lost sight of it."

"Some kind of drone?" I asked.

"No, it wasn't a drone: too big, too fast. This thing was round, at least fifty meters across, and hovered. It was absolutely silent. No engine noise at all, but it took off too fast for a balloon. An F-22 has a max speed above Mach 2. This thing accelerated away at least twice that."

"Could you see if it had markings?"

"It was dark, and we didn't want to shine lights on it," said Michael. "It's funny: It happened, and yet it was so long ago that I just kind of forget about it. A lot happened after that. The enemy had seen the lights."

Michael didn't talk about his military service often. I was surprised he'd say anything at all in front of Taylor. I guess he trusted her more than I'd realized.

"I've seen things, too," said Marie. "In the sky. There's a lot of weird, around here."

"Well, I guess maybe I'll see something, as well," I said, "when I take the UFO tour."

"We," said Marie. "When *we* take the tour."

"You don't have to go."

"I want to, and besides, the locals know me. Without me along, no one will talk to you."

"She has a good point," said Taylor. "We need intel from inside the groups."

"Have you ever been on one of these things?" I asked.

Marie hesitated and then nodded.

"How do we make contact?"

"You call the number and show up at the designated location. They collect the money there, everyone climbs in a van with blackened windows, and then they drive you out into the desert. At least the one I went on."

"This sounds like a setup for a human trafficking ring," said Michael.

"I was thinking that, too," Taylor said. "I want you guys to be careful."

"I'm always careful," I said.

"Uh-huh. Don't kill anyone, either."

I sighed. "You still don't trust me?"

"I trust you. I also know you have a tendency to react violently when pushed."

"I'm not planning to take my pistol."

Taylor snorted. "Like you need a weapon."

"I would think that if the killer makes a move," said Michael, "you'd want Michelle to neutralize the threat."

"I want the killer to face justice in a court, not be *neutralized*."

"If I'm attacked, I'll defend myself," I said. "I don't expect anything to happen. I'm looking for answers. I can't help it if trouble finds me."

"Sometimes I think you lot are just trouble magnets," said Taylor.

"I've never even had a speeding ticket," said Marie.

"You don't have a driver's license," Taylor replied. "I do my homework."

"Michael is a deputy federal marshal—"

"Retired," Michael interjected.

"—and I'm specialist in occult crime who regularly works with law enforcement tracking serial killers. How could we *not* get in trouble sometimes?"

"Oh, you know I'm on your side, Michelle," said Taylor. "I just worry that your luck is going to run out, and I'm going to be consulting with you in a jail cell."

"I won't take a gun, okay?"

"Thank you."

Taylor was right: I don't need a weapon to defend myself. I suppose that was one reason why I was so overconfident. I couldn't imagine then that anything would go wrong.

CHAPTER TWENTY-EIGHT

The meeting place was about an hour northeast of Taos, outside a place called Eagle Nest. We were to travel through to the south side of town and meet at the RV park. I already wished I hadn't agreed to leave my gun in the hotel. It wasn't anything like a premonition; I just wanted the comfort of knowing that I was safe.

I did have my boot knife. I hoped I wouldn't have to use it. Killing with a knife is a little too up-close and personal. I'd be happy if I never had to kill again, but if I did, I hoped I didn't have to use a knife.

About a dozen vehicles were already waiting when we arrived. I glanced at the dash clock; we were fifteen minutes early. The sun was down, but the sky was still smoldering in the west. It wouldn't be full dark for another hour.

"Last chance to run," said Marie.

"You really think these people will be that bad?"

"Not at all, but you're clutching the wheel so hard that your knuckles are white."

I sighed. "I'm fine. I just wish I knew what we were getting into."

"They're just normal people. Some of them have seen things they can't explain. Some of them are just hoping to see something extraordinary, to give their lives meaning."

"I can understand that. I've had a lot of weird experiences, but I wouldn't trade them for anything."

"Exactly."

We got out of the Jeep and joined the others.

A couple of people knew Marie, which helped. I sensed curiosity about me, but nothing antagonistic. One of the women said they were still waiting on a few more people to show.

Three cars pulled in together a few minutes after eight.

I took an immediate dislike to the balding guy who got out of a dirty white pickup truck.

"That's Ralph," Maria said. "He can get a little touchy-feely. Just ignore his comments and don't end up alone with him."

"Why do they let him come around," I asked, "if they know he's a problem?"

Marie shrugged. "I think that when you've been ostracized, outcast from society, you don't want to be like the normies and drive people away. Even if they deserve it."

"Okay, well, I can't promise I won't break a few fingers if he touches me."

"That's fine. Just don't kill him unless he really deserves it."

"I'm not a killer, you know," I said. "I don't just kill people."

"You've got a temper. I remember what you were like. After what Taylor said, I figured you still had a problem with it."

"I've shot a few people," I admitted. "But they were all bad."

Marie giggled.

"Can I have your attention, please?" a man called out. He was standing on the bumper of a blue truck. "I'm Ricardo. I'll be your guide tonight. I see a lot of familiar faces – thanks for coming back. To those of you who are new, welcome. I'm hoping we have good night. Those of you with us last time will remember we saw some very interesting things. Leslie will get you signed in. Please give her the license plate number of the vehicle you'll be in. We like to keep track of everyone."

Leslie was polite and professional as she took our money. Fifty bucks each seemed like a lot for what we were getting, but I suppose they knew what people would pay. On the other hand, it wasn't much money to receive validation of what they believed.

I didn't care. I was planning to expense it to the FBI.

"Marie! I'm so glad you're back with us again," said Ricardo as he walked over to us. He was a good-looking Hispanic man, about my height. "Who's your friend?"

"Michelle, my brother's fiancé," said Marie.

News to me.

"You're ex-military?" Ricardo asked.

"I'm not at liberty to say."

Ricardo chuckled. "Welcome. You're not from the Southwest?"

"No, Kentucky."

"Watch out for snakes. Most of them will be sleeping, but you might step on one and piss it off. Don't wander away from the group. People get lost out in the desert. We've lost some from other groups."

That got my attention.

"I won't wander," I said.

Marie and I got back in the Jeep. I was glad we wouldn't be in a van.

The bald guy, Ralph, had been watching us intensely. He creeped me out. I hoped he'd do the smart thing and leave me alone. I didn't have much faith in his intelligence, though. Everything about the guy screamed *incel*.

"How well do you know him?" I asked.

"Ricardo or Ralph? Ricardo is harmless. He's a schoolteacher."

"I thought what he said about people going missing was interesting."

"That was the first I'd heard of it," said Marie. "You think it's connected to the murders?"

"Without knowing who went missing, or when, I couldn't say."

"I'll keep my ears open. People will talk tonight. As for Ralph, he's not a local. He showed up a couple years ago. He's a creep, but people mostly ignore him. You don't think he's the killer, do you?"

"No. The killer is intelligent, skilled. I can't imagine Ralph performing surgery."

"The guy looks like he'd have trouble opening a beer can."

"Probably has trouble with some of the cans having a tab on the bottom instead of the top."

We laughed a bit at that.

A few minutes later, Ricardo pulled out in his blue truck. We all followed him. He led us deep into the mountains, up steep roads and around sudden turns. I suspected he was taking a long way to get to his destination, to obfuscate where it was. After all, he was selling us his knowledge of good places to watch for UFOs.

We finally pulled into a desolate area with a lot of large rocks, where we all got out of our vehicles.

"Okay, everyone, listen up. Find a rock, get comfortable, and watch the skies," said Ricardo. "Don't wander off."

"Oh! I just saw one! Look!" a woman yelled.

Everyone looked where she was pointing.

"That's a meteor, idiot," Ralph said loudly.

"No reason for name-calling," said Ricardo. "Everyone has a first time as an experiencer. I had almost forgot: the eta Aquariids meteor shower is still going on. We missed the peak, but you should still see some good meteors."

"I came here to see UFOs, not meteors," someone muttered.

"Tonight, with luck, we'll see both," said Ricardo.

A bloodcurdling scream echoed through the mountains around us.

"That was a mountain lion," said Ricardo. "It won't bother us, but don't wander into its territory."

"You're sure it safe?" someone asked.

"I come here all the time."

Marie tugged on my arm and led me to some flat rocks nearby. The rocks were at a good angle to recline and watch the sky. Marie and I lay back to wait for something to happen.

CHAPTER TWENTY-NINE

The night was cold, but I was wearing a jacket, and the rock was still warm from the sun.

The moon was down, and there weren't any clouds. It would be a nice night to stargaze, even if we didn't see anything weird. To be honest, I wasn't expecting anything to come of our trip. I hoped that maybe we'd hear something, pick up some impressions from the other people on the tour. There wasn't much chance of that, though. These people didn't know anything that we needed.

A mountain lion cried out in the distance. It reminded me uncomfortably of Pikeville. I'd heard one there, too: the night that policeman had been possessed, and I'd shot him.

"What are you thinking about?" asked Marie.

"Other nights like this one," I said.

"I sensed a change in your mood. I didn't mean to intrude."

"You weren't," I said. "This last year has been something else. There's been good, but a lot of bad. There's so much about the world I don't understand. So much that has changed since last year. Even just the stuff that's changed since I came out here. I never suspected there'd been other projects like ours."

"You really didn't remember anything from before?"

I shrugged, a useless gesture in the dark. "I had bad dreams."

"I still do," said Marie. "I can't imagine being around death as much as you are. I'd have nightmares all the time."

"For better or worse, you get used to the death," I said. "I don't have nightmares about my work. I do still sometimes have them about the past. I remember little bits from the project. I remember Michael, and trying to escape. I remember the machine."

"The chair, yeah," said Marie. "What did the mountain lion remind you of?"

I sensed she wanted to change the subject away from the project. I did, too. "I last heard a mountain lion on a cold night last fall, when a police officer, who may or may not have deserved it, was possessed by a demon and murdered his family. I shot him. It didn't make me popular with the local police."

"I can only imagine." Marie laid back on the rock. "How do you know he was possessed?"

"I found the magic circle in a hotel room, with corpses. He entered the room and broke the circle. Later, before I shot him, I saw a shadow riding him."

"That's creepy. Do you think anyone can be possessed?"

"No. I think he was involved with the criminals who set up the circle. He was willing to be possessed, or the entity – demon, whatever – couldn't have gotten him."

"Do you deal with thing like that a lot?"

"More than I care to."

"I thought your life sounded glamorous. Now I'm not so sure."

We saw six meteors during the next hour, but nothing extraordinary. No fireballs, no UFOs or UAP, nothing. The air smelled clean, with a hint of pine and sage. That was a nice change from the air around Cincinnati, where burning of coal is the primary source of power. The skies back home are always tinged with yellow smog.

"How long do you usually stay out here?" I asked.

"Until dawn."

"It's going to be a long night."

A little after midnight, according to my phone, Ricardo called out to everyone. "Look to the south – that's to the right from where we pulled in here."

I could see a light moving slowly along.

"Notice anything special about it?" said Ricardo.

I studied it more. The light was moving north, and then it turned to move west, to fly over the mountains. I could see more detail as it came closer. There were unblinking red lights on both sides.

"Military jet?" I asked.

"Why do you say that?"

I mentioned the lights.

"Military jets only have a solid red light on one wing," Ralph said sneeringly, "to make it clear which side to pass on."

I was getting really tired of that guy.

"That's partly true," said Ricardo. "However, experimental military aircraft have solid red lights on both wings, sort of a do-not-pass sign. You don't see a lot of planes with two, but here in New Mexico, where planes are tested, you do see a few."

The plane slowed as it neared the mountains. Suddenly it lit up. I didn't want to believe it, but it looked like a flying saucer: bulbous in the middle and then out to form the disk. A glowing, luminous shape. It was nearly silent as it moved past us. It didn't sound like a jet or a helicopter. Bright lights speared the mountainside as it hovered maybe three miles to the north of us.

"What is it?" someone asked, her voice full of awe. "It that actually a *visitor*?"

"That is an aircraft I believe was reverse-engineered from alien technology," said Ricardo. "Those of us who study such things call planes like that a *Manta*, because of the shape. If it gets closer, you'll see the glow of the engines and the twin tail booms."

"How is it silent?" I asked.

"The engines are on top, with horizontal vectored thrust along the belly. I first got a good look at one of these about a decade ago. I even found some pictures on the dark web of one sitting in a hangar at the Groom Lake facility, Area Fifty-One. At least the plane in the pictures looked a lot like what I'd seen."

"How does it look like a flying saucer," the excitable woman asked, "if it isn't one?"

"It has a cluster of lights in the front and on the wings. I suspect the Feds made it that way to fool people into thinking they'd seen a UFO. Since people are often ridiculed for reporting UFOs, it makes the perfect cover."

I had to admit, I was impressed. Ricardo didn't claim it was alien, even though he could have. I did think the part about it being reverse-engineered from alien tech was bullshit, but then, the guy did need to make a living. I hadn't heard of horizontal vectored thrust, but it made sense. It had to be more stable than the vectored thrust from a Harrier.

I wondered what the plane was looking for on the slope of the mountain.

To me, that was a far more interesting question than how it was built.

CHAPTER THIRTY

We watched the aircraft comb the mountainside for about an hour before people started losing interest. It was mysterious, but it wasn't the alien craft they'd been hoping to see. I didn't care either way. I was just cold and needed to piss.

The other people there seemed to feel similarly.

Small cliques had formed.

From what I could overhear of their conversations, the groups were composed of like-minded people: the people who wanted to be abducted, the ones who thought they had been and wanted answers, and the people who just wanted something interesting to happen in their lives.

"I think I might wander around and talk to people," said Marie.

"Be careful," I said. "The killer could be here."

"I'll be discreet."

"Hey, before you go, where the hell do you relieve your bladder in this place?"

Marie chuckled. "I just find someplace out of sight. I've already gone once."

"I never saw you leave."

"You were watching the fake UFO. Just dig a little hole and do your business. Do you need tissue?"

"I have some," I said. I keep a little travel-size pack in my jacket.

Some of the rocks to the southeast looked promising, away from the cars and the people, downslope, and not in line of sight to the aircraft. Most people would be looking at the plane, if anywhere.

I dug a little hole with a stick and dropped my pants. Guys have it easier; they can just whip it out and whiz, and not have to worry about anything. I felt really vulnerable and exposed, even though it was dark. As I squatted over my little cat hole, I couldn't help but think of a snake biting my coochie. It wasn't a pleasant thought.

I cleaned up, buried my wet spot, and stood, pulling up and buckling my pants. It was too damn cold tonight. I shivered. A feeling of dread worked its way up my spine. I dropped into a defensive stance.

A shadow moved across my line of sight.

I knew it was Ralph.

"Can we not do this?" I called. I hoped someone would hear me. Just in case, I pulled the knife from my boot and straightened. "This isn't going to end well for you."

"You shouldn't have come here," said Ralph.

There was something odd about his voice. It sent shivers up my spine again. I'm not easily spooked, but this guy was seriously creeping me out. I realized my hands were sweating, and adjusted my grip on the knife. That wasn't normal, either.

"I know what you are," said Ralph.

As far as misogynistic rants go, this wasn't what I expected. I'd expected him to call me names and then try to make good on some threat. This whole mysterious thing didn't seem in character. Nothing about this seemed normal.

"I have no idea who you are or what you want, but you need to get out of the way before you get hurt."

I'm fast, but I was almost too slow to get out of his way when he charged. I expected Ralph to swing on me. He didn't have a weapon in his hand. His hand was open and empty – at least, that's what I thought. The sudden, unexpected pain in the side of my head and neck was almost overwhelming.

I could feel blood gushing down my face and knew I was in shock. I didn't know what just happened. Ralph was still here, but he didn't look much as he had before. There was something bestial about his face, and his hands... His fingers ended in blade-like claws.

"I'll take my time and make an example of you," the Ralph-thing said, "for daring to come here."

He moved at me again, and my instincts took over. I didn't know how badly I was hurt, and I was bleeding a lot. I couldn't take the time to do anything about it, though. I did know that whatever Ralph was, it could and would kill me if I didn't fight back.

I swung at it, and there was a sudden pain in my right arm. It wasn't as bad as the pain in my head. I think my leather jacket took most of the damage. I tossed the knife to my left hand, spinning to cover the exchange.

I took a hit across my back, and then I was on the offensive. My knee to its groin took the Ralph-thing by surprise, and as it doubled over, I drove my knife into an eye socket with all my strength.

The scream tore at my mind.

The Ralph-thing dropped to its knees and clawed at the knife before falling back. It lay there twitching. I jerked my knife clear, ready to strike again, but it was dead. I could hear people yelling and calling out. I wiped my blade clean and tucked it back in my boot.

Absurdly, all I could think about was that Taylor was going to be pissed at me for killing the thing, after I'd promised her that I wouldn't kill anyone. I hadn't had much choice. I never have much choice, but I don't go seeking people to kill.

I stumbled back up to the others.

Grey fog was closing in on my vision.

Without the adrenaline from the fight to sustain me, I was fading quickly into shock. I heard someone calling 911. I think it was Ricardo. He was saying something about a mountain lion attack. I wanted to tell them that it hadn't been a mountain lion, but my tongue wasn't mine to command.

Marie caught me as I sagged to the ground.

My body wasn't working all that well, either.

Marie was saying something about help being on the way, and to stay awake. Yeah, that wasn't going to happen. Between the pain and the blood loss, I was on my way out. My last thoughts were that it was good that I hadn't been able to say anything about what attacked me.

I couldn't afford to spend a week or two in a psych ward.

CHAPTER THIRTY-ONE

Unfortunately, I never quite lost consciousness.

Passing out would have been a welcome relief from the pain. Instead, I was sort of awake but not very responsive as they rushed me to the nearest regional medical center. Fluids and pain meds helped with my awareness. I still wasn't quite sure how I'd gotten to the medical center, but I was happy Marie was here with me.

It took the doctor a while to stitch me back together. I had a lot of cuts. Most of the wounds weren't too deep, but they hurt and bled a lot. The doctor numbed the cuts before cleaning them, which I appreciated. I declined the rabies shot, took the antibiotics.

Taylor and Michael showed up as the doctor finished working on me, there in the emergency room.

"Oh, my god," said Taylor.

Michael froze, then moved to my side and gripped my hand.

"That bad?" I asked. I hadn't seen a mirror. "How many stitches?" I asked the doctor.

She finished tugging at my back and pulled my gown up over my shoulders. "Who are these people? Who let them in here?"

"Special Agent Taylor, FBI," Taylor said, flashing her badge. "And Deputy Federal Marshal Delling. Dr. Fredericks is one of ours."

"Oh, well, your agent here was attacked by a mountain lion."

I shook my head at that. "How many stitches?" I asked, touching my face. Someone at the hospital had shaved the side of my head. I didn't remember them doing that.

"I used butterfly Steri-Strips on your face, head, and neck," said the doctor. "Leaves less of a scar."

"And the rest?"

"Three hundred thirty-six."

"That's a new record for me," I said.

Michael smiled and shook his head.

"Well, don't go making a habit of it," said the doctor. "I appreciate the stitching practice, but I'm good now."

"Thanks, doc."

"I'm Dr. Aguilar," she said. "Nice to make your acquaintance."

"What the hell happened?" asked Taylor.

"I'd rather not talk about it here. Can I get discharged?"

"I'd advise against it," said Dr. Aguilar. "You lost a lot of blood and suffered major trauma. We'd like to keep you a couple of days for observation."

"I'm sure you would, but I need to get back out to where it happened."

"I really don't think that's a good idea."

"The patient is declining further treatment," Michael said in a tone that didn't brook argument.

Dr. Aguilar glanced between Taylor's and Michael's faces. "I'll have the discharge nurse bring the AMA paperwork." She left, shaking her head.

"Are you okay, Marie?" asked Michael.

"No, but I'm not injured. This blood is all Michelle's."

"Sorry about bleeding all over you," I said.

"I'm just glad you're okay."

"You really want to go back out there this morning?" asked Taylor.

"What time is it?" I said.

"Around 0700," said Michael.

"Should be light enough."

A nurse came in and had me signed several forms, and then took out the IV. I hate those things. I felt really thirsty, and I needed to pee. I signed another form, and was given discharge instructions and a prescription for antibiotics and pain meds.

"Where are your clothes?" asked Taylor.

"Bloody and torn up," I replied. "I think I saw the nurse put them in a red bag under the bed."

"I see them." Taylor whistled. "Damn, were you mauled by a whole pack of lions?"

"It wasn't a mountain lion."

I stood up, and my vision greyed out a bit. I took a few deep breathes to steady myself, and everything stabilized. My jeans weren't too bloody, so I put those on. Michael helped me with my socks and boots. I felt weak and dizzy, which irritated me.

I don't like feeling vulnerable.

Only as we were leaving did I remember that I hadn't driven my Jeep here. I had no idea where it was. For that matter, I wasn't real sure where *I* was. The sign said *Holy Cross*, but one hospital is much like another.

"We're in Taos," said Marie. "Ricardo had Antonia drive me and your Jeep back here. They wouldn't let me in the helicopter with you. I've got your keys."

"Helicopter?"

"You don't remember being airlifted out of there?"

I shook my head.

"Well, I've got your keys, but I don't think you should drive."

"I'll drive," Michael said. "Where's her Jeep?"

"Over this way."

"I'll follow you guys over," said Taylor.

Michael dropped me off at the hotel. Taylor had to help me inside my room. I was feeling pretty shaky. Michael took Marie home to get cleaned up and change clothes.

I wished I could take a shower but contented myself with washing up in the sink.

I looked terrible. I was pale, with dark bags under my eyes. I had no idea how much blood I'd lost, or been given, but it didn't equal out. I was going to need to eat more meat for a couple of weeks.

The wounds on my face looked raw and swollen. The doctor had done a good job with the butterfly strips, though. The edges of the wounds were lined up well. I doubted I'd have strong scars, just faint lines. The emergency room staff hadn't shaved my head, just buzzed the hair off one side. They *had* then carefully shaved on either side of the cuts themselves. It looked a little punk.

Under the light bandages, the cuts on my right arm weren't too bad, but the ones on my back were deeper. I don't know what I'd been thinking, turning my back on an enemy. I know better than that. I'd paid the price for my foolishness, even though my counterattack had worked.

My back itched. I could see a lot of stitches there, and patted the bandage back down into place. Wearing a bra was out of the question, so I just wore a couple of layers of shirts. At least I'm not too large in the chest to go unsupported. At least not for too long. I was probably going to have to sleep on my stomach for a while, too.

"Well, you look a little better," said Taylor. "You going to tell me what happened?"

"I'm rather wait for Michael and Marie to get back and tell you all at once."

Taylor nodded. "Can I do anything for you while we wait?"

I sat down on the bed and carefully leaned against some pillows. I was too weak to just sit up, but it hurt too much to sit back. "There should be Cokes in the fridge, and some beef jerky and chips around here somewhere."

I definitely needed the protein and salt.

"I'm sorry, Michelle."

"For what?"

Taylor gestured at my face, the rest of me.

"I'll heal. I'm not too worried about this. I'm more worried about what happened. We'll need to get back out to the site ASAP. Oh, and uh, there's a body there."

"Not a mountain lion, huh?" Taylor sighed. "You promised not to take a gun."

"I didn't take my gun. You didn't say anything about a knife, though."

Taylor shook her head.

"I'd be dead if I hadn't taken it."

"Well, I'm glad you're not dead."

CHAPTER THIRTY-TWO

Michael and Marie arrived a few minutes later with breakfast.

I ate my sausage-and-egg burritos quickly. I wasn't hungry. I just felt that I should eat. I'd lost a fair amount of blood. I still felt weak.

I knew time was pressing. I needed to get back to the site of the attack, and it was over an hour away. Each minute that passed was one too many. I couldn't say why I felt that way, though.

"Everyone ready to go?" I asked.

Michael drove. I settled into the passenger's seat and tried to get comfortable. It was difficult, with the wounds across my back. I've been hurt before, more times than I care to count. This was different somehow.

"Well, are you going to tell us what happened, or not?" Taylor demanded from the back seat.

"I wasn't attacked by a mountain lion," I said.

"You said that. You've got the claws to dispute it, though."

I told them about Ralph and what he'd said. I told them how he'd changed and attacked me. I can imagine how it must have sounded. I'm not sure I would have believed such a story, if it hadn't just happened to me.

"I have to say, your story is really out there, even for you," said Taylor.

"So, the man turned into a monster?" Michael asked.

"I know how crazy it sounds."

"It was dark, and you were hurt," said Taylor. "Given the sensitivity of your abilities, I could imagine you sensing him being a monster inside and then seeing it."

I shook my head. They didn't understand. Maybe they couldn't.

We pulled into the small parking area. Ralph's beat-up truck was still there. I could see the signs of a hasty evacuation. A few blankets still lay on rocks. There was some trash around, and someone had lost a shoe.

Gravel crunched under my boot as I got out the Jeep. The air was cold; I could see my breath. The side of my head felt naked with my hair buzzed.

"We were sitting on those rocks," said Marie, pointing.

It was easy to follow the blood trail back to where I'd been attacked. There was a lot of blood to follow. My blood. I had to fight against dizziness as I saw it. Blood doesn't normally bother me. I see a lot of it in my line of work. I guess it was just the memory of how it got here.

The smell hit us first: rotting meat and cabbage mixed with sewage.

There was a body right where I thought I'd been attacked, where the blood trail ended. The body was old, though. *Weeks* old, at least. The flesh had rotted and decayed, peeling away from the bones. I forced myself to get closer to the reeking remains. The clothes had mostly rotted but looked like what Ralph had been wearing. There were signs of a wound in the eye socket. There were no maggots, and there should have been.

"I'll need to call this in," said Taylor. "Get a team out here."

"Wait just a minute," Michael said. "I think there's another body behind those rocks."

There was a body: Ralph's.

The clothes were the same. This body had been clawed open, ripped up, and torn apart. His guts had spilled out. Both of his eyes were intact. It wasn't who I'd stabbed the night before.

"Any idea who this is?" asked Taylor.

"Ralph," said Marie.

"I thought Ralph was who attacked you," Taylor said to me. "You said you stabbed him in the eye."

"I did, but it wasn't over here. It was over there by the rotting body."

"Michelle, you can tell that body has been there for weeks. It's almost decayed away."

"And you should be able to tell from the blood trail that I was attacked over there, not here."

"You're sure it wasn't a mountain lion? Maybe it dragged the body."

I growled in exasperation. "Then where is the blood? It wasn't an animal."

"If it wasn't a mountain lion, what was it?"

"I *don't know*. I *told* you what I remember. I do know that other body wasn't here last night."

"We would have smelled it," said Marie. "The wind was from this direction. The whole parking lot would've stunk of it."

"Okay, I'm going to call in the bodies," Taylor said. "*Don't touch anything*."

I went back to Ralph's body. The wounds looked similar to mine. Whatever attacked him had also attacked me. There were no bite marks, just deep slashes from claws. Ralph had a look of utter terror on his face. I could only imagine what it must have been like, to have been murdered by someone who looked just like him.

"Michelle? What are you thinking?" asked Michael.

"I don't know. It's farfetched, but you said your friend Harrison saw someone who looked just like him. Like a twin or something. Look at the clothes on the two bodies. They're the same."

Michael nodded. "I noticed that. They're the same size and build, too. Harrison didn't mention claws or shapeshifting. I don't think this attack is the same thing as what he saw."

"Maybe not, but something is going on." I told him about the aircraft we'd seen.

"You saw that here?"

"The plane was looking for something. We saw it combing the

mountainside with searchlights."

"I don't know what to make of that. It's... odd."

"Could whatever attacked you have been something that, I don't know, escaped from a lab or something?" said Marie. "You just though it was Ralph, in the dark, because he gave you the creeps?"

"He spoke to me," I said. "It sounded like Ralph. At least I thought it did. I thought it *was* Ralph, even as he started to attack me. That was why I got hurt so badly. I thought Ralph was going to slap me. I wasn't worried until the claws hit me."

"You mentioned that before. What he said was kind of creepy."

"This whole thing gives me the creeps," I said. "I know what I remember, but it couldn't have happened. Could it?"

"If you say this man changed shape, then I believe you," said Michael. "You aren't easily fooled. Something very strange is going on."

No shit. "Thank you," I said instead. "I wish I had some kind of answers, though."

"I don't know how up on Southwest folklore you are," said Marie, "but have you heard of skin-walkers?"

"Shapeshifters, right?" I asked. "Navaho?"

"Or doppelgangers," said Michael, "if you prefer European folklore. Mythology is full of things like that, all around the world."

"Ralph was a creep," I said, "but whatever attacked me felt... demonic. It definitely wasn't a spirit, though. Not like any I've ever encountered before, anyway. Obviously, this thing's claws were very real, and don't forget the rotting body."

"Let's assume for a moment that something killed Ralph and took his form so it could get close to you. You stabbed it. Where is the body?"

I gestured to the rotten corpse. "As crazy as it sounds, I think that's it. Look at the eye socket."

"That body had been here weeks," said Michael.

"Has it?" I asked. "Where are the maggots? Why haven't the ants stripped the body of flesh? This isn't one of the alien abduction bodies. This isn't irradiated. Insects would have reduced it to bones by now if it was weeks old."

"Can we be certain it isn't radioactive?" asked Michael.

"You think the body might be radioactive?" Taylor said as she walked back.

"No," I said. "The M.O. is all wrong. This isn't related to the other case. At least, I can't imagine that it is. I'm not ready to accept aliens just yet."

"Good. Me, either," said Taylor. "Well, just to be certain, let's fall back to the parking lot."

We went back and sat in my Jeep, waiting for the FBI and police to show up.

I couldn't get comfortable. My back hurt, and the stitches pulled, no matter how I turned. At some point, I dozed off.

INTERLUDE

My dream is different from most of the others, because this time I'm aware from the beginning that I'm dreaming.

I am both my adult self and a child, lost in a strange place.

Most of my dreams – or nightmares, if you prefer – are about the Providence Project. In those dreams, I'm usually a teenager, trying to escape the facility or being tortured in that damn chair. There's nothing of that kind of fear in this dream. I am not afraid, even though the military instructors with us are.

I can feel their anxiety, and somehow it pleases me.

I am not normally someone who enjoys the fear of others. However, in this instance, I am very happy about that dread for some reason. The instructors call where we are camp, but we all know it's something else. Kids aren't taught how to kill at camp. At least, I don't think they are. As far as I know, I've never been to a normal summer camp.

In my other dreams, I am older and in a hospital gown. Here, I am younger but dressed in a tank-top, loose military-style pants, and black combat boots. My hair is buzzed short, and my chest is flat, so I know I have to be a pre-teen: I started getting boobs when I was twelve.

Despite our youth, I recognize several of the other children. The taller redhead is Michael, standing close to a red-haired girl whom I only belatedly recognize as Marie. She looks so young and different with red hair instead of white. The horrors that changed her hair are still in her future.

In all our futures.

Julia, Amy, and Victor are here, as well.

Victor has a permanent sneer, even as a child. I hate him, but oddly, I like both of his sisters. Future me, watching the dream play out, couldn't help but wonder what had happened to us all, that Julia would hate me so much. I remembered that we had been close as children. I was sure it had nothing to do with where we were in this dream, and much to do with what happened later. From what Julia said before, she hated me because I'd gotten out and she didn't, which is hardly fair. That wasn't my fault.

Someone begins screaming behind me.

They aren't the kind of screams that I know all too well from the other nightmares. These aren't screams of losing one's mind to the pain of being tortured. No, these screams are even more animal, bestial. There's pain in the screams, but there's also an intense rage, more than anything else. I can certainly understand the rage. I feel that inside me all the time.

The door behind our group slams open. The screaming thing stumbles out. I'm suddenly afraid then, because I recognize this. It used to be Tom, one of the other kids in our group. Tom was given the injections, the same as the rest of us, but something must have gone wrong with his.

Or maybe the injections went right, depending on what our captors wanted. I remember that the doctors seemed excited when they led him away to inject him. As if they were trying something new. I'd heard one of the doctors mention a new batch of serum. I was relieved they hadn't picked me.

I'm popular with the doctors.

Tom's face is swollen and contorted in agony. He claws at his face, tearing the skin open in a gory spectacle that I can only stand and watch, frozen in horror. I am an unwilling witness to what's happening to him. I feel bad for him, but I'm mostly relieved that it isn't me. I feel ashamed of that.

Under skin and red gore is another layer of skin. He is becoming something else now, wearing a flesh mask that only looked like Tom. I can see part of his face lying on the floor. The blood runs in the grooves of the tiles.

Tom screams in madness, horror, and pain.

Without thinking about it, I spin, driving the heel of my hand into the temple of the nearest instructor, just like they taught us. The man falls, and I have the instructor's pistol in my hand before his corpse hits the floor, before anyone else can react. I check the safety and chamber a round.

Tom is no longer screaming. The sounds he makes are bestial. He growls and snarls as his old skin falls away. His eyes blaze red, and the skin under his skin is not human any longer, but dark and scaled.

The sound of the pistol is loud.

CHAPTER THIRTY-THREE

"Michelle!"

I awoke suddenly. Michael was shaking me, looking worried. I could see cars and trucks parked all around us. The vehicles had federal government tags. State police were parked farther out.

"What's going on? How long was I asleep?" I asked. My back hurt.

"A couple of hours," said Michael. "We thought you needed the sleep. I wouldn't have woken you if it wasn't important."

I nodded. "I know, and I did need the sleep. I was having a really fucked-up nightmare, though."

"Something's happened that I think you'll want to see."

I groaned and got out of the Jeep. I wished I'd worn a bra, despite the discomfort. There were a lot of people here. Oh well, at least it wasn't too cold anymore. Michael, perhaps reading my mind, handed me his jacket. It was too large but nice and warm from being worn. I felt safer, feeling his warmth around me.

Taylor was down the hill, past the rocks, by the first body.

I didn't see Marie anywhere.

"What's up?" I asked.

"You didn't touch the body, did you?" asked Taylor.

I shook my head. "No, why?"

"Take a look."

There wasn't much flesh left. The soft tissue was almost completely gone, and even the bones were starting to crumble. The strong rotten smell was gone, too. The grass and weeds for a meter around the body were turning black, dead, and brittle.

"What the hell?" I asked.

"We think someone dumped something caustic on the body," said Taylor. "We're sending a sample off for analysis."

"So this really *is* the guy I stabbed?" I asked.

"Yeah, not so loud with that," Taylor replied. "I don't need the paperwork. We don't have an ID on the perp, and probably won't. I don't think those teeth are going to last much longer."

"But you believe me now?"

Taylor nodded. "I didn't think you were lying before. One of our forensics guys mentioned that the wounds on Ralph Garcia were too wide apart to be from a mountain lion. They were also too clean and deep. He suggested the killer may have used long, metal claws. Apparently, you can buy crap like that on the internet."

"I suppose that could be what happened. It was dark," I said. I didn't believe my attacker had been using metal claws, but I couldn't prove otherwise, either. Anything I said would sound crazy. Even thinking about what I believed had happened felt crazy. I've seen some shit, but never someone just *changing* like that.

A nagging memory of my nightmare crept in then, but I ignored it.

Whatever happened in my past wasn't relevant to what was happening now. I couldn't even be sure if that nightmare was something that actually happened. I'm sure it was triggered by what I'd seen the not-Ralph do. That's the problem with interpreting dreams.

How do I know what's an actual memory and what's just nightmarish embellishment?

"Our current theory is that someone sent this guy to kill you, ran into Mr. Garcia first, and killed him because he was a witness. Then he went after you. Whoever sent him then dumped lye or something else caustic on this guy to cover up any evidence. The one who covered up the body could have taken the metal claws then."

"Lye wouldn't do it," I said. "Maybe some kind of strong acid. Can you ask your forensics guys if any acids smell like rotten cabbage? I thought that was an odd smell this morning. It didn't fit with anything else."

"I will. Thanks." Taylor called the guy over and explained.

"Rotten cabbage smell?" The man scratched his head. "Could be dimethyl sulfide or a methanethiol release. Those are usually bacterial byproducts, though. I suppose someone may have dumped a load of hungry bacteria to dissolve the body. Odd choice, but evidently effective. I'll tell the lab to look for bacteria in the samples."

"You get that?" asked Taylor.

"Yeah. It doesn't make sense, but I suppose it makes more sense than that some monster did this."

"Oh, it was definitely a monster," Taylor said. "It was just the normal, human kind."

"Wow, I just saw the side of your head. Did you get attacked by the same guy?" the forensics guy asked excitedly.

"Gorman, don't make me regret calling you over."

"Right, right, right. I'm going. I'll go look at the other body. We did get pictures of those wounds, though, right? It would really help with the comparative analysis."

"Gorman."

"Right. Nice to meet you, miss."

I just smiled and shook my head. The guy probably didn't talk to many women. He seemed to know his science, though.

"He means well," said Taylor.

"No worries. So this dead guy is our perp? The one who attacked me? I'm not crazy?"

"You're asking *me*?" She shook her head. "You know I think you're crazy. That doesn't make you wrong, though. I think this is the guy who attacked you. We still don't know why, or who sent him. I'd be a lot happier if we had the weapon."

"Taylor, you do realize there wasn't a weapon, right?"

Taylor sighed loudly. "I know what you said happened, and I

believe that's what you think you saw, but I can't put that in a report, Fredericks. Think about it."

"My DNA is probably all over this guy's fingers," I said. "And no dirty jokes! I'm not in any shape for those."

"Like we're going to get any useful evidence from this body. Besides, you aren't thinking clearly. If he'd had blades, your blood would still be all over his hands. Why don't you head back to the hotel?" Taylor suggested. "I don't think there's anything you can do here."

"You don't need a lift?"

"We've got enough FBI here, I'll find someone."

I couldn't resist harassing my friend. "I'm sure Gorman would be happy to give you a ride."

"Okay, get out of here. Go. Go now."

I found Michael and Marie up the hill, away from all the commotion.

"You guys ready to get out of here?"

"More than," said Marie. "I was just trying to see where that aircraft was last night."

"I'd almost forgotten about it," I said.

"You were pretty out of it, but the plane swept up along this ridge right after you stumbled back. It hovered over the area where that body is for a few minutes before turning off its lights and blasting out of here."

"That's *very* interesting," I said. "You think they were looking for what attacked me?"

"How could they have known?" asked Michael.

"Well, that's the question, isn't it?"

CHAPTER THIRTY-FOUR

I made Michael stop and buy me a steak when we got back to town. People stared at me, at my claw marks. I didn't care. I was hungry and wanted some red meat. I also wanted a beer or two but refrained; I didn't know how it would interact with my meds. Rather, I had a pretty good idea of how it would interact with my meds, and I didn't want to risk it.

Speaking of which, we picked up my pain pills and antibiotics at the pharmacy. I bought a bottle of iron supplements, as well. I still felt weak and a little dizzy, but I think that was mostly just blood loss and exhaustion. I took my pills and crawled face-first into the bed, where I slept for six blissful hours, devoid of dreams.

The wonderful smells of garlic and butter woke me up.

Taylor was waving a breadstick under my nose. "I think she's alive."

I groaned and sat up.

"Wow, that hairdo really works for you," said Taylor.

I flipped her the bird and went to the bathroom. I splashed water on my face and managed to get what was left of my hair under control with a hairband. Some of the puffiness had faded around the wounds. They really were clean cuts. Maybe I'd just imagined they were from claws.

Taylor had picked up pasta: rotini in red sauce with meatballs. It smelled and tasted wonderful. We didn't talk much as we ate. Michael and Marie seemed a little restrained.

"What?" I asked, munching on the last breadstick.

Michael glanced at Marie but didn't say anything.

Taylor wouldn't meet my eyes.

"Seriously, you guys are freaking me out."

"They feel guilty," said Marie, "that you got hurt."

"Oh, for god's sake," I muttered. "This is hardly the first time I've been injured doing my job."

"Well, it looks pretty bad," said Taylor.

"The blade almost got your jugular," Michael said. "It only missed by millimeters."

I sighed. "It wasn't a blade. I know you guys don't believe me. I have trouble believing it myself. It isn't your fault, though. I let my guard down. His hand was open as he swung on me. I thought he was going to slap me, and I was moving closer to punch him."

"I don't think we're going to get an identification on the perp who attacked you," Taylor said. "The skull crumbled to dust when they tried to recover it. No fingerprints, of course. The DNA sample looks like it was corrupted, too. Probably by whatever was used to dissolve the guy."

"So all of this was for nothing?"

"I wouldn't say that," said Marie. "I got invited to an alien festival here in town, over Memorial Day weekend."

"Alien festival?"

"A few thousand people descend on Taos every year. It isn't anything like the huge festival in Roswell, but it gets a few celebrities."

"Why here?" asked Taylor. "I get Roswell, with the supposed crash back in the forties."

"In the late sixties, there was a freakish storm here," said Marie. "Supposedly, a green meteor fell from the sky and crashed near here. The buzz is that the government covered it up with the construction of the Angel Fire Air Station."

Taylor glanced over at me. "Isn't that the airport you were worried about?"

"It was also the location of a government black project," I replied, "that somehow connects to Project Providence back in Ohio."

"Project Wormwood," said Michael. "No doubt named for the green meteor."

"So you think something actually fell out of the sky?" Taylor asked. "Other than a rock?"

"I don't know," I said. "I think we should try to find out, though."

Taylor leaned back. "Do you know that I had four *blissful* months without anything strange happening? Four nice, quiet months where all I had to worry about were serial killers and a bank heist."

"So, what? You're saying is that you missed this?" I asked. "Missed me?"

Taylor rolled her eyes. "Okay, so what now? The clock is ticking. We need to find who's killing these people. Do we have any leads?"

"Well, we know that the murderer is someone connected to the alien fans," said Michael. "We have a major event coming up next weekend. We know someone didn't like Michelle going on that sky-watching retreat. They tried to kill her and then got rid of a body to cover their tracks, which means they're scared. We must be closer to catching them than we realize."

"The man leading the tour last night, Ricardo, mentioned that other people had gone missing," I said.

"We got a last name?" Taylor asked. She was taking notes.

"Estevez," Marie replied. "He's a schoolteacher."

"I know you guys are personally invested in finding out about this special project shit," Taylor said, "but my focus is on stopping the killer. I'm going to bring Ricardo in for questioning. Do you want to be there for that, Michelle?"

"I don't think I should be in the room," I said. "We want these people to trust me. They won't if they think I'm working with the FBI."

"You can watch through the glass. I'd like to hear what you think of his responses."

"You don't think Ricardo has anything to do with the murders, do you?" said Marie.

"I don't know," Taylor said. "I doubt it, but sometimes you don't know about people. He wouldn't be the first schoolteacher to snap."

"How are you going to explain the FBI being involved?" asked Michael.

"Oh, that's easy," Taylor said. "Those two bodies we found this morning are on federal land."

"When are you going to pick him up?" I asked.

"We'll probably aim for tomorrow morning," said Taylor. "I'll need to talk to the local police chief. We'll need to use their secure interview room. I've spoken to the chief a couple of times since I got here. I hope she's okay with this. I don't want a repeat of the problems we had back in Pikeville."

I shuddered. Having the local police actively impeding our investigation had been no fun. Not to mention them harassing me and trying to arrest me for the murders.

"I'll try to think of some questions for you before then," I said.

"Okay." Taylor stood up. "I'll give you a call in the morning. Get some rest."

After they left, I washed in the sink. I really wanted a long, hot bath or even just a good shower. I couldn't do either with stitches. Michael helped me with the bandages on my back. There was some blood there; I'd been moving around too much. He gently washed around the wound and put fresh bandages over the four long cuts.

His hands were warm and gentle. I wanted him then, quite urgently, but was too tired to do anything about it. He kissed my forehead and helped me to bed. I knew he wanted me, too. I fell asleep feeling him next to me.

I felt safe.

CHAPTER THIRTY-FIVE

Taylor called at around ten in the morning.

Michael helped me get dressed. I'd decided on the one sports bra I had with me, along with my brown suit. I was going to need a new leather jacket; mine wasn't wearable.

I'd have to go shopping. So it wasn't all bad. I decided then that I'd ask Marie if she'd like to go with me. I wanted to get to know her better, without Michael along. I had a feeling she'd open up more to just me.

"How does that feel over the stitches?" asked Michael.

"Well, it isn't comfortable," I replied. "Not too bad. How did the cuts look?"

"They're healing nicely. Do you want me to drive you over to the police station?"

"No, I'd like to try driving on my own. I haven't taken any pain meds this morning, so I should be fine."

"Do you feel up to that?"

"I feel better," I said. "I'm not dizzy. I think all the food and sleep yesterday helped."

"Okay, the police station isn't far, so call me if you don't think you can drive back."

I gripped his arm. "I'm fine, Michael. I got hurt, but I'm not out of the fight, by any stretch of the imagination."

He nodded.

The police station wasn't hard to find. I parked and went in. Taylor introduced me to Police Chief Tapia, a stern-looking woman with wide cheekbones and dark hair and eyes; I thought she might be Native American. We spoke briefly, and then Taylor directed me to the observation room.

There was a familiar figure standing by the one-way mirror.

"Agent Oliver?"

"Dr. Fredericks! I'm glad that you're doing – Oh, my god, what happened to you now?"

I laughed. "Taylor didn't brief you on the new murders?"

"She didn't tell me you were almost a third," Oliver said. "Just your head, or…?"

"Head, right arm, and back. The back is the worst. Well, the deepest, anyway. The head wound was scarier."

Oliver shook his head.

"How are *you* doing?" I asked.

"Oh, they let me out right after you. I'm not real comfortable with what happened, but I can't spend my life worrying about something that might never come to be. The doctor assured me that it only raised my risk factors for cancer by a little."

"I'm glad you're okay."

Oliver gestured at the table in the other room. "Do you know anything about this guy? Are we thinking he's the perp?"

"Taylor hasn't told you anything, has she?" I was surprised.

"I just got back into town this morning. We haven't really had time to get acquainted."

"Oh. Well, no, I don't think Ricardo is the killer," I said. "He's a schoolteacher. He led a small alien watching tour last night – no, two nights ago. Two people died, and I was attacked."

"Wow," said Oliver. "You're like a cat; you've got nine lives. Try not to use them all up, okay?"

I smiled. He had no idea. "Thanks, Oliver. I'm glad you're doing better, too."

Taylor entered the other room with Ricardo. The man looked a little scared, but that was normal. Anyone who isn't intimidated by being in a room and questioned probably has something to hide.

Oliver turned on the speaker next to the window.

"Please state you name for the record," said Taylor.

"Ricardo Estevez."

"And you're a schoolteacher?"

"That's right. I teach middle school English. What's this all about?"

"You called 911 and reported a mountain lion attack, two nights ago."

"Yes. Is that so wrong? That poor young woman had been attacked."

"Does he mean you?" asked Oliver.

"Yeah. I'm pretty sure I'm older than him."

"You were attacked by a mountain lion?"

"No."

"Mr. Estevez, were you aware that two other people were missing from your group?" asked Taylor.

Ricardo frowned. "We couldn't find Ralph. I told the police that. No one else was missing, though."

"We found two bodies the next morning, Mr. Estevez."

"Oh, my god, Ralph's dead?"

"Why would you assume that?"

"Because he was missing," said Ricardo. "And you found a body. What is this?"

Taylor pushed a picture across the table. "Can you identify this man?"

"Oh, god, that's Ralph."

Taylor pushed another picture over.

Ricardo's face took on a greenish cast. "I'm going to be sick."

"Can you identify the man in that picture?"

"I can't… I'm sorry, I can't look at that again."

Taylor took the pictures back. "Care to revise your statement about someone missing?"

Ricardo took a deep breath. "I don't know what to tell you. No one else from our group was missing. Was Ralph killed by the mountain lion that attacked that woman?"

"We're uncertain at this time if a mountain lion was involved."

"What else could it have been?" asked Ricardo.

"You tell me."

"Seriously, what is going on here?' Ricardo demanded. "You asked me to come in and answer a few questions. I'm here voluntarily. Do I need a lawyer?"

"I haven't accused you of anything, Mr. Estevez. Do you feel guilty about something?"

"What?"

"You're going to want to think about your answers, Mr. Estevez. Two people are dead, and I think you know a lot more about all of this than you're saying."

"I don't know anything."

"That remains to be seen."

"Wow, she's kind of a hard-ass," said Oliver.

"You have no idea," I replied.

Taylor left the room and came over to where we stood. She'd acquired a coffee cup from somewhere. She had an instinct for finding coffee.

"Oliver, Fredericks, what do you think of this guy?"

"I don't think he's the killer," I said. "I was pretty sure of that already."

"He is hiding something, though," said Oliver. "He knows something."

"The other night he mentioned that people sometimes went missing," I said. "Try lying about the other body. Make him think it had been there a while. Ask him how often he goes up there, and if anyone has gone missing before."

"Good idea," Taylor said. "I'll let him stew a little and then go ask."

"So, just to be clear," said Oliver, "you don't think the attack was a mountain lion?"

"No," Taylor said. "Take a look at Fredericks' wounds. What do you see?"

"Four clean slashes." Then he nodded. "Animal attacks aren't that clean. Claws tend to rip a little along the cut."

"Exactly. The first dead guy, Ralph Garcia, was killed by the same attacker who wounded Dr. Fredricks. That attacker was killed on scene. Sometime later, someone dumped something on the body to make it dissolve."

Oliver glanced between Taylor and me. "What aren't you telling me? What do you mean, he was killed on scene?"

Taylor nodded to me.

I didn't want to lie to Oliver. "I killed the attacker," I said.

CHAPTER THIRTY-SIX

"Excuse me?" said Oliver.

I sighed. "I was attacked that night. I defended myself."

"We believe the attacker was armed with a multi-bladed weapon," said Taylor. "The weapon wasn't found on site. The current theory is that whoever dumped solvent on the body also took the weapon."

"So you fought against an armed man? With what? Did you shoot him?"

"I carry a boot knife," I said.

"Well, you are full of surprises," said Oliver. "This wasn't in the report."

Taylor looked pained. "I left it out deliberately."

Oliver glanced between us. "Okay, I think we're going to have to talk about this later. What about Mr. Estevez?"

"I have a few more questions for him," Taylor said. "How about we do lunch after and discuss the case."

"I think that's a good idea."

I had mixed feelings about telling Oliver what had been going on, and yet I also felt that he deserved to know. We'd been through a harrowing experience together, with the body and the radiation. I felt as if I could trust him. He might not believe me, but I didn't think he would turn on me, either.

Taylor finished her coffee, gave me an inscrutable look, and left. A minute later, she entered the secure room and sat across from Ricardo. She looked through her files as he grew more agitated.

I'd seen Taylor questioning suspects before. In Pikeville, she'd used similar tactics of not giving anything away and letting the suspect squirm. It was often an effective tactic.

"So, Mr. Estevez, is there anything you'd like to add to your statement?"

"Look, I'm just an English teacher, okay? Yes, I run a side gig giving UFO tours. Most of the time, people just point and gawk at satellites, okay? I don't know what happened the other night. I've never had anyone hurt."

"But people have gone missing?" asked Taylor.

Ricardo sighed. "Sometimes, like Ralph, yeah."

"I don't see any record of you reporting anyone else missing."

"Look, I just take people out to dark places and let them look at the sky. Sometimes we see weird stuff. If someone goes missing, they often turn up the next day. I used to worry about it, but it's mostly just people sneaking off to have sex, you know?"

"And when it isn't?"

"Drugs, usually," Ricardo said frankly. "Look, I just don't want to get involved with that kind of people. I've heard about the bodies in the desert. I figured some cartel had moved into the area."

That was an angle I hadn't considered.

Drug cartels did some pretty sick shit to make examples out of people. On the other hand, making an example of someone doesn't really do you any good if no one knows who did it. I couldn't see a cartel not leaving a signature or calling card. Not to mention the question of how they could have done it.

"You see, the problem with that is we have two bodies, and a woman in the hospital," Taylor said. "At least one of the bodies had been on site for a few weeks. You're saying you never noticed anything? There was a pretty strong smell."

"I didn't smell anything last night. No one mentioned anything, either. It was cold, though. Something like that might not smell as bad in the cold. I don't know. How is the woman doing?" Ricardo asked. "I felt so bad that something had happened to her."

"She isn't your concern."

Ricardo sighed. "Look, lock me up if you want to. I never saw anything there. I never suspected anything would ever happen there. You say it wasn't a mountain lion. Okay, but I have no idea…" Ricardo trailed off and then looked scared. I could feel his sudden spike of anxiety, even from the next room.

"Do you have something to add?" asked Taylor.

"You're carefully not saying what you think it was that attacked her. Well, I didn't see anything or come into contact with anything. Can I please go now? I don't think you can hold me any longer with charging me with something, and I would really like to leave."

"You may leave. Thank you for your time, Mr. Estevez. Please don't leave town. We may have some more questions for you." Taylor escorted him out, and then came over to where we stood.

"That was… *odd*," said Oliver.

"I'd bet you that he thinks an alien attacked me," I said.

Given what I'd actually seen, maybe it wasn't so far-fetched. I work with the supernatural all the time. I don't know why the thought of aliens was where I drew the line. Maybe because a line has to be drawn somewhere, or you start believing in everything. That's tinfoil-hat territory.

"As strange as it seems, I agree with you, Fredericks," said Taylor. "I don't think he knew anything, either. The drug angle is a red herring. So, what now?"

"Now? We have lunch," said Oliver, "and you two explain to me what the hell is going on."

I drove us all over to the Mexican restaurant that had become our favorite. Michael and Marie were already there, having lunch. I shook my head slightly. Michael nodded almost imperceptivity and bent forward to whisper something to Marie. They both glanced at us as we sat at a booth near them.

"Who wants to start?" asked Oliver.

"There's a lot. Where do you want to start?" I asked.

"Start with what you told me back at the station."

Taylor slid a thick folder across the table. "This is the case file for the attack. There you'll find pictures of Dr. Fredericks' injuries, taken at the hospital."

Oliver looks through the photographs. "Jee-*zus*, Fredericks. How are you walking around? This definitely wasn't an attack from a mountain lion."

"No, it wasn't," said Taylor.

"Then what?" He flipped through the file to look at the other bodies. "What the hell is this?"

"The person who attacked Dr. Fredericks dissolved after they were killed. We don't know how or why."

"What did you kill him with? A water gun full of acid?"

"Just a boot knife," I said. "We think someone dumped something on the body before we got back out there."

"You're not just an occult specialist, are you?"

"That's where it gets complicated," said Taylor. "I don't know how much to tell you."

"Because you don't trust me?"

"Because we do, but we don't want you getting hurt," I said. "Some of the information about me is classified."

Oliver shook his head. "You are so weird. Okay, what the hell. I have suspicions. Let me ask you a question."

"Okay."

"You took the full dose of radiation back there in the desert, didn't you?"

I nodded. "Four hundred plus rads. They had to destroy my clothes and phone."

"You two have worked together before?"

"Eastern Kentucky serial killer case."

"That doesn't explain why you didn't report that Dr. Fredericks killed a man, Special Agent Taylor."

"I'm not completely convinced that it was a man," said Taylor. "No weapon was recovered."

"Or a mountain lion, either. Why don't you tell me what happened?"

I glanced at Taylor. She shrugged.

My back itched as I told Oliver about that night, and what had happened. Telling it all again, it seemed even crazier. Food came, and we ate while I told my story. Oliver had good control of his emotions; I couldn't tell what he was thinking. I expected him to stand up and walk out on us.

Oliver thought for a few minutes about what I'd said. Then, "Well, this case just keeps getting crazier."

CHAPTER THIRTY-SEVEN

All things considered, I thought Oliver took what I told him pretty well. I mean, I kind of thought he would, or I wouldn't have told him the truth. Oliver and I had bonded while in the hospital together. His opinion of me mattered more than I'd realized.

"I guess I can see why you wouldn't report all of that," he said. "Normally... Well, nothing about this case has been *normal*. I'll be honest with you, Taylor. I was irritated when they told me a hotshot special agent from back East was taking over my case."

"I'd have felt the same way, but I did specifically ask that you stay on the case," said Taylor. "I liked the work you'd done on it up to that point. I didn't want you to feel like I taking over, per se, just joining you."

"Oh, I'm glad you're here," said Oliver. "No offense, but this case is too weird and getting too much scrutiny from Washington for me to want to be the lead."

"If you can, just ignore the weird for now. I think the important thing is to focus on stopping the killer," I said. "What happened to me was unfortunate, but I'm not convinced it had anything to do with the other murders."

"*Unfortunate*, she says, after almost dying," said Oliver. "Again. Why do you think the attack and murder have nothing to do with the others?"

"Because it was sloppy," I said. "Killing a man and then openly attacking me: those seem to be aggressive, unplanned actions. Whoever is behind the other murders is methodical. Look at us. Even after weeks, we have no real leads. No, whoever or whatever attacked me in the desert wasn't related to the rest of the case. Not directly, anyway."

"Okay, anything else you want to tell me?"

"Nothing that's relevant to the case," I said.

"That isn't exactly comforting. You're surrounded by a lot of mystery, Dr. Fredericks. Anyway, tell your friend to come on over and stop staring."

I looked around. I'd seen Michael leave a little earlier. He hadn't come back in. There was a gaunt Middle Eastern man over by the bar, looking at me. I'd never seen him before.

"Who?" I asked, continuing to look around.

"The guy by the bar."

"I don't know him."

Perhaps aware of our scrutiny, the man walked over to our table. He seemed curiously intent on the cuts on my head. He didn't creep me out like Ralph had, but there was definitely something not right about him.

"Help you with something?" Taylor asked mildly. I saw her hand slip into her jacket.

The man barely glanced at her. "No."

He reached for my throat.

I don't react well to things like that.

I grabbed his wrist and was almost bowled over. The guy was scarily strong and could have easily overpowered me. He stopped, though, and we just looked at other. I let go, and he dropped his hand, then stepped back. Taylor kept her hand on her gun, under her jacket.

In all fairness, he was probably reaching for my chin, to turn my head. He seemed fascinated by the cuts. On the other hand, it's my head, and I didn't want him touching me.

"Who are you?" I asked.

"My name is Hollis," he said. "Your wounds – how did you survive the attack?"

"What do you know about it?" asked Taylor.

He stepped back farther so he could look at her, too. "Nothing, until I saw your wounds. I'm surprised they're healing. I also didn't realize any of them were active here. I suppose it didn't use the fire?"

"Cuts are usually made with blades," said Taylor.

"Or claws," Hollis said.

I couldn't help it; I flinched.

"Who the hell are you?" Taylor demanded.

"I told you, my name is Hollis."

"First or last name?"

"Just Hollis."

"Are you a friend of Erin?" I asked, following my intuition.

"Friend?" He seemed to think about that. "I don't know, actually. I hadn't thought about it. I think she would say… that yes, we are friends. She asked me to check in on how things are going here. I see that I will have to report that things are not going well."

"I'm fine," I said.

"It won't stop now. They don't ever stop."

"*They*?" I asked. "You mean the man who attacked me?"

"Do men normally have claws?" asked Hollis.

"No, I suppose not," I said. "But what hurt me isn't around anymore."

He raised his eyebrows in a comically exaggerated expression of surprise. "You killed it?"

I nodded cautiously. This whole situation was really weird. It was stranger, even, than the encounters with Erin, and those had been bizarre. This guy just didn't read right. He didn't seem human. I didn't get a bad feeling, though, like I would if some entity was riding him.

"There are things I am still learning. I see, perhaps, Erin's interest in you. I shall report favorably, then. Erin wanted me to tell you that she still wishes to help, and that you shouldn't attempt to find the source until she returns."

"We're going to need a lot more than that," said Taylor.

"I have said what I must, and now I will be going. I would not advise attempting to stop me."

He turned on his heel and walked away. I watched as he passed a column. He didn't walk past it; he just vanished. I got up and looked around. He was *gone*, as if he'd never been here. The waitress hadn't noticed him. I sat back down with Oliver and Taylor.

"Okay, what the *actual* fuck?" asked Oliver.

"I wish I could answer that," I said.

"Who is Erin?" Oliver looked back and forth between Taylor and me, waiting for an answer.

"Before we say anything, you need to decide if you really want to know," said Taylor. "That information is dangerous. This is one deep, dark, rabbit hole you won't ever be able to escape."

"I think at this point, I *need* to know. To preserve my sanity."

"I'm not sure that knowing more will help preserve your sanity. Look at me."

Oliver chuckled. "Hit me with it anyway."

I held up a hand. "Maybe we should wait. Go back to the hotel and talk to Michael and Marie first. This affects them, too."

Oliver shook his head. "You are so... bizarre. Okay, yeah, let's go and talk to the others."

I hoped we were doing the right thing.

I trusted Oliver. He'd had a rough time dealing with his feelings after the radiation poisoning, and we'd really connected in the hospital. I didn't want to lie to him, and I didn't want to withhold the truth. Taylor had come around to believing in me. I hoped he would, too.

CHAPTER THIRTY-EIGHT

I called Michael and let him know we were thinking about telling Oliver the truth.

Michael was at Marie's house, so we went there to talk. It was more comfortable than the hotel room, which would have felt crowded. I was thinking that I might have to rent an office space if this case went on much longer.

Oliver declined refreshment and sat carefully in the armchair. I think he still didn't feel all that great. It made me feel a little guilty. I didn't have any lingering effects from the radiation and was quickly healing from my cuts.

"Okay, so what's going on with you guys?" asked Oliver.

"That's kind of a big question," I replied. "Can you narrow it down a bit?"

"I'll start at the beginning: Why did someone from Homeland Security recommend you for this case?"

"I told you before," I said, "I worked with Henderson on a case last fall, and again in the winter."

"Who does he really work for?"

"We wish we knew the answer to that, ourselves," said Michael.

"Who do *you* work for?"

"I'm currently on leave-slash-vacation from the Federal Marshals

Service."

"Okay," Oliver shook his head. "So who is Hollis, really?"

"Hollis?" asked Michael.

I explained what happened back at the restaurant. That brought up Erin, and I told Oliver about what had happened with her since I'd taken on the case. I told him the truth: I had no idea what she was talking about.

"So we're talking some kind of secret military project?" said Oliver. "And you're all involved?"

"I'm not," said Taylor.

"But you know about all of this, and it isn't bullshit?"

"Fredericks first told me about it during the case over the winter," Taylor replied. "It sounded pretty crazy to me, but it added up. I've managed to find out just enough from other sources to know it's real. Most of those sources said I was crazy to get involved at all."

"What *are* we talking about?" Oliver asked.

Michael and Marie nodded.

I sighed. Might as well.

I told Oliver about the Providence Project. Then I told him about what Erin had said, and that we still didn't know how it all fit together. It isn't an easy thing for me to talk about. Oliver was hard to read, but I think he believed me.

"Let me see the cuts again."

I turned my head.

"And these were just yesterday?"

"The night before, but yeah."

"Must be nice. I stub my toe and limp for a week. Any drawbacks?"

"You mean other than people noticing I'm not normal? Yeah, I get involved in this kind of shit all the time."

Oliver laughed. "Okay, so what are those other projects you named?"

"We don't know, exactly," said Michael. "That's part of the problem."

"What does this have to do with the murders?"

"We don't think it has anything to do with them," I said. "Maybe the attack the other night, although it doesn't seem to be related, but I can't say that with any certainty. It does seem as if the attack might have been because I'm getting too close to something."

"Too bad we don't know what," said Taylor. "Oliver, I've got to say, you're taking this better than I did."

"Who, me? I'm gibbering inside," Oliver said. "Part of me doesn't want to believe the government would experiment on kids. Part of me knows they have. You read about shit like the Tuskegee study, and it's like, yep, I can believe it."

Back in the 1930s, the US government conducted a study on the effects of syphilis on black men. The participants weren't given treatment, and the experiments went on until the 1970s, when a reporter broke the story to the world. It was just another sad, horrible chapter in our nation's history of unethical medical experiments.

"Project Providence, or possibly Project Absolution, used the children of military personnel," I said.

"What was done?" Oliver asked.

"We wish we knew," said Marie. "In vivo injections while we were in the womb. Special vitamins for our mothers. Injections while we were children. After that, a lot of testing and training. I remember that many of our cohort were tested to destruction."

"You mean killed? That's… *horrible*," said Oliver.

"We've learned to live with it," I said. "There is one other thing you should know."

"Just one?"

I smiled. "I have a special ability."

"Other than radiation resistance and fast healing?"

"I can touch objects and sense strong feelings and emotions associated with them."

Oliver nodded. "Given what else you've told me, that doesn't even faze me."

"Good, then we can get back to the case," said Taylor. "Ricardo didn't know anything useful."

"I'm glad to hear that," Marie said. "He always seemed okay."

"Unfortunately, that doesn't leave us with many leads."

"I have a few suspicions," I said.

"Well, spill them, Fredericks."

"I think we're on the right track. We know the victims were alien believers, right?"

"I still think it's an abduction cult," said Michael.

"Those guys," said Taylor. "Religion without a moral code. Great."

Marie bristled a bit at that. I'd talk to her later and smooth it over. I'd noticed Marie was quick to side with the alien hunters. I couldn't say why, but I could guess. She'd been called crazy for her beliefs most of her life. I imagine she felt the alien hunters were kindred spirits.

"Was that why you were on the sky-watching tour?" asked Oliver.

I nodded. "People go missing from those tours, and no one reports it. I'd really like to know if our victims went on any of those tours."

"I can look into it," Oliver said.

"That's going to be difficult," said Marie. "People usually pay cash."

"Did you discover anything useful?" I asked. "I forgot to ask, with the hospital and all."

"I may have," Marie replied. "Several of the little cliques were talking about two people who went missing. They were well-to-to experiencers. That wasn't the odd part. Apparently there was a small group of people who all claimed to have been abducted. These two were part of that group. I couldn't discover much about it, except that Dr. Munson was the leader."

"Dr. Munson?"

Marie shrugged. "I've heard of him, but not a lot. He's some kind of doctor from California. Big believer in alien abductions. Pushed an alien hybrid theory about a decade ago. I was surprised to hear him mentioned, since I hadn't heard anything about him for a few years."

"That sounds like something that could be important," I said. "I'd love to know if he was a surgeon."

"I think he was a psychologist, but I'm not sure. I may have one of his books around here."

"Anything you can find out," I said.

"I'll look into him, too," said Taylor.

We broke up our impromptu group after that.

I think Oliver took it all pretty well. Maybe too well. I don't think he'd really processed everything we told him. I'd expected him to ask more questions. In his place, I would have.

CHAPTER THIRTY-NINE

At Taylor's insistence, I took a few days off.

I'd already put a lot of energy into this case. I needed to rest and recover from my injuries, and Taylor and Oliver needed time to do some old-fashioned detective work. I was certain they'd call me if anything interesting developed, and I welcomed the chance to spend more time with Michael and Marie, without having the case looming over our heads.

I even found time to call Lawrence.

"Hey, Michelle, how's your vacation?" asked Lawrence.

"About the same as the last one," I replied.

"Ouch."

My last vacation had been going with Lawrence to Pikeville and getting caught up in a mess with a demon, a serial killer, human traffickers, hill witches, and a vampire cult. I was beginning to think I should never take a vacation. It wouldn't do me any good, though. Trouble would always find me.

"Want to talk about it?" he asked.

"Not really. How's Jean?" I asked. Jean is Lawrence's sister. She was staying at my place for now. It was useful to have someone to watch my cat. Not to mention that the poor girl had been isolated in Eastern Kentucky and really needed a good friend.

"Doing well. She just finished her first semester and is very excited to keep going. She's thinking about taking summer classes. Samson is doing well, by the way."

Samson is my cat. I missed the furry little bastard. I hadn't asked, because I trusted Jean to take care of him.

"Have you made any progress on that thing I asked you about?"

Lawrence was decrypting files we'd gotten from Julia. It was slow going. Military-grade encryption is no joke.

Lawrence was silent for a minute. "I have, but I'd rather not discuss such a private matter over the phone."

"I understand completely. A few things have come up recently that put a different spin on what we've learned in the past year. We should talk in person when I get back."

"You know, Jean could use a vacation, and I could, too," said Lawrence. "I hear the skiing is great in Taos."

"So I've heard. Not really my thing."

"You think Mark and Jen would watch Samson?" he asked.

"Probably. You might have bribe them with wine."

"I have just the bottle. I'll see what Jean says, then call Jen. Talk to you tomorrow?"

"Sound good. Thanks."

I lay back against my pillows and tried to get comfortable. My back didn't hurt much, but it itched like crazy. Michael had looked at the wounds earlier and said they were healing well, about the same as the ones on my head. Those itched, too, but were easier to ignore.

I'm not the kind of person who really knows how to relax.

Oh, I can meditate, do Tai Chi, I enjoy reading – you know, *relax* – but I have to be doing *something*. I've never liked going to the beach, because I don't like laying around and doing nothing. My friend Mark says it's a result of my Protestant work ethic.

What would he know about it? He's Jewish. Not to mention that he's also a workaholic.

I tried to play a game on my laptop but couldn't get into it.

I finally got up and washed my hair in the sink, and bathed as best

I could. I hated not being able to take a long bath or even a shower. I didn't know how much longer I could hold out.

After getting dressed, I glanced out the front window of the room. My Jeep was still sitting there, so Michael must have walked to Marie's gallery. I was glad they were spending so much time together.

Michael had told me about how close he and his sister been as children. He deeply regretted the rift that formed between them, and his part in it. I told him it wasn't his fault, and Marie would understand, but he'd been really worried about seeing her again.

Fear of rejection affects us all.

I texted Michael to let him know I was going to wander. He'd understand.

I didn't have any plans when I left the hotel. I just hopped into the Jeep and drove. I stopped to get a breakfast burrito even though I wasn't hungry. I ate it while driving.

It wasn't until I pulled off the road that I realized I'd driven back to where I was attacked. It wasn't deliberate. I hadn't even been thinking about it. I got my pistol out of the console and stepped out of the Jeep.

The air was cold up here on the mountainside.

I still hadn't bought a new jacket.

My blood was easy to find, dark stains against the sandy soil. The trail led to where the body of my attacker had lain. The FBI forensics team had cleaned up the area as best they could. A faint, lingering smell of rotten cabbage still hung in the air.

The memory of that night was still fresh in my mind: the pain, the fear, the desperation. I had been afraid, since the attack was unexpected. I closed my eyes and remembered. The man's hand had been open, as if he was going to slap me. He hadn't held a weapon.

The shock of pain made me wince. It was just the memory of the claws, though. The impossible claws on the hands of a man with the face of one who was lying dead a few meters away. Well, dead or dying – people usually take longer to die than you might think.

Ralph had been an asshole and a piece-of-shit excuse for a human being, but he hadn't deserved to die, gutted and bleeding out in the desert. I found where he'd been killed easily enough. Dried blood had splashed for a considerable distance from his body. At least one major artery must have been hit.

I touched the spilled blood, hoping for a flash of something, but it was just blood. It held no secrets it was willing to share with me. A final act of defiance from a troubled man.

Marie had said the military plane hovered over the body of my attacker. Could they have sprayed the body with whatever made it dissolve? I didn't think it likely.

I couldn't imagine what the plane had been looking for on that desolate slope.

What actually happened that night?

I couldn't say.

Shapeshifters, skin-walkers, monsters: I didn't really think any of that was real. I've met plenty of monsters, but they were all of the human variety. The few demons and other entities I'd encountered were immaterial. Demons don't have flesh; that's why they have to ride people.

I call them demons, but I don't think of them as demons in the traditional sense. Or maybe I do, but in the older Greek meaning of the word. A daemon was a disembodied intelligence. I'd seen them ride people, to drive bad people to commit worse crimes. I'd never seen one actually made flesh.

What I had seen under the starlight was a demon made flesh.

I shivered.

That thing was going to haunt my dreams.

INTERLUDE

Marissa has been sick for a few days.

We've been trying to cover it up, to hide her illness from the doctors, but it's no good. She's too sick. The boy with the amazing green eyes, Michael, thinks it might be cancer. Marissa has two growths on her back. There's something wrong with her hands, too.

The pain torments her.

Marie thinks it has something to do with the injections they give us. We're all changing inside. We can feel it, even if we don't know what it means.

It's Julia who tells the doctors. She does it out of mercy.

The doctors take Marissa away, and we all know we'll never see her again.

Then the soldiers come back with the doctors, and they make us all strip. It's humiliating. We are all of us together in our misery. No one snickers or makes rude comments, the way we might at other times.

We know who the enemy is.

Johnathon, a boy who has some lumps on his back, is taken away. We didn't even know he was afflicted. To judge from the look of fear on his face, he knows they're taking him to die, to be dissected.

One of the medical techs pats me down. He isn't supposed to. He's supposed to only check the boys. There are women techs to check us girls, but the doctors and techs are busy with Johnathon, who is resisting being taken.

I catch a glimpse from the tech's mind. He has disgusting thoughts about what he'd like to do to me and the other girls. I see what he has done to some of the ones they took away, how he hurt them. I can't take it longer. The core of darkness inside me wells up, and I straighten, slamming my head up into his face.

He stumbles back with a cry, and I'm on him. Before the soldiers can move to intercede, I reach down and grab the man by the testicles. One hard squeeze, and I feel them pop, like small, rotten eggs. The man screams, and sudden pain flashes through my skull as one of the soldiers slams the butt of their rifle into my head.

I twist out of the soldier's grasp. One, two, three, strikes to the solar plexus, and I feel something tear under my hardened fingers. The soldier is gagging as he sags to the ground, heart stopped, drowning in his own fluids. The tech is still nearby, screaming, but I'm not done with him yet.

I lift the rifle into my hands with a foot. I have no intention of shooting the tech. That would be too easy for him. I reverse the rifle and bring the stock down in a smooth arc that ends at a knee. The other soldiers are on their way, but I'm fast and methodical. I manage to break most of his bones before the soldiers get close to me. My last swing crushes the man's skull.

The soldiers beat me.

I don't care.

They'll hurt me, but I will haunt their dreams.

One day, I will be free, and I will hunt them.

I have become an angel of death.

CHAPTER FORTY

I can't tell if my dreams are memories or just nightmares.

I suppose they could be a mixture of both.

It isn't that I really remember all that much about the things done to me as a child. I remember Michael and I trying together to escape from the later project. I suppose the nightmares I'd been having since I was attacked could've just been nightmares. I think, though, that there's a grain of truth somewhere in them.

I may not like it, but I recognize the darkness inside me. I know what I'm capable of, and I know the things I've done in those dreams were things I would do now if in those circumstances. I acknowledge that I'm a killer. I know what they made me. However, I hope to only ever use that rage to help people.

Sometimes I'm haunted by Henderson's comments to me about all of us survivors of the project being killers. I know what I'm capable of. Sometimes it gives me comfort, knowing I can kill if I have to. Most of the time, I worry that I'll become like Julia, driven by rage. Insane with grief and remembered pain.

We are more alike, Julia and I, than I'd like to admit.

Michael came out of the bathroom is a cloud of steam. He'd taken a shower. I envied him.

"I drew you a bath," he said.

"You know I can't take a bath or a shower," I replied.

"Sure you can. You just need to keep your stitches dry. I'll help you wash your hair and wash your back for you."

"I love you," I said as I quickly stripped out of my pajamas.

"I love you, too," Michael said. "Now get in the tub before I grab you and ravage you."

"Hmm, sounds good to me."

Michael pointed into the bathroom.

It felt good to finally be clean.

After I dressed, we drove over and met Marie at the gallery. No one came in while we were there. Marie said the economy had taken a downturn, and it was always difficult to sell art in times like this.

Consuela came in to cover lunch, and we went out to eat at the Italian place.

"You feeling okay, Michelle?" asked Marie. "You're looking a little rough today."

"Well enough," I said. "I've been having nightmares since the attack."

"About what happened?"

"Strangely, no. About other stuff. Things that may have happened when we were children. I don't know. It isn't like the memories of the Providence Project. These are weird."

"Want to talk about it?"

"Sure. Why not?"

I told them about what I'd dreamed. Both of the dreams had been strange. They'd both felt as if they had at least some truth, too.

"You know, I don't actually remember *everything*," said Marie. "I think I do from the later Providence stuff, but what they did before? No, only some of it. I do remember Tom; he was nice. I didn't care for Marissa. It wasn't anything personal. We just didn't get long. I don't remember them dying. I do remember them being gone, though."

"For all I know, these were just bad dreams," I said.

"I didn't realize it, but I think I've had dreams about what happened to Tom," said Michael. "At least, I've had dreams where someone I knew, a young man, suddenly turned into something else."

"I wonder how many kids died in that program," I said.

"Well, I remember dozens of us at first, but by the time we were in Providence, only a little over a dozen were still alive," Marie said.

"How could they do it?" I asked. "How could the doctors, techs, nurses, and soldiers torture children to death? We were the children of other soldiers – they had to know that."

"You know psychopaths are always drawn to positions of authority and power," said Michael. "I'm not saying everyone in power is, but the positions do attract the scum who like to hurt people. Look at how bad police brutality has become."

"You think the government just found a bunch of psychos willing to do that?" I asked.

"Not all of them were bad," said Marie. "Some tried to shield us from the psychos. I remember some nurses who always insisted they be in the room with us. I think they were trying to keep some of the horrors at bay."

"They still participated in the torture, the drugs, the injections of god-knows-what."

"I wasn't condoning any actions of the personnel. I just meant they weren't all psycho. They can't use that excuse."

"Well, what do you think about the dreams?" I asked, dropping the other subject.

I wasn't ready to forgive any of the people who'd hurt us as children. I wasn't going to hunt them down, as Julia had, but that didn't mean I wouldn't kill them if I ever met one of them on the street.

As I said, Julia and I are more alike than I'd like to admit.

"I think they could actually be memories," said Michael. "I know you fairly well at this point. Normal dreams and nightmares don't linger for you. The strong ones like these are probably at least partially based on memory."

"That's a scary thought," I said.

"You mentioned that Tom had been given an injection. You thought it was something new. What's scary to me is that what they did to us might not have been as bad as it could have been."

That was something to think about.

"I wonder if they used it on others, though," said Michael. "Maybe the guy who attacked you was one of the kids injected with that shit. Whatever it is."

I was spared having to respond by the server bringing our food to the table.

Michael had a good point. If I'd seen something like that before, in the first project, then what attacked me in the desert could have been related. I couldn't rule it out, anyway.

For some reason I couldn't define, I didn't think that was right, though.

The boy in my dream, Tom, had been torn apart from within. The changes wrought upon him had been involuntary and had driven him mad from the pain. The thing that attacked me in the desert had changed to appear and sound like Ralph. It had also changed its hands into claws almost instantly as it swung on me.

Whatever had attacked me, it wasn't the same thing.

Hollis, the strange associate of the enigmatic Erin, had known that I'd been attacked by claws. He had known what attacked me, and he was surprised that I'd not only survived but killed the thing. I had no idea what I'd gotten myself into out here in the West, but I knew that somehow, it was all interconnected.

CHAPTER FORTY-ONE

Lawrence and Jean surprised me the next day by calling in the late morning from the Albuquerque airport. I offered to drive down and pick them up, but Lawrence said he already had a car rented. He said they'd be here in a couple of hours.

"I thought you didn't drive," I said.

"I'll make Jean drive."

I warned him not to speed. He'd be passing through several reservations on the way, and they take their sovereign laws very seriously.

I knew Lawrence would be tempted by the casinos along the way, but I was confident Jean would keep him on track. He revised his estimate to three hours, and we agreed to meet for lunch.

The phone rang again just as soon I disconnected.

I answered it without looking. "Forget something?"

"Yeah, where I left my consultant," said Taylor. "You got your walking boots on?"

I groaned. "I thought you were giving me a few days off."

"I did. Now we have another body. Chop, chop. We'll be there in five to pick you up."

No rest for the wicked.

I sent Michael a text and then changed into my second-best suit.

My shoulder holster rubbed uncomfortably across the healing wounds on my back. I wasn't ready not to have a weapon handy, though.

Taylor pulled up in Oliver's SUV, although it had government tags, so technically it belonged to the FBI. Oliver waved from the passenger's seat. I got in behind Taylor; she's short, and I have long legs.

"No fair calling shotgun before you get here," I said to Oliver.

"The early bird gets the worm," he replied.

"Uh-huh, and the second mouse gets the cheese," I said with a grin.

"Don't make me come back there," said Oliver.

"Try it, G-man."

"Settle down, children, or I'm turning around," said Taylor.

"Oh, no, I'd have to go back to bed," I said. "Please don't send me to my room..."

"Now that that's out of your system, let's get down to business."

I restrained myself from bursting into song. Taylor didn't seem to be in the mood. I had no idea if she'd ever seen *Mulan,* anyway. Probably not.

"Oliver, you want to fill her in?"

"As Taylor told you, we've got another body," he said.

"Yep, not real eager to get there to it, either," I said. "Not after the last one."

"A team with a Geiger counter has already assessed the body and surrounding area," said Taylor. "We're clear to take a closer look."

"Any ID on the victim?"

Oliver handed me a slim folder. "Her name was Sofia Lucia. Lived in Roswell with a boyfriend, Lucas Hernandez. We've asked state police to round him up for questioning. She was never reported missing."

"Any connection to the other victims?"

"We're not that lucky, Fredericks," said Taylor.

"How about any connections to the UFO tour groups?"

Oliver shook his head. "She was in the Roswell chapter of MUFON, but that isn't unusual."

MUFON, aka the Mutual UFO Network, is a club that researches and reports UFO activity. I'd thought about joining once, myself, years ago. I'd been interested in seeing if there was a paranormal aspect to UFO sightings. Other things had come up, and I never joined. The members I'd met had been enthusiastic but harmless.

"Still, it means she was connected to the other victims," I said.

"A connection other than just being killed in the same fashion?" said Taylor.

"Yeah, other than that." Taylor was definitely in a mood.

"Washington has been up her ass." Oliver didn't sound very sympathetic.

"Maybe we'll learn something from the boyfriend," I said, relenting. If Taylor had been getting reamed by Washington, she didn't need me giving her shit. "At the least, he'll know when she vanished."

"I want to know why he didn't report it," said Taylor.

"I can think of a couple of reasons," I said. "A lot of people in this country don't trust the government."

Taylor snorted. "No, really?"

"If he thought she'd been abducted by aliens, he might have been afraid to report it."

"Fair enough."

"Do these people really believe that?" asked Oliver.

"Some of them."

"You're still on track to go to that convention thing, right?" Taylor asked.

"Yes, with Marie." Oliver looked confused. "Taos has an alien festival every year."

"When's that?" he asked.

"This coming Memorial Day Weekend, three days of fun."

Taylor rolled her eyes.

"I went to the one in Roswell a couple of years ago with my husband," said Oliver. "Total chaos. It *was* kind of fun, actually, now that I think about it."

"We're here," Taylor said.

We were northeast of town, in the foothills of the mountains. There were more trees, and some pueblo houses nearby. I hadn't been in this area before, but I recognized the Taos Pueblo from pictures.

"We're on tribal land," said Taylor. "Be respectful and watch what you say. We're guests here. Remember that this is foreign soil. The body is to the north of the pueblo. We may have some trouble from the local authorities."

I could see a few sheriffs' trucks in the distance.

"The victim isn't a local," I said. "You said she was from Roswell."

"I said the victim lived in Roswell." Taylor shrugged. "She may have been related to someone here. In any case, we need special permission to investigate any body found on tribal land."

"I assume we have that," I said.

"More or less."

I could see this going poorly.

We got out of the SUV. A few of the local police glared at us. Oliver led Taylor and me unerringly to the sheriff, so he must have dealt with him before. The sheriff was a heavyset man with a wide hat and a long colt .45 revolver on his hip in a tooled leather holster. He didn't look friendly. I couldn't really blame him.

"Special Agent Taylor, Agent Oliver, and Dr. Fredericks," Taylor said. "FBI."

"Yeah, I remember you guys," the sheriff said. "I don't remember calling the FBI, though."

"Sheriff Romero, the victim lived in Roswell, which makes it our jurisdiction."

"She was found here, which makes it ours. This is our land, fed. Don't forget that."

I touched Taylor's arm to get her attention, since she was about to try to bluster. It might work in the long run, but it wasn't going to get us results quickly. We needed to examine the body and the surroundings without delay.

"Sheriff, we aren't here to make trouble or step on your toes," I said. "From what the initial report said, this victim has the same injuries as the other recent victims. We just want to stop the killer from hurting anyone else."

"You're a doctor?" His eyes flicked over my injuries with interest.

"Forensic. I want to examine the body, with your permission. We won't disturb the victim. We want justice for her."

"Justice isn't something we see a lot from the federal government."

"We just want to stop the killings," I said. "If our investigation leads back here, we'll contact you first and coordinate as to what you think the best course of action is."

The sheriff sighed. "Be quick, and don't disturb the body."

"Thank you, sir."

CHAPTER FORTY-TWO

"We'll coordinate with the sheriff?" Taylor said quietly as we walked over to the body.

"No one here killed these people," I said.

"You can't know that. And I don't like you make promises for me."

I shrugged. I trusted my intuition. Whoever the killer was, they weren't living anywhere near where the bodies were being found. The killer was too methodical for that.

"I'm sorry, Taylor," I said. "I just felt time pressing. We need stop this bastard."

"On that, we agree."

Someone had thrown a wool blanket over the body.

A short woman in uniform stood near victim. She smiled when we approached. It was the first time I got the sense that anyone was happy we were here.

"I'm Deputy Conchas," she said. "You must be the feds. I'm surprised you got past ol' grumpy so quickly."

"Dr. Fredericks here has a silver tongue," said Taylor. "Why was the body covered?"

"It would be disrespectful to do otherwise," Conchas said. "And it is pretty disturbing to look at. We didn't want people to see what had been done to her."

"May I look?" I asked.

"I'll hold up the blanket so no one else can see."

The injuries were consistent with those on the other bodies. This woman had been dead for a couple of weeks, at least. Despite that, there wasn't much rotting. The abdominal cavity wasn't distended, either. I wondered if the radioactive substance the murderer used had killed off the bacteria.

"Thank you," I said, standing back up.

Conchas covered the body respectfully.

"When was the body found?" I asked.

"This morning," she replied.

"This woman has been dead for weeks," I said.

Conchas shrugged. "This is a high-traffic area. If the body had been here longer, it would have been noticed."

I nodded. The killer had moved the body to the pueblo. Why? So it would be found? That seemed the most likely explanation. I don't like things that seem obvious, though.

"Who found the body?" I asked.

"A local farmer, José," said Conchas. "He doesn't speak English."

"Could you translate Tiwa for us?" I asked.

Conchas grinned. "Yeah, I can do that." She waved to another deputy.

The deputy led an elderly man over. The man was small and wrinkled. He had to be over hundred years old. I wouldn't have been surprised if I was told he was two hundred. Hell, if he'd told me he was twice that, I'd have just nodded agreement.

Conchas spoke to him briefly.

He replied with a nod.

"Hello," I said. "Can you tell us what happened?"

Conchas translated.

The man shrugged and replied.

"He says he found the body this morning, reported it, and what more do you need to know?"

"Did he see or hear anything... unusual?"

"He says you won't believe him."

I pointed to the cuts on my face. "These were not from a mountain lion. I'll believe you."

The old man squinted at me for a few minutes. I'm not sure how good his eyesight was, but I could tell he knew something. He started breathing harder, and looking around. Finally, he spoke for a few minutes to Deputy Conchas.

"He says what hurt you wasn't what killed this woman."

"I didn't think it was. I just pointed it out so he'd know I would believe what he tells me. What else did he say?"

"Look, he's very old and very traditional. I don't really think it matters what else he said. It won't help. It doesn't have anything to do with the body."

I glanced at Taylor and Oliver, and jerked my head. Taylor nodded and the two of them walked back to talk to the sheriff. I figured the deputy didn't want to say anything in front of the feds.

"I'm not with the FBI," I said. "They've hired me because I work with the strange and abnormal. I can… see what others can't."

"What did you mean when you said the wounds weren't from a mountain lion?" Conchas asked.

"I was attacked a few nights ago by what I thought was a man. He attacked me and suddenly had claws. The FBI says it must have been knives. I know it wasn't."

Conchas took a deep breath and blew it out. "Okay, yeah. Not many people would tell me something like that. Maybe you're legit, or just crazy. He said a bad shaman must have attacked you, but that wasn't what killed the woman. He doesn't know what killed her, but he has suspicions."

"So do I," I said. "I think what attacked me wasn't natural, but the one who killed the woman just wants us to think he isn't."

She spoke to the man again.

"He agrees. He says there was a bright light in the field last night, and a loud growling. He was afraid to come out and look, because people have found animals dead out in the fields when that happens.

Sometimes those who find the bodies get sick."

I nodded. "The bodies are sometimes radioactive," I said. "That's why we had someone check this body first. I think this woman was moved from somewhere else. I think the killer must have come and dumped the body here."

Conchas nodded. "No tracks near the body, though."

"That can't be covered up?"

"Maybe." Conchas asked the man something, then nodded. "He says to look over by the river. Sometimes the growling comes from there first, when they find animals."

"Thank you," I said.

The man nodded and returned to where he'd been before.

"I'll walk with you," Conchas said.

"Thanks. Are you from here?" I asked.

Conchas nodded. "I grew up over in the new village. I have an aunt who's traditional, though."

"It's a beautiful place."

"We got lucky. No one ever found any gold or valuable minerals on our land. So we never had to move."

I nodded. Too many of the First Peoples had been driven from their lands by the ruthless expansions of Europeans across America. It was a story as old as time, for many people around the world, but the memories were recent and painful for the people living here in the Southwest.

Conchas and I walked away from the body in a loose, spiraling search pattern. The ground here was hard-packed, with a fine layer of dust over it. There was more vegetation, even trees, as we got close to the river.

Back in Kentucky, it would have been called a small stream or creek. Here, where water is scarcer, this was a lifeline. I recalled that the map had labeled it the Rio Pueblo de Taos. It didn't look very deep.

"There," I said, pointing. "Those look like tracks."

Conchas led me over to the riverbank. "Good eyes. Not much to go on, but yeah, that's definitely tracks from a truck or SUV," she said. "A wide, heavy one, too."

"Looks like maybe a Humvee," I said. "Or a civilian Hummer."

"You ex-military?"

"Something like that."

"Well, no one around here owns anything like that," said Conchas. "Let me call the sheriff."

CHAPTER FORTY-THREE

A few minutes later, the sheriff, Taylor, and Oliver came through the bushes south of us. I waved, and they made their way over to us. The sheriff looked annoyed. I wondered what they had been talking about.

"What ya got?" the sheriff demanded.

"Tire tracks, sheriff," said Conchas.

"So? Probably just some city boy hot-rodding. There weren't any tracks near the body. How do you explain that?"

Taylor must have really pissed this guy off.

"Sheriff, if you don't mind following me for a moment." I walked up the bank. "You can see here that several small bushes were cut down. There are no tracks after that."

"So?"

"You think they used the creosote bushes to cover their tracks?" Conchas asked me. "It could work, if they tied the bushes to the bumper."

I nodded. "The tracks we do have lead in the right direction. We also have a witness who saw a light and heard a growling in the field. That could have been the Humvee lights and engine."

"Witness? You mean old José? He's blind and senile."

"He didn't seem either, to me," I said. "In any case, casts should be taken of these tracks. At the least, good clear pictures."

"We don't have the resources or the time for that."

"Luckily, we do," said Taylor. "As we discussed earlier, this is a *federal* crime scene. We'll take it from here. Just leave a couple of deputies here to liaison with the locals. There's no need for you to stay, since you're so busy."

I winced a bit at that. Taylor was making an enemy, for no good reason. I had a feeling it was going to come back and bite her on the ass. The sheriff could make life very difficult for us all. I didn't know what had gotten into her.

It took a couple of hours for the FBI forensics people to scour the area between the river and the body. It was early afternoon before I got back to Taos. I had completely forgotten about meeting up with Lawrence and Jean.

My phone showed I had missed three calls: two from Lawrence, and one from Michael.

I called Lawrence back first. "I am so sorry," I said as he answered.

"Hey, Michelle, no worries. We saw Michael walking down the road as we came into town. We had lunch with him and his sister. Marie is *so* nice. I can't hardly believe she's Michael twin sister."

"I got called away on a case," I said. "No cell reception."

"No problem. Say, we're all here at the gallery. You should come on by."

"I'll be right there."

There was a white BMW convertible parked outside the gallery. I knew it had to be the car Lawrence rented; it seemed like just the sort of ostentatious thing he'd do. He was always trying to run from his impoverished Eastern Kentucky roots.

I knew Lawrence didn't drive. I wondered what Jean had thought about driving a car like that. She'd probably hated it. Jean didn't like to call attention to herself.

"Oh, my god, Michelle, what happened to your head?" Lawrence exclaimed as I walked in.

I'd forgotten to tell him about the attack. "Long story," I said.

Jean came over and gave me a hug. "Missed you," she said.

"I missed you, too," I replied. "How was your first semester?"

"Amazing. Looking forward to going back."

"Love your hair, by the way."

Jean blushed and ducked her head.

She'd gotten her long, cinnamon hair cut to a chin-length bob. It suited her somewhat round face. She'd put on a little weight, too. I was glad. She'd been too thin, back in Pikeville. She was probably giving the freshmen boys at university heart palpitations. Not that she'd notice.

"You're going to make me beg, aren't you?" Lawrence said as he gave me a hug.

"I got attacked a couple of nights ago," I said.

"By what? A cougar?"

I shook my head.

Lawrence sighed. "Okay, I'll ask later. Just the head?"

"Also back and right arm, so don't squeeze too tight."

"You should have said something," Jean scolded. "I wouldn't have hugged you."

"That's why I didn't say anything," I replied.

Jean smiled and shook her head.

Michael came out of the back room. "I thought I heard you out here. Everything go okay?"

"I think so. I learned some interesting things about the case. Are we alone in here?" I was usually comfortable in the gallery. Now, I felt as if I was being watched. I didn't like the feeling.

"There's no one else here," Michael said.

Marie came out of the back and looked around. I think she felt whatever it was, too. The last time I'd felt like this had been back in Pikeville, but I'd taken care of that problem.

"Just a feeling. As for the case, we found some tire tracks from a Humvee nearby. We think that's who dumped the body."

"A Humvee or a Hummer?" asked Michael.

"Definitely a Humvee."

"Those aren't street legal in most states. Any video surveillance feeds?"

"It was on the Taos Pueblo Reservation, so no."

"That's unfortunate. Maybe Taylor can find a list of people who own one."

"I'm sure she's on it. You're assuming it was civilian."

Michael frowned. "You think the military could be involved?"

"I don't know. Something about the whole thing didn't feel right. No one has seen anybody dumping the bodies, but last night a farmer saw a bright light and heard a growling noise from the field. The tracks were nearby."

"That's why you think it was a Humvee."

"Exactly. The victim had been dead for weeks. Someone moved the body to the reservation. Why?"

"You're thinking the military moved the body because it was too close to something sensitive?" Michael asked. "There aren't any bases in the area."

"That we know of."

"You still think the civilian airfield might be a cover?"

"I think it would be easy to hide the transfer of personnel there."

"Maybe it would help if we knew what you were talking about," said Lawrence.

"We should go somewhere else to discuss it," Marie said. "Like my place."

"It's still early afternoon," said Michael.

"No one is going to buy anything today," Marie said. "If they really want something, they can come back tomorrow."

We drove over to Marie's place. Lawrence checked for electronic bugs, which might have seemed out of the ordinary once but now just seemed normal. I caught everyone up on what had been going on. It took a while. A lot had been happening. I think Lawrence and Jean were a bit overwhelmed by it all. I know Jean was.

Sometimes there just isn't an easy way to tell a friend you're a freak.

CHAPTER FORTY-FOUR

Marie's cats took an instant liking to Jean, showing they had good taste.

"My turn, I guess," Lawrence said. "I finished decoding the rest of the data on those hard drives we got from the van. Julia must have gotten the information from the CIA – it was really tightly encrypted. However, the data was somewhat haphazardly arranged. I think Julia just grabbed everything she could off a server. I can only imagine from where."

"Anything about the special projects on there?" asked Michael.

Lawrence nodded. "Quite a bit about Providence, actually. There's security camera footage of several attempted escapes. Which, I have to say, is very scary stuff."

"Some of us lived it," I said. Somehow I knew it was me in those videos. "We don't need the details right now. Anything about those other projects?"

"Yeah. Not a lot, though." Lawrence opened his laptop. "As you suspected, Project Wormwood was based out of Angel Fire Air Station. The drives don't contain much else about it. Project Absolution was some kind of outgrowth of the research from Wormwood. Providence was a different project that – and I quote – used assets from Project Absolution."

"No idea what it was, though?"

"No, just the names and history of the projects. I don't think Julia was interested in the other ones. The note files on here show she was looking for the personnel from Providence."

"I think it's clear that Absolution must have been some sort of super soldier program," said Marie. "It wouldn't have made sense to train us to fight otherwise."

I was surprised Marie was speaking up; she was usually shy. Lawrence and Jean must have made a good impression on her when they first arrived. I wished I hadn't missed that. That was the downside of taking this case. I felt as if I was missing spending time with Michael and Marie.

Mostly because I was.

"I suppose it makes sense. I used my combat training against the guards at Providence enough times. I did wonder why they trained us. They had to know we'd use the skills against them. The military just shuffled all of us kids into the Providence project because we're tough enough to survive that damn chair."

"Yeah, about that," Lawrence said. "Your cohort was just the first group of kids in Project Absolution. The military started new cohorts every two years, up until 1980. You were part of the first group, born in seventy-two. I don't know what happened to the other groups of kids. Julia was only interested in your cohort, since it was the only one transferred to Providence."

"She might have been looking for her sister Amy," said Marie. "Owens."

"There wasn't anything in the data about an Amy Owens," Lawrence said. "There were a lot of names, but not that one. I'll do a general search for an Amy."

"Try looking for an Amita," Marie said. "I sort of remember Julia calling her that once."

"Okay, thanks. I will."

"There was nothing at all about Wormwood?" I asked.

"Just that Absolution was an outgrowth of the research."

"Which doesn't make sense," said Michael. "I know Wormwood was a project to develop rapid-transport technology. Project Brimstone, a current project, is using the tech developed at Wormwood. The person I spoke to about it wouldn't have lied."

Lawrence shook his head. "I don't know what to tell you. The files are clear on the subject – look for yourself."

"I believe you," said Michael. "I just don't understand the connection."

"How did you guys even figure out any of this?" asked Jean. "It's so crazy. I mean, you knew some or all of this already, didn't you?"

"The memory caps put on us as children are slipping a bit," I said. "We didn't have names for the special projects until we ran into a strange woman out here named Erin. She seems to know a lot about all of these projects. She indicated that she needs our help with something. I think it has something to do with Project Wormwood, although I have no idea what."

"She could be from one of the later generations of children," said Michael. "I couldn't tell how old she is, but I thought maybe she was a little younger than us."

"Maybe," Marie said. "Her soul felt immensely old."

"Whoever she is, I think we should get her on our side," I said. "She obviously knows a lot, and since she's stronger than any of us, she could be useful in a fight."

"We have no reason to trust her," said Michael.

"And yet I do," I replied. "I couldn't tell you why, though."

"She's going to have to answer some questions before I trust her. I know it's tempting to believe her, since she's obviously one of us, but remember Julia. Not everyone who survived the experiments did so sane."

Michael and I were usually in agreement on things. I think the dissonance between us now could be felt by the others. It was uncomfortable for me, and *I* knew it was just Michael being cautious.

I also think Michael was holding a bit of a grudge at having been overpowered. That had probably never happened before. I was confident he'd come around. I trusted my instincts where Erin was concerned.

"So what's next?" asked Lawrence.

"Well, there's the alien festival this weekend," I said. "There was a meteor here in the late sixties that some people believe was a UFO. People come from all over to celebrate it."

"That sounds like fun," Jean said and then blushed.

"It could be," I replied. "I'll be busy trying to catch a killer."

"Well, when you put it that way…," said Lawrence.

I smiled. "Seriously, go have fun. Festivals are always a good time. You guys are on vacation. I'm the one who took this job."

"We don't mind helping," said Michael. The others nodded.

"I appreciate that. I may take you up on it. I'd really like to get a better look at that old air station, too."

"You still think the military has something to do with this?" Michael asked.

"It could just be some murderer with a Humvee. Those might not be street legal, but killing people isn't legal, either. I don't think the scumbag would care."

"We should be careful, though. The government has a bad habit of handing special projects off to private companies."

"Sure, then they don't have to comply with Freedom of Information requests," I said.

"My point is that there could be a PMC involved. We need to be careful."

Private military companies, PMCs, are mercenaries. I was pretty sure the troops Julia employed had been mercs. For that matter, the guards in the Providence Project probably had been, too.

"Maybe we should put off exploration of the former air station until after the festival," Marie said. "You never know what kind of information we might learn from people who collect conspiracy theories like stamps."

"That sounds like a good idea," said Michael.

I nodded.

I didn't agree with them, but I wasn't going to argue, either. If I had the chance, I'd run over to Angel Fire and poke around. There was something over there, something that filled me with dread, but I wasn't going to rest until I figured out what it was.

INTERLUDE

We are, all of us, ill.

I suspect the latest series of injections didn't go as planned. In the past, when they injected us, it might make us feel a little sick for a few hours, but nothing like this. None of us were able to get out of bed this morning, even when they used the prods. We are all weak and feverish.

It's getting worse.

The doctors are confused, but I sense excitement from them, as well. They detect what I can sense: that there are changes occurring in us children. I am terrified of what those changes could be. What happened to Tom still haunts me.

It's strange, because that feels as if it was a lifetime ago. I don't know when Tom was with us. I suspect it was last year, because other, more normal changes have occurred in my body since that time. I am older than I was. However, when I am here in the camp, all my memories bleed together.

It feels as if I'm always confused.

My life during the rest of the year is a blurry recollection. Every summer, I come to the special camp that no one talks about. Here in the camp, some of the other children remember me, even though I don't really remember them. Each time it feels new to me.

I am wracked with cold chills.

I think it's the medicine they've given us. The doctors say they're giving us inoculations. I don't think anyone believes that. A few of the children might. I know the doctors don't.

The fever worsens, and the changes inside me are more painful. The doctors told us that we might begin to hallucinate if the fever gets worse. I think it must have, because I can see a nimbus of fire around most of the other children. When I raise my hand, I see flickering blue-white fire there, too.

The doctors remove those without the fire. I think the children without the fire have died. I know I will never see them again. I didn't know any of those kids. They were the weaker ones. I mostly spend time with the powerful children.

The burning pain is unbearable.

I cannot help but scream.

I am not the only one doing so.

In the night, when the lights are out, the effect is more noticeable. I remember from my classes that the human body radiates in both the infrared and the ultraviolet. Our eyes can't normally see into those spectrums, but what is normal anymore? I wonder if I see the heat in our bodies. I feel my mind touching the minds of the other children.

It helps to know I'm not alone.

I feel a cool hand on my head and hear a whisper in my ear.

The pain and the fire subside. I see someone moving among the beds. Normally I would be afraid. Visitations in the night are usually unpleasant, but this person has beautiful wings with dark feathers, and is helping us. Surely she is an angel.

I think I must be hallucinating, and there is no one here.

Either way, I begin to feel better.

Hallucination or not, the relief from pain is a gift, and I cherish it.

CHAPTER FORTY-FIVE

People started arriving for the festival on Friday.

The town had put up banners and streamers. A small tent city was going up at Kit Carson Park, and the convention center was a hive of activity. Marie was kept busy at the gallery, although most of the visitors just wanted to gawk at the local art without buying anything.

I had lunch with Jean and Lawrence. It was nice to catch up with them. We hadn't really just had time together since they came out here. We talked about Jean's classes and Lawrence's lack of a love life. Jean wasn't dating anyone, either, but didn't seem as bothered by it.

I kept hoping Erin would show up at lunch. I wanted to talk to her about her involvement in the projects. I wanted to know what she knew. We needed to know more about these special projects, and I thought Erin was the key. She knew more than she'd told us.

I walked down to the park after lunch, but the venders weren't open yet. I did get a glimpse of the kitschy crap they were selling. One vender had things that looked like green, blow-up sex dolls with bug eyes. I avoided eye contact and quickly walked past.

Without much to do, I walked back to my Jeep and started driving around. Before too long, I found myself headed east. I didn't really think about what I was doing until I saw the sign for the Colfax County Angel Fire Airport.

Michael didn't want me to poke around the airport alone, but since when do I listen to what anyone else says? I pulled into the gravel lot outside the main building. Two small planes and an old helicopter sat out on the tarmac. I wondered how many people in Taos owned their own planes.

I stepped out of my Jeep. It was colder in Angel Fire than it had been in Taos. The feeling of something wrong crept up my back, too. I felt something the last time I'd been to the airport, when I picked up Taylor, and before that when I drove past. I hadn't gotten out of my Jeep either of those times.

It made a difference.

My Jeep is an extension of my home and therefore shares some of the same protective properties. Outside my vehicle, I had nothing except my own mental shields to protect my mind from whatever psychic impressions were in the area.

There were a lot of psychic impressions.

Tragedy had stalked this field. People had died here. I could even sense a faint echo of future horrors, which I normally can't do. Planes crash sometimes. It happens less often than car crashes but tends to kill more people at once. I didn't sense a large number of deaths, but even small groups dying in flames leaves an impression.

"Can I help you, ma'am?"

I turned toward the speaker, a young man in greasy coveralls. He probably worked on the planes. I gave him my best smile. It might even have worked if I didn't have big scars on my face.

"I'm just checking out the field," I said. "I've always wanted my own plane."

"I don't think any of these are for sale."

"I wasn't looking to buy right now. I was just checking out the airfield, in case I do move here."

"Oh, okay. Yeah, the Colfax County Airport is pretty cool. It's the highest airport in the country."

"Cool. Do you mind if I ask you a few questions about it, Fred?"

He started. "How did you know my name?"

"It's on your coverall," I said. "My name is Michelle."

"You a reporter?'

"No, why would you think that?"

He shrugged. "You're good looking and asking questions. We don't get a lot of visitors."

"I'm just interested in the airport," I said. "Marie Delling is my sister-in-law."

Fred frowned. "She runs the gallery down in town? White hair?"

"That's right."

"Oh, okay. Well, what do you want to know? I got to get back to work on the plane in the hanger."

"Can I walk with you? I'd love to see the inside of the hanger."

"Sure."

Fred seemed curiously indifferent to my charms. Young men usually fawn a bit over adult women. I wondered if he was gay. It didn't make any real difference – I was getting into the main building without having to deal with him being a horn dog – but I thought it odd. Maybe it was due to the cuts on my face. People are often embarrassed by others' injuries.

"You worked here long?" I asked.

He shrugged and began working on an engine.

It was like trying to squeeze blood from a turnip.

"I heard this airport used to be a military air station," I said.

"I'm not old enough to remember that."

Ouch.

I decided to leave him alone, since he obviously wasn't interested in having a conversation. I wandered around the hanger. There wasn't much to see. A couple of planes were undergoing maintenance. There were grease spots on the concrete but nothing that looked like blood.

Curiously, I felt watched. Careful glances in Fred's direction showed that he was keeping an eye on me. I didn't think he was worried about me stealing anything, either. Something odd was going on here.

I cut across the hanger. Fred wasn't working on the engine any longer. I crept closer to where I could hear a low voice. He was talking quietly into a landline phone next to a metal door set in the floor. He nodded, hung up, and stepped outside through an open doorway.

Carefully, I followed him.

I wasn't careful enough, though. As I stepped out, I felt a pistol suppressor press against the side of my head. I froze. I hadn't sensed anything from Fred, but I could see that it was him, out of the corner of my eye.

"Who are you?" he asked. His voice was cold.

"My name is Michelle," I said. "I told you that."

"I.D.," he demanded. "And don't try to draw that piece under your jacket. You aren't that fast."

I drew my wallet out of my pocket and handed it to him. He glanced at my license without the gun wavering, and pocketed my wallet. His eyes were emotionless.

"So what now?" I asked.

"Now we step back inside, and it's your turn to answer questions. Go through the door, take three paces, and stop. I'll be right behind you. Don't try anything."

I did as he told me.

"Carefully remove your pistol and lay it on the ground. Kick it back to me."

I sighed. "Look, can we talk about this? I think if you were going to shoot me, you'd have already done it. This doesn't seem like a robbery. So what's going on?"

"Don't try to be cute. Remove your pistol."

"I'm not giving you my only means of defending myself just so you can rape me," I said. I knew that wasn't what was going on, but I figured it was what most women would be worried about.

"What? That isn't… Drop your gun!"

"No."

"Damn it."

I heard the man step up behind me, felt as much as heard the *swoosh* as he raised his pistol to hit me with it. I waited just a moment longer, for him to commit to bringing the pistol down on my head.

I spun, caught his wrist with my left hand, and jabbed him in the throat with my right. I didn't hit hard enough to kill him, just hard enough to gag him. Surprisingly, he didn't drop the pistol.

He brought his knee up. I dodged and slammed my own knee into his groin. As he gasped, I spun him around and jerked his right arm up behind his back as I hit him low, in the kidney.

His knees buckled. I twisted his right arm up harder. He still wouldn't let go of the damn gun.

"Drop it," I said. If I applied any more pressure, I was going to break his arm. I was trying to avoid that.

CHAPTER FORTY-SIX

Fred finally let go of the gun, twisting to relieve the pressure on his arm. I snatched the pistol out of the air and stepped back, keeping a bead on him. He just sat there on the ground, rubbing his shoulder.

"You're a lot stronger than you look," he said.

I frowned. I'd expected him to make a move. Instead, he was settling down to sit on the concrete. I suddenly wondered if I'd misjudged the situation, and he'd just been trying to rob and rape me.

Not that it made much difference.

"Why did you attack me?" I asked.

"Well, I didn't exactly attack you," he said. "Hell, I'm the one with the sore shoulder."

"And I'm holding the pistol you were threatening me with. I'd like to know why."

"You were trespassing," Fred said. "I was just asking you to leave."

"Bullshit."

Fred shrugged.

He was stalling.

I suddenly remembered that he'd made a phone call. I glanced over at the metal doors in the floor. They were quietly opening. Fred took my moment of distraction to surge to his feet and charge me.

I spun his pistol around my finger by the trigger guard and slammed the grip like a hammer into his head. Fred slumped to the ground with a gasp. He wasn't quite unconscious, but he was definitely stunned.

I could hear boots on concrete coming from below, where the doors were opening.

My wallet was still in Fred's pocket. I checked, but he didn't have any identification of his own. I tucked his pistol into my waistband to free my hands and grabbed him by the scruff of his shirt and his belt.

He wasn't all that heavy, maybe a hundred fifty pounds.

I lifted him over my head and threw him into the opening doorway in the floor. I didn't stick around to see what happened. I punched the button to close the doors and ran like hell out of the hanger.

No one chased me, but I didn't feel comfortable until I was out of rifle range from the place.

I pulled Fred's pistol out of my pants and tossed it onto the seat next to me.

The pistol was an unremarkable Glock 17 with a suppressor and a light on the underbarrel rail. Lots of people use Glocks, so it didn't tell me anything about who the man worked for.

Taylor could have probably run the serial numbers for me, but I didn't want to involve her in this unless I had to. She was in enough trouble. Besides, this thing with the special projects was kind of private.

The farther I drove away from the airport, the better I felt.

I'd been a little worried about that helicopter. I figured if someone was worried enough to put a gun to my head, they might just chase me from a helicopter. No one chased me, though, in a helicopter or in a car.

Whatever was going on under that airport, it had left lingering echoes of horror and pain. The guard – Fred, or whatever his real name was – hadn't known anything. At least, he hadn't revealed anything when I picked him up. All I got from his mind was that he'd escorted others through those doors at gunpoint. None of those people had ever returned. He hadn't been real concerned about that.

I wish I'd gotten a better image from his mind of those people he'd sent to their doom. I couldn't tell if the people he'd seen were those the

FBI and I were investigating. I didn't think the two things could be related, but I knew I was going to have to tell Taylor about the attack and the airport, and what I had done about it, even if the information caused her more problems. Fred was definitely part of a private military company.

There were even more people crowding the streets when I got back to Taos. I estimated a few thousand wandering around. The rubbish bins were overflowing, and trash was blowing around the streets.

I hated it.

Taos was too nice a town for something like this to happen to it. On the other hand, tourism was the lifeblood of the community. If not for the tourist money, Taos would have dried up a long time ago.

I pulled into the parking lot of the hotel and called Taylor.

"What's up, Fredericks? Solve the case yet?"

"Not quite. Are you back in town?"

Taylor laughed sourly. "Yeah, I'm back in town. I'm at the alehouse right down the road from the hotel. Come on by and have a drink."

She sounded as if she'd already had a few. "I'll be right there," I said.

I pulled away from the hotel and circled back to the alehouse. It was an unassuming place that so far appeared to have avoided the tourists' attention. I know that technically I was a tourist, too, but I didn't think of myself that way. Tourists were *swarm, swarm, selfie, selfie.*

Taylor sat at the bar, nursing a beer and laughing at a balding guy who was trying to talk her up. The guy was fit and looked more than a little drunk himself, or he'd have realized Taylor was out of his league. Of course, a lot of guys in bars think more highly of themselves than you might expect.

"Excuse me," I said, pushing past him. "My friend isn't interested, pal."

"Fucking dikes," the guy muttered as he stumbled away.

I just sighed and settled onto the stool next to Taylor. "Wanna talk about it?"

"Fuck, no, but I'm gonna anyway," said Taylor.

I ordered a dark beer.

Taylor glowered at me. "Did *you* need to talk about something?"

"I did a quick recce around the airport," I said. "I had a little run-in with a PMC guy."

Taylor groaned. "Where's the body?"

"I left him alive," I said. "He drew a gun on me just for looking around the airport."

"Want me to call it in?"

"There's no point. He won't be there. None of the cameras will show anything. You know how this works."

"Yeah, I do." Taylor sighed. "Damn it, Michelle, why did you go alone?"

"I didn't think anything would come of it." I took a long pull on my beer. "So what has you in this state?"

"The fucking Bureau of Indian Affairs. They formally complained to the FBI. I had to go and apologize to that damn sheriff. I just got back an hour ago."

"Well, that sucks."

"Yeah. I have a deadline now. Solve the case this weekend, or I'm off the case. Can you believe this crap?"

"Yeah, I can. Nothing the government does surprises me."

"I guess that makes sense, from you," said Taylor. She knocked over her beer. "Shit."

The bartender gave me a look that said I'd better cut her off before he had to.

"Come on, Taylor, let's get you back to your room."

"Let me finish my… Shit. Right, no beer."

I settled up the bill with the bartender and helped Taylor stand up. She was drunk, but not badly. She took a couple of deep breaths and nodded.

"I'm good."

I stayed close enough to catch her anyway. I helped her over to my Jeep. It was getting dark outside, and I was distracted with Taylor. I didn't see the guy from the bar and his two friends until they stepped out of the shadows. The other two guys were younger looking, but in even better shape.

Somehow, I didn't think they wanted to talk.

CHAPTER FORTY-SEVEN

Taylor saw them first and laughed.

I glanced up and sighed. "Come on, guys, don't do this."

"We know what you need, bitch. You just need a man to straighten you out," Baldie said.

The guy said the right crap, but his body language was wrong. He also didn't radiate any kind of anger, which I can usually sense. Baldie just felt... blank.

Taylor sat down on the curb. "Fredericks, wait for them to swing first, and don't kill them."

Oddly, they didn't even flinch.

"Come on, boys," I said. At this point, I was resigned to a fight. "Who's first?"

Baldie stepped in and swung at me. I evaded his haymaker and put him down with a fist to the temple. He dropped to all fours. I followed up with a kick to the ribs that lifted him off the ground.

The sound of a flip knife is distinctive and always gets my attention.

I jumped back from the swing of the other young guy, who had a long skinning knife. These guys had come prepared. I caught his hand on the next swing and broke his wrist. He dropped his knife into his other hand and tried to gut me.

These weren't just random locals.

I spun the man around, breaking his arm, and shoved him at Baldie, who was just getting up. They tripped over each other and fell. The third guy leapt over them and swung at me with a hunting knife.

I deflected the slash, feeling a burning pain along my left arm. I punched him then, hard. The man grunted and staggered back, obviously startled by my strength. I followed it up with a sweeping kick to his knee and then drove my palm into the side of his head.

I heard his neck snap.

Baldie was up and going for a pistol in a shoulder holster.

The sound of Taylor's gun was absurdly loud.

Baldie staggered and looked down, unbelieving, at the hole in his chest. Taylor carries a forty-caliber loaded with hollow points. I couldn't believe the guy was still standing. He took a step toward me, still trying to draw his pistol. Blood gushed from his mouth, and he fell to his knees and then onto his face.

The man whose arm I'd broken was trying to stand. I kicked his good arm out from under him, and he fell with a cry. He'd fallen onto his own knife. Somehow, I couldn't find it in my heart to feel sorry for him.

People were coming out of the bar, so I didn't have a lot of time.

"Who do you work for?" I asked.

He spat blood at me.

I grabbed his sleeve and tore it from the shoulder seam. He cried out. There was a tattoo on his shoulder for a private military company. I didn't recognize the design, but I had a feeling it was the same one that my old friend Fred had. The man gasped and rolled over, his sightless eyes gazing at the sunset.

"You okay, Fredericks?" Taylor called.

"Yeah, just getting tired of being jumped."

"You're bleeding."

I glanced at my arm. My sleeve was hanging open. The suit jacket and blouse had been cut cleanly. Now that I was thinking about it, the cut started to throb and burn. I sat down on the curb. Blood dripped steadily off my hand.

"FBI," Taylor said loudly. "Get back."

"I'm a doctor," said a familiar voice.

"Dr. Aguilar, right?" I said.

"Yeah. I thought I told you I had enough practice with stitches."

"Sorry, doc."

Aguilar stopped when she saw the bodies of the men. "Anything to save there?"

I shook my head. "They're dead."

The doctor sighed and gripped my arm. "Let's take a look at this."

"Okay."

"You're going to need stitches," said Dr. Aguilar. "Looks like it was a sharp blade, maybe a razor. Cut through skin and muscle but didn't sever any tendons or arteries. I'm going to need to apply pressure, though, and that's going to hurt."

"Go for it, doc."

I winced as she gripped my forearm with both hands. I could hear sirens in the distance. I was glad it had been Taylor who shot the guy. I didn't envy her the paperwork, but at least she wouldn't get in trouble for it. This was a pretty clear case of an officer defending a civilian.

The ambulance got here quickly, but then, we were close to the hospital.

"You okay, Fredericks?" asked Taylor. She'd been talking to the police. I hadn't noticed them arrive. I was feeling a bit groggy from shock and the aftermath of adrenaline.

"Yeah, Dr. Aguilar here is taking good care of me."

The doctor rode with me to the emergency room.

"I'm sorry, doc."

"Don't worry about it. They would have paged me anyway. Faster this way."

She helped me out of my suit jacket and shirt. Then she washed up and changed into scrubs. A nurse cleaned the wound with an iodine solution. I started bleeding again then. The doctor came back in as the nurse was finishing up.

Dr. Aguilar numbed me up, poked around in the wound, and then started stitching. I watched the monitors, since I was feeling a little lightheaded. I looked back as she was tying the last stitch.

"Want to talk about what happened?" asked Dr. Aguilar.

I sighed. "Not much to say. I was helping Special Agent Taylor out of the bar. She'd had a bit too much to drink. Those three guys jumped us. I fought them. Two had knifes, the third a gun. Taylor shot the guy with the gun."

"Adrenaline can really sober you up. I know this isn't something most people want to talk about, but do you need any other sort of examination?"

"I wasn't raped. Yes, we were attacked, but it escalated quickly and was over just as fast. I got cut during the fight."

Dr. Aguilar nodded. "I had to ask. Do you mind if I take a look at your older wounds? I have a feeling you haven't exactly been taking it easy like I ordered."

"Apparently it's difficult to take it easy during a murder investigation."

"Hmm. The cuts on your face have healed really well. Your back, too. In fact, I wouldn't have believed it, but I think you can have these stitches out now, if you want."

"I would love to have them out. They itch."

Dr. Aguilar carefully cut and removed the stitches. The stitch holes itched, and oddly tickled just a little. She wiped down my back after she was done, then wrapped my forearm with a bandage.

"Wrap your arm with plastic wrap, and you can take a shower," she said.

"Oh, thank god."

She laughed. "Don't push your luck, Dr. Fredericks. Your body has been pushed to the limits in the last few weeks. You obviously heal quickly, but don't push it any further."

"Well, I can't really help it if guys are going to pull knives on me and my friend."

"I don't know who you really are," Dr. Aguilar said, "but I don't think for a second three guys just jumped two FBI agents because they got spurned in a bar. You take care of yourself, okay?"

I met her eyes and then nodded.

I wished I could tell her everything. She seemed like a nice person, and trustworthy. It would have been a relief to get it off my chest. I couldn't, though. If she knew everything, she'd be a target. Even if she didn't believe me.

"I'll try my damnedest, doc. I really will."

CHAPTER FORTY-EIGHT

Taylor picked me up at the hospital.

She'd brought a spare shirt, which told me Michael knew what happened. I was a little surprised that he wasn't with her. I knew why, though.

"The police are going to need a statement from you," said Taylor.

"I figured. Are you doing okay?"

Taylor sighed. "I just shot someone, so no, I'm not okay. Are you?"

"Other than having more stitches? They were mercenaries, Taylor. This wasn't some random attack."

"I sort of suspected as much. I may have had a bit too much to drink, but those guys didn't act right. Oh, they said the right words to piss me off, but it seemed like a show."

"I think it might have been retaliation for me snooping around the airport."

Taylor shook her head. "I told you not to go up there alone. Do you think they'll try again?"

"Good question. I think after this very public fuck-up, they'll back off, at least for a little while. I don't intend to give them time to regroup and think up a better plan, like a sniper rifle."

"Promise me you won't go back there alone."

"I promise. Now, what story should I tell the police?"

"Are you suggesting that I'd groom a witness?"

"Come on, Taylor."

"Tell them as much of the truth as you think they'll believe."

Talking to the local police wasn't much fun.

They had difficulty believing one small woman – I'm not that small – could have fought three buff guys. I responded that the guys had been very drunk. They weren't, and neither was I, but whatever. Taylor had shot one guy. One broke his neck when he fell, tripping over his feet. The other fell on his own knife.

Moral of the story: Don't play with knives when you're drunk.

Or, you know, attack a couple of women. Don't do that, either.

I don't know if the police really believed me, but they didn't have any reason to charge me with anything, either. I was obviously just a victim. Insert eye roll here.

Taylor drove me back to the hotel and dropped me off.

Michael was sitting in bed, reading. He started to get up, but I waved him back down. I wanted to snuggle, and he was in a good place for that.

"What happened?" he asked.

"It's complicated, and I'm not entirely sure, because some of it just doesn't make sense."

"That sounds pretty normal."

I laughed. It wasn't all that funny, but I was way past the breaking point. The day had been far more eventful than I ever wanted. Also, I may seem tough, but killing someone is never easy for me. I hope it never *becomes* easy. I was responsible for those men being dead. It hurt, even if it had been self-defense.

I told Michael about the airport, the guard, and what happened at the bar. He asked a few questions, mostly clarifications or requests for more details. He was very interested in the tattoo on the shoulder of the last assailant.

"CNI," Michael said. "Control de Negocios Internacional. Mercs."

"Business Control International? Never heard of them."

"No reason for you to have heard of them. They provide corporate security in hotspots around the world. They have a reputation for being somewhat ruthless. They also have a reputation for crimes against humanity. They torture, kill for sport, and generally give other mercs a bad name. They aren't supposed to be operating on US soil. These guys are not to be messed with."

"I took down a couple okay," I said.

"You got lucky. No offense. I know how good you are, but these guys underestimated you and paid the price. They won't make that mistake again."

"So how do we deal with them?"

"*We* don't," Michael said. "I'll make a couple of phone calls. Focus on the job for the FBI, and I'll deal with this."

I nodded. When Michael gets like this, I listen. I knew he was going to call in some favors with his old commanding officer. Michael had been Special Operations before becoming a federal marshal. He knew what to say, to whom, to get things done. He left to go make the calls.

It had been a hell of a day, and I still hadn't processed what happened.

The guard at the airport had reacted all wrong.

There was no reason to jump me just for poking around the hanger. I hadn't found anything at that point. I wouldn't have dared to go into the basement, or whatever it was, beyond the metal doors on the ground. I had been ready to give up and leave when he jumped me.

Why?

Why would the CNI show their hand that way?

I'd sensed that the guard had escorted others into the facility in the past. Had it been the people who later turned up dead? The murderer's MO didn't fit with the mercenaries' actions.

And yet, somehow, the alien murders and the mercs *were* connected. I didn't have enough information to understand *how*, but I knew they were. The body on the reservation had been dumped there from a Humvee. That had to be the mercs. Of course, all I knew was that they dumped the body there. I still didn't know who was actually killing people.

Michael returned a little later. He'd walked to the store and bought plastic wrap for me. He helped me undress, which wasn't as much fun as it should have been, and then he wrapped up my arm so I could take a shower.

It was blissful.

CHAPTER FORTY-NONE

Michael and I met Oliver, Taylor, Marie, Lawrence, and Jean for breakfast the next morning.

The restaurant was crowded.

I had to do a double take a few times – many people were wearing outlandish costumes, some of which looked very real. I've been into renfaires all my life, but these people were taking costuming to the next level. I felt a little envious, I have to admit. I love cosplay.

"What's the plan for this event?" asked Lawrence.

I realized they were all looking at me.

We had an amazing array of talent sitting at the table: two FBI agents, an ex-Special Ops, semi-retired Deputy Federal Marshal, and an expert in corporate espionage. Three of us sitting here were survivors of government super soldier experiments. Not to mention Marie and Jean, whose best talent may be just being really great people.

Don't knock it. Being a good person is *hard*. Those two have more empathy in their little fingers than I do in my whole body. Just giving a damn is a hell of a superpower. God knows most people on this planet don't.

It humbled me a bit to think they were all relying on me and my meager intellect.

"We'll wander around, together or individually," I said. "Just take in the sights, listen to what people are talking about. If you hear anything about mutilations or abductions, relay the information to me. Feel free to pass on anything else you think is interesting."

"Check in with Michelle at least once an hour," said Oliver. "Don't let yourselves be drawn by anyone into out-of-the-way areas. There's a very good chance the killer is here today. Don't say or do anything to give away that you know that, and don't be the next victim."

"That's a scary thought," Jean said. "I don't really know what you guys are looking for, but I can certainly promise I won't wander. I got kidnapped once. I ain't looking to have it happen again."

I squeezed her hand. Back in Kentucky, Jean and Lawrence had been abducted by the serial killer who called himself the Preacher. I almost hadn't been in time to save them.

"You two should stick together," I said. "Don't worry about what we're doing. Go have fun taking in the sights. Do check in with me, though. If I don't hear from you guys, I'll to come looking."

"Michelle on the rampage," said Lawrence. "It's a scary thought and yet cool, too."

"You know that the rule about not trying to solve every problem on your own was made for you, right?" Taylor said, looking at me.

I grinned. "Trust me, I'll call you guys if I see anything weird."

Just then, a person dressed as a xenomorph walked by. The costume was very realistic. Scary, even. I wondered who would go to so much trouble and expense. More so, why? Why *that,* of all things? It's like the people who dress as *Star Wars* Storm Troopers at cons. Why? I'd understand dressing as an X-wing pilot or a rebel commando. Hell, even a *Star Trek* Starfleet officer. Why dress as a bad guy?

Not to mention the difficulty eating, drinking, and trying to go to the restroom.

It was a fucking *epic* cosplay, though.

We split up then.

Michael gave me a quick kiss. We'd decided it would be better if I walked around alone. Not only can I sense things better alone, but people react to a single woman differently. I suspected I'd get better results alone than if I had Michael glaring at all the men who got too close.

I fell in with the crowd of people making their way to the park.

I'd seen venders setting up the day before, but it turned out that only a small number of the booths were actually selling anything. The others had people handing out pamphlets, flyers, and other information about their own brand of strange.

In a way, I could respect what they were doing. These people had experiences they couldn't explain. They were looking for answers and maybe a connection to other people who'd had similar experiences. I could almost see myself doing that, to find others who'd survived the projects.

Just walking around and taking it all in was interesting. People were talking openly about the strangest things. Not to mention the complete non-sequiturs. I overheard some very odd conversations.

"I almost ran over a Wookie on my way in here."

"Sure it wasn't a Sasquatch?"

"Yeah, I'm sure. She had a bowcaster."

Weird.

"Did you see the chick with the angel wings? They moved, man!"

"I thought it was strange. I mean, *black* feathers?"

"I thought the wings made her look hot."

"Everybody has their own kink, man."

I didn't see anyone with angel wings. I would have liked to. Angel wings would be a cool addition to a costume. I just never could figure out how to attach them properly. I didn't even want to think the last part of that conversation.

"I'm telling you, the government has been experimenting on children since the seventies!"

That caught my attention.

The guy in the tent was talking animatedly to a guy who looked bored. I looked through the pamphlets on the table: *Aliens Among Us! Genetic Hybrids: Monsters or Saviors?* And my favorite, *How to Nurture Your Alien Cat.*

I'll give him that one; most cat *are* aliens. I say that in the most respectful way possible. I love my cat Samson, but he is a true bastard sometimes. He definitely has an agenda. Not to mention that he seems to understand everything I say, except when he doesn't like what I'm saying. Ask him if he wants some tuna, and oh yeah, he's *there*. Tell him no, and he just gives me that *no comprendo* look.

If I woke up one day and someone told me cats had taken over the world, I'd just nod. Yep. That sounds legit.

"The government has been experimenting on children since the seventies!"

"I've heard that," I said.

"Exactly! That's what I'm talking about. Everyone knows about it, but no one wants to talk about it."

"I meant I heard you tell that guy," I said. "Tell me about it."

He leaned closer, in a conspiratorial fashion. He needed some deodorant. "Well, you see, back in the sixties, the government realized that other countries were outpacing the United Stated in super soldier research programs."

I nodded.

"Well, Russia had gotten ahold of Nazi scientists, just like we did, after the war."

"Project Paperclip," I said.

"You've heard of it?"

"Yeah, go on."

"Well, anyway, the USSR was outpacing us in super soldiers. After Soviet super soldiers turned the tide of war in Vietnam, the US decided we needed super soldiers, too."

"Okay, I can buy it," I said. "When did it start, here in the US?"

"Oh, the first batch of enhanced kids was born in 1972."

CHAPTER FIFTY

Soviet super soldiers in Vietnam?

What had this guy been smoking?

"When did you say?" I asked.

"1972."

I tried not to react too much, having been born in 1972.

"I've heard that, too," I said.

His eyes got really large. "Where did *you* hear it?"

"Back East," I said. "I heard there was a project around Cincinnati."

"Cincinnati?" he laughed. "Why would anyone think *that*? That is so stupid."

"Just what I heard." The guy was kind of a dick, but he did seem to know something. It wasn't as if the military was required to have only the one project. "So where do you think it was?"

"Everyone knows Project Chimera was in Seattle," the man said.

"Okay, thanks. Know anything else about it?" *Project Chimera?* That was bit on the nose. The government was usually much more ambiguous with special project names.

The guy looked around, as if worried someone would overhear his crazy theories.

"There were a lot of kids taken into the project. The children of military personnel. They took them in every two years, starting in 1972.

They genetically altered them, made them hybrids."

"Okay. So the government genetically altered kids in the seventies? Isn't that a little advanced, technology-wise?"

The man shook his head. "The Nazis did it in the war, with their inhumane experiments. Also, the first mouse genetically altered to have a human immune system was in 1970."

I did not know that. "You said the experiments made the kids hybrids?"

"Yes, with cats and dogs!"

"What?" I was already looking around, for an exit route.

"The first generation, born in seventy-two, looked like dog-people and cat-people. That's where the idea of cat-girls got into popular culture, from the sightings of some of them who'd moved to Japan with their parents, back when the US still provided military protection for Japan."

"Cat-girls?" I said. "Okay, I'm out."

He was still talking, but I wasn't listening.

It was weird, because the guy obviously had *some* actual facts. I wondered if the government had deliberately leaked a little information, just to discredit anyone who might actually come forward. I wouldn't put it past them.

If that man had known what I know, he'd have gone even more nuts. I knew the government had experimented on kids; I was one of the damn kids. The things they had done to us were far worse than this guy's cat DNA crap. Whatever Project Absolution had been based on, whatever they had used to change us, it wasn't genetic material from cats and dogs. Not if half of the dreams I'd had were based on real suppressed memories.

I listened for a few minutes to a woman on a soapbox telling everyone that we shouldn't eat fish because they were aliens. I'd expected her to say it was because they're meat, or contain fat, or too much mercury, or something. I was used to people trying to push the vegan lifestyle on me. To hell with that; I like my beef, pork, and chicken.

"It's actually cephalopods that are alien," I said loudly. "Like cuttlefish."

That shut her up, confused. She yelled after me as I walked away: What did *I* know?

Very little about that, actually. Although I probably wasn't wrong. I'd recently read a pre-release paper on the subject. There's evidence that cephalopod DNA is alien. Gotta love meteors, man.

I called and checked in with the others. They were having the same sort of luck as I was. Lots of interesting things were being discussed at the festival, but none of it was particularly useful.

The guy selling the alien sex dolls was doing well, to judge by the number of people at his tent. The female sex dolls had three breasts, and the males had two tentacle-like penises. That freaked me out a bit, not because of people wanting to get their thing on with an alien – I couldn't care less about that – but because those dolls appeared to be made from the same material as vinyl pool floats.

It would smell bad, squeak strangely – which could be a turn-on for some, I suppose – and have rough or even sharp edges. I had gotten cut badly on a pool float once when I was a kid. No way was I going to let something like that near my coochie or any other hole.

I met up with Taylor a little after that. She looked exasperated. I didn't blame her. She had to be hearing that ticking clock in the back of her head. We were running out of time to solve this case.

"Anything, Fredericks?"

"Nothing useful," I said. "This reminds me of Octoberfest back in Covington."

"This isn't like any Octoberfest I've ever been to."

"I just meant the wild party nature of it, and the numerous street vendors selling anything and everything."

"You see the sex-thing?" she asked.

"Yeah, I almost bought you one."

"Oh, fuck you," Taylor said, laughing.

"I thought if I bought you a doll, then you'd stop pining away for me."

Taylor rolled her eyes. "I'm headed over to the convention center. There might more exhibits and less crazy there."

"I wouldn't bet on the latter," I said. "Some of the panel discussions and lectures could be interesting, though. I haven't seen a program for them yet."

"Me, neither. I just know I can't take much more of this. Some crazies stopped me a while ago and tried to convince me that there was an angel walking around. What the hell does that have to do with aliens?"

"Everything is included," I said. "Some of the Ancient Alien believers think stories of angels are about visitations from aliens in the past. The people here aren't completely wrong, though. There *is* an angel walking around."

"What the hell are you talking about?"

"I heard some people talking about a woman in an angel costume," I said. "They were talking about how realistic her wings are."

"And some other kook saw her and thought she really is an angel?" Taylor shook her head.

"Most of these people don't get out much," I said.

"Yeah, I can see that."

"That doesn't make them bad people."

"I didn't think it did."

"I think most of them are just lonely."

"Who isn't? Shit, give me another five years of working with you, and I'll have my own booth here."

I joined her in laughing.

Oliver joined us then. "I'm glad someone is having a good time. Did you see that booth selling the sex dolls?"

Taylor and I laughed even harder.

"That shit freaks me out," said Oliver. "Why the hell does the male one have two penises?"

I put my hand on his shoulder. "Oliver, you may not be aware, being gay, but women have two holes down there."

"Spare me the biology lesson. Even if you do have two, I can't believe you'd want to have something in both of them at the same time."

Taylor shrugged. "All the crazy around this place, and *that's* what bothers you?"

"I'm not prudish," Oliver said. "I just draw a firm line about some things."

"We're getting ready to head up to the convention center," I said, "if you'd like to join us. Probably fewer sex dolls there."

"I sure as hell hope so."

It was nearly time to check in with the others. I called them and let them know we were headed up to the convention center. Jean and Lawrence were having fun where they were. Michael said he'd meet us there with Marie.

CHAPTER FIFTY-ONE

There was a long line to get in.

It cost thirty dollars, which I didn't think was that bad, but some people argued about it. Apparently there had also been a five-dollar coupon in the swag bag the year before, which the people running the ticket booth didn't want to honor. Apparently it only applied to pre-order tickets bought last year.

All in all, it took about an hour to actually get inside.

Just inside the main foyer was a display; I can't quite bring myself to call it art. The display was of a full-size flying saucer – how do they know the size? – and three buff grey aliens standing over a terrified woman in a torn dress that just barely covered her nipples and groin. I suppose it could have been some sort of homage to fifties science fiction films, but I thought it was tasteless and tacky.

All around the room were tables with people hawking their books. Local chapters of UFO organizations – and the Society for Creative Anachronism, for some unknown reason – were handing out pamphlets and flyers. There were even a few celebrities signing autographs and taking pictures with people, for a price.

"Hey, it's the big-haired aliens guy," I said, pointing.

"Why is he dressed like a lounge lizard?" asked Taylor.

"Maybe he's a reptiloid," Michael said. "I thought he'd be taller, though."

I had, too. He looked as if he'd barely be up to my nose, even with the hair. They always made him look taller on TV. Hell, just how short were some of those people? This guy towered over people sometimes on his show.

"What now?" Taylor asked. "I feel like a fish out of water."

"How do you think I feel?" said Oliver. "How many brown people do you see in here?"

That was true. The crowd was almost exclusively lighter-skinned. I had thought a few times, while watching the aliens show on the History Channel, that there was some racism present in the idea that aliens were responsible for all the amazing accomplishments of other civilizations. They never said the French, English, or Germans had everything handed to them by extraterrestrials. Except maybe during World War II.

I pulled out the program they'd given me when I bought the tickets. "Well, the most interesting lecture for us, for the case, has to be *New Evidence for Alien Abductions and Medical Experimentation in Taos, Rio Arriba, and Colfax Counties, NM.*"

"When's that?" Taylor asked. "And what the hell is up with the name?"

"This afternoon," I replied. "I think the researchers like to present so-called evidence as if it were a paper for a scientific journal."

"For the love of god," said Taylor. "Why all the pseudo-science trappings?"

I shrugged. "It's presented by a Dr. Munson, which rings a few bells."

"Munson is a person of interest, a psychologist or something."

"Anything interesting before then?" asked Michael. "We might as well learn what we can while we're here."

"There's a lecture about the 1972, Taos UFO," I said. "Starts in just a few minutes. Could be interesting and useful."

"The meteor?" Taylor asked.

"I think some people claim it was something else," said Michael.

"Without evidence?"

"Well, why don't we go to the lecture and see what the evidence is?" I said. "It could be something other than how someone *feels* about it."

The lecture hall was mostly full when we got there, but we managed to snag some seats by asking a person to move to let us sit together. Most of the people in the room were well-dressed. A few looked like reporters.

Of course, that made the people dressed like grey aliens stand out more.

The speaker introduced herself as Dr. Garcia. I wondered what she was a doctor of. She began by discussing the strange weather phenomenon that preceded the green anomalous object – her words. The storm clouds had rolled in quickly, followed by lightning and torrential rains. I knew that in a place like Taos, two inches of rain an hour was a lot. It had probably caused severe flooding and damage to personal property, although that wasn't mentioned.

Dr. Garcia had pictures of the storm.

The first slide was dramatic. It showed a massive supercell storm wall, silhouetted against the mountains at sunset. Intense, forked lightning played around the bottom of the storm like the legs of an insect. Fairly high above the storm, red sprites and tendrils could be seen in the mesosphere.

It was a hell of a picture.

The second slide was almost identical, except a green, glowing object was falling through the storm, leaving a faint trail behind it. I heard gasps from around the room. I suppose people see what they want to see. I saw a one-in-a-million photo of a meteor falling through a storm, if it wasn't doctored. Other people in the room saw aliens.

The next slide showed a green flash from behind some hills. That slide was followed by slides of the object's proposed impact site. From the maps, I realized that the meteor must have gone down around where the airport is now.

Dr. Garcia made a big to-do out of the fact that the military had moved in and built an air station at the location of the supposed impact.

She didn't have any pictures of the military operation, any object she said was recovered, or even of the base. She ended the lecture with a slide of the airport, saying that many mysteries were left to be resolved.

Yeah, no shit.

That was one of my big problems with supposed alien researchers. They might present a few things as evidence, but then they never follow through with anything. Worse yet, suppositions and conjecture are often treated as facts.

The lecture hall burst into applause as the lights came up. I saw people actually hugging each other and saying things like that they finally had proof. I didn't get it. The only things I'd seen proof of were a storm and a meteor.

I worked my way through the crowd. I had questions.

"Dr. Garcia? I'm Dr. Fredericks," I said, extending my hand.

She had a weak, limp handshake. "How can I help you?"

"First, I'd like to thank you for the informative lecture," I said. "I'm quite interested in the meteor."

"UFO," she corrected.

"Of course," I said. "I was just wondering why you think it's anything other than a natural phenomenon."

"You saw the slides, right?"

"I did, and they were very impressive, especially for pictures taken in the sixties. The photographer was a true artist."

Or whoever had doctored the pictures up on a computer was.

"Well, there's your answer." Dr. Garcia was packing up her books. I could see another lecturer eager to take over the front table and podium.

"Was anything ever recovered?" I asked.

"Look, you saw the slides and heard my lecture. If you want anything else, you'll have to wait until my book comes out. I'm not going to just *give* you the information so you can swoop in and steal my research."

"I think you may have me confused with someone else," I said. "I'm a forensic anthropologist. I'm not interested in writing books. I'm just interested in that meteor."

Dr. Garcia stamped her foot like a child. "UFO!"

She didn't know anything.

"Thanks for your time," I said.

"Don't think I won't be watching! I'll talk to my publisher about this! You won't steal my work!"

I shook my head and left the room. The woman was obviously paranoid and obsessed. Those were two traits I *did not* want to deal with just now. If Dr. Garcia had talked about mutilations or abductions, I might have thought she was our killer.

As it was, I just thought she was crazy.

CHAPTER FIFTY-TWO

"That went well," said Taylor.

"Well, at least we learned a little bit about the storm and the meteor," I said. "They really were unusual events. I can see why they captured these people's imaginations."

"I don't," said Michael. "Other than the coincidence of a meteor falling through a storm, and someone managing to take a picture of it, I didn't see anything unusual."

"These people thrive on coincidence and conjecture," Taylor said. "We don't even know if there *was* a meteor. The picture could have been doctored."

"I've heard about the meteor since I moved here," said Marie. "I think *that's* real. The locals talked about it a lot before this festival sprang up."

"Don't forget that there was a project named Wormwood out here," I said. "A green meteor falling from the sky on the eve of the project could have been the source of the name."

Michael looked unconvinced. I have to admit, I wasn't all that sure, either.

"Did you notice that the green trail the meteor left behind didn't extend up through the cloud?" asked Oliver.

I hadn't. "Damn. I guess the picture was doctored." I shook my head. "Okay, the next lecture is in half an hour. I think it has some promise."

"Yeah, I'm going to skip that one," said Marie. "The program says it contains graphic images. I don't want to see anything like that."

"I think I'll head back with you," Michael said, "if you don't mind."

Michael was being gallant and walking his sister home.

Oliver was going to a different lecture. He didn't want to look at anything graphic, either. I couldn't blame him. I'd seen enough blood and gore to last a lifetime. It was funny: the pictures of the mutilated cows I'd seen bothered me more than the photos of mutilated people.

The sign outside the lecture hall said New Evidence for Alien Abductions and Medical Experimentation in Taos, Rio Arriba, and Colfax Counties NM – Warning: Graphic Content.

I settled into a chair next to Taylor and prepared myself for ambiguous images of dead animals. I was disturbed by the general feeling of the room. The people filing in and taking seats around us were excited. It churned my stomach a bit.

Dr. Munson came in, and some people actually stood and clapped.

I was beginning to think that being a researcher into UFOs and related subjects was more a cult-of-personality thing than anything resembling real research. How many cancer researchers can you name? Any medical researchers at all? I suppose a few of us know of Jonas Salk and the polio vaccine; not many people know of Edward Jenner and the smallpox vaccine. I'd be hard pressed to name any others, though. Most people who spend their lives trying to improve the lives of others never get any recognition.

This glory-hound scarecrow didn't impress me.

"Thank you all for coming today," said Dr. Munson. "It is truly humbling to see so many people interested in my research."

He didn't seem very humbled. Also, his voice had an annoying, nasal drone and slur to it that made me grit my teeth. I seldom take an instant dislike to someone. This guy, I immediately hated.

"Before I get started, I want to impress everyone with the seriousness of my research. Also, anyone who didn't take my graphic images warning seriously should leave now. I've had people pass out before."

Munson sounded pleased about that.

He droned on for about half an hour before he showed the first slide. He knew his audience would sit through anything to see something even slightly suggestive of aliens. He was right; no one left.

He started with images of cattle mutilations from around the world. The pictures were uniformly disturbing but nothing new to me. I'd seen a few of the same pictures online. Dr. Munson spoke for a while about possible reasons why those areas of the body were being targeted. It was all the same tired speculation I'd already read.

Some of the crowd were getting restless.

This wasn't what they'd come here to see.

Dr. Munson noticed. "Our next slide is the most graphic so far. I want everyone prepared for it. Not all of the aliens' victims have been bovine."

This slide was also one I'd seen before. A man had been found in Argentina with the same injuries as his cows. It was graphic but not new. Someone in the audience gasped. I thought it sounded like a ringer, since there was no burst of emotion. Munson had people in the crowd paid to work for him.

"The images get more graphic as we move toward bodies that have been found in the surrounding counties."

This was what I'd come for. What information did this vile man have about the murders? Were we looking at the killer?

The first three slides were pictures of old bodies found in the desert. The injuries were consistent, but the pictures must have been taken a few decades ago. I could see the film grain.

The next slide made me flinch. I recognized the victim. I'd looked at pictures of the woman every day since taking the case. I recognized the bone structure, and the arrangement of fillings in her teeth. The tattoo of the butterfly under her ear was the clincher.

This *doctor* had pictures of a body the FBI had found in the desert.

That didn't mean he'd killed them, but he certainly had some explaining to do.

I gripped Taylor's arm to call attention to the slide. She nodded. She'd noticed. I started to get up, but she stopped me. She wanted to see what else this guy knew.

For the next half hour, Munson showed us pictures of mutilated bodies. He spoke about the injuries with the glee of a zealot. One of the bodies, we hadn't found yet. All of the other pictures were of victims we'd recovered.

Taylor waited until after the lecture to approach him.

"Can I help you ladies?" he droned. "I'll be doing book signings later, if that is what you're after. Anything else, and I feel compelled to tell you I'm a married man." He laughed a little, as if he were joking.

I'd rather have fucked a corpse.

"Actually, I was hoping you'd make time to answer a few questions," said Taylor.

"Nothing is free, darling. As I said, I have a book signing to attend."

Taylor showed him her badge. "I must insist. I'd rather not turn this into a public spectacle, but I will cuff you and frog march you out of here if that's what it takes."

"Am I under arrest?" He didn't seem concerned. He unhurriedly disconnected his laptop and put it in a briefcase.

"Not yet, but after what I just saw, I think it's probable," said Taylor. "I can read you your rights and cuff you, if you wish."

"What agency was it? The FBI? Fine." He seemed bored. "I'll come along and answer your questions. I was wondering when you'd catch up to me. I'd heard weeks ago that you were in town investigating. I offered my services but was turned down."

"I'm not offering you a job," said Taylor. "I'm taking you in for questioning."

I flanked Munson, and Taylor took the other side. We got out of the building without incident. I'd half expected the man to try to incite a mob to save him. Taylor called Oliver and had him bring the car around to the closet place the road wasn't blocked.

I kept expecting something to happen, but we made it to the car and climbed in, Munson between Taylor and me in the back. I didn't like being this close to him. The doctor didn't say anything on the way to the station. He just sat clutching his briefcase.

I called Michael and filled him in.

The whole time, I could feel Munson's fear growing.

He wasn't afraid of us, though.

CHAPTER FIFTY-THREE

Oliver drove us straight to the police station.

Once inside, Taylor took Munson's bag away from him and handed it to me. She then cuffed him to the table in the interrogation room. Munson sat there with a smug smile on his face. The darkness inside me wanted me to beat that smile from his face, and then his face from his head.

I did neither.

Taylor sat across the table from him, with the case file folder. Oliver and I stood guard in the corners of the room, just behind Munson. I wanted the bastard to squirm and think the worst.

"State your name, please," said Taylor.

"Dr. Edward Jacob Munson. I am a licensed clinician in psychology in California."

"This isn't California. You showed slides at your presentation today. I'd very much like to know where you took them."

"I didn't take them from anywhere," Munson said smugly.

"You don't seem concerned," said Taylor. "To be clear, you are potentially facing murder charges."

"Don't be ridiculous. I haven't murdered anyone."

"You had pictures of bodies from an active murder investigation. At least one of the bodies in your little slideshow of horrors, we haven't found yet. If we search your apartment, will we find more pictures? Will we find the personal effects from the victims?"

Munson sighed. "If I cooperate, I'll expect protection," he said. "I'll also need assurances that I have full immunity from prosecution."

Taylor laughed humorlessly. "Why would we do that?"

"Because I know who – or rather, what – killed those people, and who covered up the murders."

"So what you're saying is that you're just an innocent in all of this?" said Taylor.

"By no means," Munson replied. "I was, however, forced to go along with the cover-up."

"Forced?"

"You may be aware that I once gave UFO sightseeing tours here in Taos. My medical license had been revoked in California, due to an unfortunate misunderstanding. You see, doctors and patients can sometimes grow close –"

"I don't care," Taylor said, cutting him off. "Tell me about the tours."

"Yes, well. I had a small group of true experiencers with me. I had verified through hypnosis that all of them had experienced actual alien encounters. I was eager to learn more. One night, we caught sight of a vehicle we'd never seen before. It was a glowing disk, more bulbous in the center."

I realized he was taking about a Manta, like the plane I'd seen before I was attacked by the weird doppelganger with claws.

"We followed it to a body. The one you never found, I imagine. You see, we stumbled upon a group of soldiers in hazmat gear dumping the body in the desert. They, naturally enough, didn't like being disturbed. We were held at gunpoint. Then they bound us with zip-ties and took us to an underground facility."

"This is bullshit," said Taylor. "Tell me the truth, or they'll find *you* out in the desert."

"I assure you I'm telling you the truth. God help me, but I am."

I nodded to Taylor. I could sense that he was being mostly honest.

He was holding something back, but I figured he'd tell us eventually. He seemed like a man resigned to his fate. He wanted to confess what he'd done.

"All right," Taylor said. "Go ahead, tell us the rest. If you leave anything out, though, the deal for immunity is off the table."

"I understand," said Munson. "You won't believe me, but I am telling you the truth."

"Try me."

"Very well. We were stripped and kept in a cell together for a few days. They didn't mistreat us, and fed us well enough. It wasn't comfortable, but it wasn't too bad, either. One day, they took one of my companions. She didn't come back. We heard the most awful screams. Each day, they took another. It was maddening. When they came for Roger, the last besides myself, I demanded to know what was happening. They laughed at me but took us both."

I realized he was crying. I couldn't bring myself to feel much for him, though. Somehow, I knew he was a part of what had happened. He wasn't innocent. Not by any stretch of the imagination.

"What happened then?" Taylor asked.

"Guards in biohazard gear took Roger through an airlock. I was taken to a room with a large window. I could see into where they had taken him. They had something in that room. Something terrible. It looked like a man, somewhat, but it wasn't. It was an alien. Or a hybrid. Oh, no, it wasn't a man. It had a monstrous hunger I could feel. It... *latched onto* Roger, like some sort of leech. The sucking noises as it drained the blood from him make me sick to this day. I still have nightmares. When it had finished, Roger was, as you may expect, dead."

Munson began sobbing. I realized he must have been talking about Roger Goring, one of the bodies the FBI had found last fall. There hadn't been any sign of violence on the body, other than the removed organs and orifices. Was that why they'd been removed? Had there been some sign of how the blood was drawn out?

"So you're saying a monster did it?" said Taylor. "Please credit us with some intelligence."

Munson just shook his head.

I didn't say anything. I was thinking of what had attacked me out on the mountainside. It had looked like a man but wasn't. I killed that one, though. Whatever Munson had faced, I felt sure it was still alive in that facility. I suddenly thought of Tom, the kid who'd turned into a monster when I was young. Could that be what this was all about? Could it be some sort of twisted, inhumane experiment?

"Taylor, can I talk to you?" I asked.

She jerked her head toward the door, and I stepped out into the hall with her. Oliver stayed in the room to keep an eye on Munson. Taylor looked annoyed.

"This guy is so full of shit," she said. "I don't think he actually feels anything. And a monster? Come on."

"I'm not so sure. I told you before, it wasn't a man with a knife that attacked me. Don't forget that someone was eager to disappear the body before an autopsy could be performed. Also, I haven't told you everything about what I remember of the military projects."

"You're talking about Absolution? You mentioned it before."

"I remember them trying out different drugs and things on us," I said. "Once, I remember, they gave something to a boy that turned him into a monster, literally."

Taylor sighed. "Shit."

"I don't think Munson is innocent, but I think he could be telling the truth."

"I'll hear him out," said Taylor, "but I'm not giving that bastard a 'get out of jail free' card."

"I don't expect you to," I said. "I don't think he does, either. You notice he didn't try to lawyer up. I think he wants to get this off his chest."

"Okay. I still think he's full of shit. How the hell could I even take this before a judge?"

"You may have to settle for some other form of justice," I said quietly. "He doesn't deserve a jury of his peers when he's already confessed."

"I won't condone vigilantism."

"Then you'll have to take your chances with the criminal justice system."

"Let's get back in there," Taylor said.

CHAPTER FIFTY-FOUR

I gave Taylor's shoulder a squeeze, and we went back in.

Taylor sat down across from Munson again.

"What happened after the monster killed Roger?"

"They made me watch the whole thing," Munson said. "They took his body out and irradiated it to kill any alien pathogens. Then they used a surgical laser to excise the tissue that had been lacerated by the creature. The flesh bore signs of what had been done. They incinerated the possibly infected tissue. I asked them what they planned to do with me. Why did they show me this? They told me they had saved me for last because they didn't *like* me."

He seemed confused by that. The man's ego was astounding; he couldn't imagine anyone not liking him. He didn't care about the horror that been inflicted on his companions. He only cared about his popularity. I wondered what he would have thought if we all told him what we thought of him. I don't think he would have liked that, either.

"How is it that you're still alive?" asked Taylor.

"I convinced them that I was more useful to them alive," Munson said. "Not only could I help cover up the potential discovery of the bodies, but..."

"Go on."

"I could bring them more," Munson said in a small voice.

"Excuse me?"

I don't think I'd ever heard Taylor sound so cold and angry.

"As a respected researcher in the field, I could bring small groups or individuals out into the desert. You see, the monster somehow feeds upon terror, and so it needed a constant, fresh supply of… sustenance. It would tolerate the use of cows, but it needed intelligent prey every so often."

"You sick son of a bitch," said Taylor. "You took more people to it. Did you watch?"

"Yes." Munson sat up in his chair. "For scientific purposes."

"Sure."

What had driven this man to turn on his own kind in such a way? I understood why he hadn't gone to the authorities. Who would have believed him? But he could have run away. He didn't have to keep… and to watch… I felt sick.

"Where was this?" asked Taylor. Her knuckles showed white around her clenched fists. I couldn't blame her for being angry. I wanted to kill Munson, too.

"It's an underground facility," Munson said. "There are several points of entry, but the most common one is through the airport in Angel Fire."

"The metal doors that lead to the subbasement," I said.

That was what the guard at the airport had been trying to do. He'd been planning to take me down to that thing. I felt a little dizzy. I had been that close to a horrific death. I was lucky. A lot of people hadn't been.

We needed to stop this.

"Yes, exactly," Munson said. "How did you know?"

"Did you take the pictures?" Taylor asked. "Of the bodies?"

"No, they are provided to me. I'm not there for every… feeding. I'm not ashamed to say that I don't have the stomach for it."

Taylor shook her head. "Okay, we're going there to stop this."

"You can't! There are lots of soldiers there. They would shoot us on sight, or worse!"

"How manty soldiers?" asked Taylor.

"I can't. They'll kill me."

I'd had enough of his whining. "You want to take your chances with us?"

"Michelle, don't. Not yet," said Taylor.

"Fine, but you're going to need to provide us with a lot more information. Do you know the history of the projects there?" I asked Munson. "How this all started?"

"Of course. Back before it went private, it was called Project Wormwood."

"Why was it named that?" I asked.

"I don't know," Munson said. "Those military project names never make any sense to me."

"Then you know of the others. Did you learn about Project Absolution?"

Munson nodded. "It was some sort of project to make super soldiers. I believe they tried to use genetic material acquired from the monster. I'm uncertain. There was talk of something else stored in the facility. Something worse. Something that truly terrified the soldiers."

It made me shudder to think I might have something like that inside me.

"Scared the soldiers?" said Taylor. "You mean more than this supposed monster?"

Munson shrugged.

There was a knock on the door, and Michael leaned in. "Michelle, would you mind?" Michael gestured out the door.

I was more than happy to get away from Munson. I *really* wanted to kill the sick fuck. I didn't want to go easy on him or make it quick, either. I don't feel that way often, and I don't want to ever feel that way again.

I followed Michael and tried to calm down. Munson couldn't hurt anyone else. That was the important thing.

"How long have you been here?" I asked.

"I walked over just after you called," said Michael, "so I've been here for most of it."

"So you know that we need to do something about that base under the airport."

Michael nodded. "I spoke to the colonel. He can have boots on the ground to support us in six hours."

"Why do I sense hesitation from you?" I asked.

"Because there's a price. That's why I didn't already have him send the troops."

"What kind of price?" I asked, although I was beginning to suspect.

"Colonel Jackson wants me to come back into the service. He wants me to take Harrison's place at Project Brimstone."

"And you're considering it?"

Michael sighed. "I don't see any way to storm a facility full of mercs and live, without more people with us. We need soldiers for that."

"And Colonel Jackson won't send them without you agreeing? That's kind of selfish."

"Asking for troops to storm a facility on US soil isn't a small favor, Michelle."

"I suppose it's not like you're leaving me."

"I'm *not* leaving you," said Michael. "I'd just be working away from home more. At least I wouldn't be far. Brimstone is based out of Jellico Mountain, on the Tennessee border."

"That's only about three hours south of Covington." I sighed. "I don't like it, but I understand."

"Thank you. I'll go call Colonel Jackson now."

Michael walked out of the building.

I was hurting. There was no way around that. I hurt so badly that I wanted to scream. I wanted to run after him and demand that he not do this. Plead that there had to be another way. I knew there wasn't, though.

Taylor came out of the room. "You okay?"

"No, I'm not."

"Well, Munson will be put in lockup until I can get him transferred to Albuquerque. He's agreed to cooperate for now. I haven't charged him yet. I don't even know how to begin to describe his crimes. I guess I'll need to reach out and find the closest SWAT team."

"They wouldn't be able to handle this," Michael said as he came back inside. "I have a team on the way."

"What sort of team?" asked Taylor.

"The kind you don't talk about. SOCOM."

"I didn't think the military could deploy on US soil."

"That was before 9-11. Things have changed."

Taylor glanced at me, then back at Michael. "I can see that."

"There's a special team for things like this," said Michael.

"What things?"

"Monsters."

CHAPTER FIFTY-FIVE

I called and checked in on Lawrence and Jean. They were fine; they were with Marie at her house. They'd all had a great time at the alien festival. I was glad someone had. Lawrence wanted to tell me something about some things he'd overhead, but I cut him off. I'd talk to him later. I wasn't in the right mood for it just now.

My nerves felt raw.

I was overloaded and now feeling a loss I hadn't expected. I knew intellectually that I wasn't losing Michael. That didn't stop it from hurting. My heart wasn't listening to my mind.

"I have a few more questions for Munson," said Taylor. "Care to come along?"

"Yeah," Michael said. "I'd like to know how many troops we're facing."

I nodded. I never wanted to see the creep again, but Michael was right. We needed to know what we were walking into.

"Go ahead," said Michael. "I have to make another quick call."

A soon as Taylor opened the door, I knew something was wrong. The light was flickering, and there was the stink of blood and shit in the air. Munson was dangling from the ceiling, with a power cord wrapped around his neck. There was a police officer holding the other end of the cord, where it looped over a beam.

The officer let go of Munson, drew his sidearm, and fired in one smooth motion as we entered the room.

I tackled Taylor, and the bullet hit the wall over our heads. I was unarmed, having just come from the festival. I still had my speed and strength, though.

I rolled under the table as he fired again. I stood, lifting the table and throwing it against the man. Taylor fired then and missed him, but barely. The bullet grazed the officer's temple.

That stunned him, and I dove forward, grabbing his pistol and twisting with all my strength. He cried out and punched me in the stomach with his left hand. I doubled over in pain, and Taylor shot him over my head.

I was still gasping for breath as Michael burst into the room, gun drawn.

Michael checked for a pulse from Munson and then the police officer. Both were dead.

Other police officers crowded into the room, trying to see what had happened, until the police chief drove them out. "What the fuck is going on in here?" she asked. My ears were still ringing from the gunshots.

"Chief Tapia," said Taylor, "is that man one of your officers?"

Tapia squatted down next to the dead man. She shook her head. "I've never seen him before. He looks a little like Martinez, whose uniform he's wearing, but Martinez is on vacation."

"Check his right shoulder for a tattoo," I suggested.

Tapia gave me an odd look, then unbuttoned his uniform. "What am I looking for?"

"That," said Michael. "It's the tattoo of a private military company. The same one that attacked Agent Taylor yesterday."

"I'm sorry, who are you?" Tapia asked. "And why are you armed in my station?"

"Major Delling," he replied, which made my heart sink. "I can't say anything else at this time."

"He with you, agent?" Tapia asked Taylor.

"Yes. He's a liaison from the Defense Department," she lied.

I thought that was very good thinking on her part.

"You want to explain what the hell is going on here?"

"I'll explain what I can," said Taylor. "Maybe in your office?"

"Yeah, okay. An ambulance is on the way."

Chief Tapia led the way back to her office. "You know, I didn't have people getting gunned down in the streets before you arrived."

"No, just people being murdered in the desert," Taylor replied. "These recent deaths are because we're close to solving the case."

"I sure as hell hope so. I'd really like to have all you FBI and whatever you are out of my town."

"Believe me, we'd like to be out of your hair, as soon as we catch the persons responsible for all of this."

Tapia shook her head. "Who shot the perp?"

"I did," Taylor said. "You can run ballistics, if you want."

"I'm not your enemy here," said Tapia. "The imposter killed the witness, I presume?"

Taylor nodded.

"Okay. I'll get a statement later. You look like you've got places to be."

"I can get it over with now. Just let my associates get on with their investigation."

"That's fine," Chief Tapia said, waving us out.

Michael and I left her office.

"Michelle, I'm sorry. I know this is all a shock for you."

"Right now, I'm just feeling kind of numb," I replied. "A lot of people have died around me recently, and I've almost died more than a few times. Let's just get back to the others and let them know what's going on."

Michael nodded.

I drove over to Marie's house. Lawrence and Jean's rental car was parked outside. I couldn't bring myself to open the car door when we got there. I was still processing my feeling about Michael leaving and rejoining the military.

Michael touched my shoulder, and I jerked away in my seat.

"I'm here, Michelle. I'm not leaving you, and we'll be able to see each other all the time. I'll just be a couple of hours away."

"I know that," I said. "I just thought..." I didn't know what I'd thought.

"That we'd get married and go into business together and solve weird crimes and live happily ever after?"

"Something like that."

"We still can. I only agreed to serve two years."

"You're hoping you can find your friend," I said.

Michael nodded. "I'd like that. Although I think Harrison can take of himself. I want to make sure we're safe from threats like what he told me about. I don't want to have to watch you die from some damn alien plague."

"I'd be fine," I said, wiping my eyes. "I'm tougher than you anyway."

"Fair enough."

"Promise me you won't get lost like your friend."

Michael sighed. "All I can promise is that I'll try. The colonel assured me that there are no more sorties to the other America planned. Harrison seems to have stopped them with the bomb. The colonel mainly wants me to try to recover technology from other places the portal device can send me to."

I nodded. That was as good a promise as I was going to get. Michael couldn't and wouldn't promise not to die. We all die. Given how close things had been recently, I was in more danger than he was.

"You better have a nice bed off-base," I said. "And I'll know if you share it with anyone else."

Michael laughed. "Who else could compare to you?"

Good answer.

CHAPTER FIFTY-SIX

The night air was cold and dry.

Michael, Taylor, Marie, and I drove out to the Angel Fire airport early, before the sun was up. Taylor was dressed in her FBI tactical gear and vest. Oliver hadn't come out. He still wasn't feeling his best, and a night op wasn't a good idea. Marie was dressed much as normal, but she wasn't planning on going in. She was just here for moral support.

Michael's team met us about a kilometer from the fence, to the south. They'd brought tactical gear and weapons for Michael.

I'd brought my own gear.

When we decided to drive out here to New Mexico, I didn't want to leave my guns in the house. Not because I was worried about Jean, but because I didn't want anyone to break in and steal them. Also, I like to be prepared in case something like this happens, and it happens to me more than you'd think.

I was in all black, with my Kevlar vest. My Sig was in my shoulder holster, knife in my boot, and a MP5 slung over my shoulder. I had extra mags for each of my guns. Michael had given Taylor and me comms, to keep in touch. I didn't expect to need any of it, though. Michael had an entire Special Operations team under his command, eleven other soldiers almost as tough and ornery as Michael. I wasn't too worried about the outcome of this engagement.

"Sir, we've got two guards," the warrant officer said. "One on perimeter patrol and another in the main hanger. No other signs of the enemy."

He hadn't told me his name. None of the solders had been pleased to see two civilians along. Taylor and I were in gear but under orders to leave the fighting to the Spec Ops team. I didn't have any problem with that. I'd seen enough blood recently.

"What are we looking at?" whispered a voice from right between Michael and me.

I barely heard Michael's knife as he drew it.

"You'll want to remove your knife, or do you need another demonstration of my strength?" said Erin.

"How did you sneak through my perimeter?" Michael asked.

"I didn't sneak."

"Give me one reason why I shouldn't zip-tie you and leave you here."

"Because you need me. Also, you might want to let your guys know there's a sniper on the ledge of that tower."

Michael stared at her for a moment. "Chief, I have intel of a cuckoo in the tower."

"I didn't see anything on infrared," the warrant officer replied.

"Thermal cloak," said Erin.

"Just check, chief."

The warrant officer sent two men to reconnoiter the tower. I could see one climb the side like it was a ladder, do something on the ledge, and then repel down.

"Right on, sitting there pretty with an M110. No IR signature. Gave him a new smile. Good eye, commander."

"Thank our friend," said Michael.

"Call me Blackbird," Erin said, getting into the spirit of things with a giggle.

Michael shook his head. "Okay, chief, take out the other two guards and move up to the hanger. *Blackbird* here will be with me and the feds. Any electronic surveillance in there?"

I realized he was asking me. "I didn't see any, and I was looking. There's a phone, and a button to open the doors to the lower level. No cameras."

"Roger. We're in the clear."

I never saw the guard on patrol. The one in the hanger was just a dark shape and a spreading stain on the concrete. No one had made any noise. Not that I had expected anyone to. These soldiers were the epitome of professionals.

"Any idea what to expect in there?" asked Michael.

"We lost our only witness before he could tell us," Taylor said.

Erin closed her eyes. "Three levels. Sixteen rooms on each level. Two other access points that lead into the desert, on the first level. One access is personnel-sized. The other is accessed from a hidden garage. There are two Humvees in there. Thirty-seven soldiers in the facility, and something else on the lower level. Only five soldiers are awake. Two of those are on patrol, one on each of the upper levels. You should keep your troops out of the lower level. They can't handle what's down there."

"How exactly do you know all that?" asked Michael.

Erin opened her dark eyes and smiled. "We all have our gifts."

"All right." Michael relayed the information to his soldiers. "We'll go and clear out the soldiers. I'll signal when each level is clear. Wait five and follow after we breech. We'll hold on the second and discuss where to go from there."

"Wilco," I said.

Michael smiled. "On my mark." He held up his hand and counted off with his fingers. His troops flowed silently past.

Suddenly, it was just Taylor, Erin, and me in the hanger.

"How did you know where to find us, Erin?" I asked.

"I keep my ears open. I heard about what happened at the police station. I listened to the recording of the interrogation. Dark stuff. You okay?"

I snorted. "Yeah, I like how casual you are about sneaking into a police station and listening to evidence files."

"Who said anything about sneaking?" said Erin. "I can be very persuasive."

"Persuasive enough to cause dereliction of duty?" Taylor asked.

"Okay, fine. I just popped in and had a listen. No one saw me. Happy?"

"I'd be happier if I knew who you are."

"A friend," Erin replied. "I am, at the least, the enemy of your enemy."

"We don't even know exactly what our enemy is," I said.

Erin nodded. "Sadly, I do."

"But you're not willing to share that information with us?" asked Taylor.

"It wouldn't make much sense to you, even if you did believe me. Sometimes you just have to have a little faith."

I was quite intrigued by Erin. She had a sort of magnetism to her. It wasn't physical attraction, although I thought she was pretty. It was more like an empathic field. I could feel myself drawn to trust her.

Of course, that was exactly the kind of thing to watch out for.

"It's been five minutes," Erin said. "We should go."

I followed Erin to the stairs into the dark basement. A shiver of foreboding rolled over me. I was afraid of what I was going to find down there.

"Let's go." Erin pointed down the stairs with her sword.

I blinked. "Where did you get a *sword*?"

"It was a gift," Erin said, "a very long time ago."

"I meant just now. I didn't see a sword as we moved up here."

"I didn't want you to see it."

"You're not good enough to cloud my mind without me knowing it," I said.

"I am, but that wasn't what I meant. We should hurry. Michael is thinking of going to the lower level without us."

Once, I would have said that she couldn't possibly know that.

Now I just took the stairs three at a time.

CHAPTER FIFTY-SEVEN

The interior of the bunker looked to be mid-century Brutalist architecture, with the typical raw concrete construction. I suppose I shouldn't have been surprised. I've never been in a bunker, but I think I expected it to look like Mount Weather in movies. Certainly an underground facility in Angel Fire, New Mexico wasn't going to be as posh as a bunker for the US President.

The air was stale and smelled like a locker room mixed with a slaughter house. I don't think the mercs had been particularly concerned about hygiene or cleaning. It could simply have been a side effect of the mental strain they were under. Even toughened soldiers couldn't face what these men had on a daily basis. Being around a monster and... *feeding* it must have taken a mental toll on them.

Don't take that as me feeling sorry for them.

There were a few bodies visible in the corridors. Blood was splashed on the walls and puddled on the floor. The blood had been walked through in some places, leaving sticky tracks of boot treads. Michael's troops had been thorough and efficient. It was clear that Michael hadn't offered any terms of surrender to the mercenaries. Given what those soldiers had been doing, they probably wouldn't have taken the offer anyway.

"Jesus," Taylor muttered.

We reached an intersection, and it wasn't clear where we should go. I caught the eye of a soldier who then pointed to the other end of the long hallway, where stairs led down. It was only as we passed her that I realized the soldier was a woman. I knew the military had opened up Special Forces combat assignments to women in 2016, but I hadn't realized any women had already made it through selection and joined teams.

Of course, that was kind of the point.

Special Operations personnel are secretive for a reason. I'd have never learned about Michael if it hadn't been for all that we went through. It wasn't something he talked about.

I could hear echoing gunfire as we reached the stairwell. It was followed by the sputtering noise of suppressed rifles with subsonic ammunition. A moment later, we got the all-clear over our coms.

"They're good at what they do," Erin said. "I could use a few troops like these."

"You plan on going to war?" asked Taylor.

"No, I just think men and women in uniform are hot."

I tried unsuccessfully to suppress my laugh.

It wasn't all that funny, but I was at the breaking point. That little bit of levity from Erin helped cut through the tension. I'm sure that's why she said it. I know it sounds odd, but I liked and trusted this woman.

Michael was waiting by the stairs to the next level. He was in full gear, with a helmet, but I recognized him by his height and build. There was a SCAR-H slung low from his shoulder. It had an attached grenade launcher. I had to admit, that forty-millimeter opening was intimidating.

"We've accounted for thirty-six mercs," said Michael. "The last one must have fled to the lower level."

I didn't like the feeling of darkness drifting up that stairwell. Whatever the monster was, it was the essence of evil. I'd encountered *demons* that didn't feel as bad. I really didn't want to go down to it. I knew that I had to, though, or I would have nightmares about this forever. I had to face that thing and at least help kill it.

"You should let me go alone," said Erin.

"Not a chance in hell," Michael replied.

"Suit yourself, but don't say I didn't try to warn you." Erin set her sword on her shoulder. "You aren't going to be able to deal with what you find down there."

"Wait – why do you have a sword?" asked Michael.

"Because a sword doesn't ever run out of ammo," Erin said. "And I like swords, this one in particular."

"I shouldn't have let you down here. You're too much of an unknown for me to feel comfortable having you on this operation."

"Think of me as an indispensable part of your team. You can't stop me anyway."

"Oh, I think I can. You're strong, but not that strong."

"If you go down there without me, you won't be coming back."

"Is that a threat?"

"I'm not your enemy," Erin said. "Try to remember that."

"Michael, let's just do this," I said. "Erin is here. We know she has as much of a stake in this as we do. Even if we don't how or why."

Michael sighed. "Fine. Let's go."

"I don't think I can," Taylor said suddenly. "I'm sorry. I've been dealing with this okay so far, but I feel like going down those steps is a death sentence. If I joined you, I think I'd be gibbering before I reached the landing."

"It's just the aura from the monster," said Erin. "There are no certainties in life, but I'm sure what you're feeling is just a normal human perception of evil."

"Well, this normal human isn't made of the same stuff as the rest of you," Taylor said. "I… I just can't. I'm sorry. All this death, and then whatever is down there…"

"It's fine, Taylor," I said. "We've got this. Fall back to the entrance. The three of us can handle it."

"The *four* of us," said Marie. "I'm going down there with you."

Michael didn't argue; he just handed her a pistol. "Only use it if you have to, and stay back."

"Of course."

"You ready?" asked Michael.

I laughed and shook my head. "Hell, no." I gestured at the stairs. "Let's go."

"Ladies first?" said Erin.

"We'll go down together," Michael said. "Erin, Michelle, take point. Marie and I will cover your six. Keep sharp. This monster is down here, but worse, there's still a merc on the loose. I suspect it's the commander."

I moved to stand next to Erin at the top of the stairs. My heart was racing, and my every instinct said to run. My tongue was dry in my mouth. I *really* didn't want to go down those stairs.

"Just stay close to me and don't engage the thing alone," said Erin.

"You're sure you don't want a gun or some body armor?" I asked.

Erin smiled. "I don't think Michael would like me to have a gun. As for armor, you don't have any here that would help against what we're about to face."

"You *do* know what it is, don't you?"

Erin looked sad. She nodded.

I studied her. Whoever Erin was, she had seen some bad shit. Worse than anything I'd seen, that was for sure. Her dark brown eyes were filled with sorrow and pain. She glanced away, and I thought I saw something for a moment. It was more of a flash of memory. Something about the way as she turned her head reminded me of something from long ago.

"Okay, my operators will hold the facility. No one else is coming up those stairs. Neither the merc nor the other thing are getting away. All the passages outside are on the first level, and being watched. There are no other means of egress."

"So we're good to go?" asked Erin.

She sounded impatient. I don't think she worked with other people all that often. I wondered who she did work for, though. I definitely got the sense that she frequently did things like this.

"Yes, let's go," said Michael.

I gazed into the darkness, sure something was gazing back. "Yeah, I'm good."

Marie murmured assent, and we moved down the stairs.

CHAPTER FIFTY-EIGHT

The stairs to the lowest level were longer than the others, with two landings. That suggested the lower level would have higher ceilings. I was surprised to find the ceiling of the corridor was a normal height. Either the rooms were taller, or there was a level in between.

"The bedrock in between sublevels two and three is porous," said Erin. "They had to cut deeper."

"I'd love to know how you know that," I said. I wasn't surprised that she'd picked up on my thoughts despite my mental shields. "Have you been here before?"

"Good guess, but no. I can sense the water in the limestone."

"Is there anything you can't do?" asked Michael.

"I don't play the piano and would probably suck at basketball. Never played it. I'd have to cheat to win. They frown on that sort of thing, I hear."

The lower landing for the stairs was marked with mud and a bit of dried blood. I was having to keep my shields tight so I wouldn't pick up things I didn't want to see, hear, or feel. Bloody, fresh-looking footprints led straight away from the stairs. The lights flickered in the corridors to the left and right, making me jump at shadows.

"It's just the field effect of the thing," said Erin. "It disrupts the electronic ballasts in the florescent lights."

"Any idea where we should go?" I asked.

Erin shook her head. "I'm not omniscient, unfortunately. However, I think following the bloody boot tracks is a good start."

"Could be a trap," said Michael. "In a similar position, I'd leave tracks and then circle back around to ambush my pursuers."

"I like your thinking," Erin said, "but I don't think you'd ever find yourself in this position. You're too good a person."

"You don't know anything about me," said Michael.

"I know more than you think," Erin replied. "We should get going, though. I have a bad feeling. I think I know what the enemy commander is up to."

"You think he'd let that thing loose?" asked Marie.

I hadn't considered that. From the look on Michael's face, he hadn't, either. That's the problem with being sane and trying to guess what someone crazy would do.

"Yeah, let's get moving," Michael said.

Erin and I moved forward together. I flipped off the safety on my MP5. Erin kept her sword drawn and ready. There was a strong sense of something waiting for us. I didn't like it.

Room after room was empty.

If the mercenaries had ever used the lower level, it had been a long time ago, but I didn't think so. Who would want to be this close to a monster? Even the most insensitive person would have felt that thing. I couldn't even imagine the nightmares the soldiers must have endured.

Well, they wouldn't have nightmares any longer. Killing them had almost been too good for them. If there was any justice, they'd have been given to the monster.

"That would be revenge," said Erin. "The best justice is swift and sure. 'Tis better to end them quickly, rather than soil yourself with their sin."

I glanced at Erin and studied her profile. She was focused and intense. I was sure then that she'd been through something similar to Project Providence. She knew pain intimately, and she also knew revenge. I wondered if she'd ever tell me her story. Somehow, I doubted it.

Somewhere ahead of us, a klaxon sounded.

"I hate being right," Erin said.

We ran forward into the next room.

This room was obviously a staging area for the horrors beyond. The door stood open to a room that stank of death and pain. I could see something through the door, but the room we were in held my attention.

Clothes, shoes, and other personal items lay haphazardly piled along the walls. There were a lot more clothes than could be accounted for by the number of victims we'd found. I kicked at the closest pile. The clothes were bright polyester and included bellbottoms and fringed vests.

"These are from the seventies," I said.

"They've been keeping it here for a long time," said Erin.

It took all of my willpower to enter the lair of the beast.

Before I'd really gotten a handle on what I was looking at, Michael raised his rifle and fired into the glass window at the end of the room. The report of the rifle was deafening and left my ears ringing. I didn't see what he was shooting at.

"Damn," said Michael. "I missed him."

"The commander?" I asked.

"Yes. At least, I think so."

"Michael, you should pull your troops out of this facility," said Erin. "That thing is loose in here. Your troops can't cope with it."

Michael turned and punched the concrete hard enough for cracks to form around the impact. He didn't seem to doubt Erin, though. He got on the coms immediately.

"Chief, time to pull out. Blow the other two entrances to seal them, then fall back to the hanger. Set charges there. If anything tries to come out other than us, blown it to hell."

Michael listened to something on his private channel. "If that thing gets to the entrance, it will have gone through us first. There won't *be* anything to come in and save."

"Are we falling back?" I asked.

"No, I want to get the commander first," said Michael. "I don't like having an armed enemy behind us when we go hunt the monster."

The door across the room, by the glass window, was locked. Michael shot the lock off and went through quickly. He called all-clear a moment later. We joined him. Looking at the suits racked on the wall, I realized this must be the airlock Munson had mentioned.

"Should we be concerned about contagion?" I asked.

"It was never a biohazard in the traditional sense of the word," said Erin.

The control room was empty except for broken glass. I thought of Munson, cuffed and forced to watch as a monster killed his companion. I wondered if Munson had been a bad man, before seeing that had broken him. Certainly the man we'd questioned hadn't been completely sane.

The next room held an odd assortment of broken machinery. It reminded me of plane crash wreckage I'd studied when in school. One of our assignments had been forensic analysis of the debris. I hated that project. There'd been a lot of pain and fear impressed on the pieces of that plane.

"What is that?" Marie asked.

She pointed at a large glass cylinder. It was filled with murky fluid, except where that had leaked out. The base of the cylinder held incomprehensible machinery. I'd never seen anything like it.

I started to touch it, but Erin stopped me.

"I wouldn't do that," she said. "A monster used to sleep in there. It's been dead for a long time, but it's the progenitor of our woes here."

I jerked my hand back.

My hand felt filthy, just from having gotten close to the cylinder.

Two muffled thumps were more felt than heard.

"My team has sealed the entrances and fallen back to the hanger," said Michael. "You'd better be right about this, Erin."

"Have I let you down yet?"

"No, not yet, but I still don't know why you're here."

Erin sighed. "I thought that was obvious. I know what happened here, and I want to stop it."

"Yes, but what aren't you telling us?" asked Michael.

"Nothing that could cause you harm by not knowing it."

Michael didn't look convinced.

I agreed with him on one thing: Erin *was* hiding something.

CHAPTER FIFTY-NINE

The third level of the installation was like a maze. Rooms connected into rooms from several different directions. The corridors were straight, with many cross corridors. We wandered for about half an hour without finding any creature.

The surgery room was every bit as horrible as I'd thought it would be. I felt sick the moment we opened the door. It wasn't from radiation; there were radiation monitors on the walls, all showing nothing. My illness was from the visions and feelings that rolled off the operating table. Not all of the victims died from what the monster had done to them. Some had lived long enough to be irradiated and then carved up on that table. A bulky, old-fashioned surgical laser sat to the side, near an incinerator.

As we left the room, Michael's second-in-command reported that there had been no activity by the entrance.

"Do we fall back now?" asked Marie.

Michael shook his head. "I'd really like to neutralize the commander before we do that. I don't want to be surprised."

"We've circled around, almost back to where we started," said Erin. "We may as well finish our sweep of these next few rooms."

She was looking for something, I suddenly realized.

The last room before the stairs, where we would have ended up if we'd turned left, held the mercenary commander. He was kneeling on the floor, muttering something that might have been prayers. The room was bizarrely appointed, lit with hundreds of candles, stacked skulls, and draped in black cloth.

A cross-like structure, also draped in black cloth, dominated the center of the room. There was something under the cloth, a humanoid shape but misshapen. At least it looked that way with the cloth over it.

The enemy commander was praying so fervently that he didn't notice we'd entered the room, until Michael pressed his rifle against the back of the man's head. The man stiffened and then raised his hands over his head. He said something that sounded like Spanish but wasn't.

"Portuguese," Erin said. *"Onde está o monstro?"*

"Nao sei. O que isso importa? Somos todos amaldiçoados por deus."

"You understand English," said Erin. "I can hear it in your mind. What is this? Why did you let the monster out?"

"It is punishment for our sins," the man said in heavily accented English. "We are cursed. Now you are, too."

"We're not the ones who gave people to a monster," I said.

"You think you are superior to me, but you have not had to face what I have," the man said. "It doesn't matter. It will come for you, and you will die scre—"

Michael's gunshot was deafening.

"He was unarmed," said Erin.

"He was never leaving here alive," Michael replied. "We've wasted enough time. We need to find this thing and end it."

"I hoped the commander would be able to tell us *where* to find it."

"He didn't know. Even if he had, he wouldn't have told us."

Marie walked past them, ignoring their arguing, and pulled the black cloth from the cross.

I couldn't help but gasp as the figure under the cloth was revealed.

The hideously burned body of a young man was bound to an atypical double-armed cross, upper arms wider than the lower ones. The cross was made of wood and roughly constructed.

The man's burns were mostly on the left side of his body. He was charred to the bone in places. Deep rents in his flesh looked much like the claw marks I had on my head, arm, and back. I couldn't help but wonder if something similar had attacked him.

His most striking features were two large, feathered wings. Those wings were pinned open, nailed to the upper arms of the cross. The feathers were cinnamon-colored, like his hair. His hands weren't normal, either: the little finger was another thumb instead. I couldn't tell how long he'd been bound there, dead. Some preservative must have been used, because his flesh hadn't decayed. It was fascinating and disgusting at the same time.

Erin let out a long, keening cry and fell to her knees in front of the man.

I had no doubt he was who she'd been looking for. She couldn't have expected to find him alive. I think she just hadn't thought he'd be pinned up like a butterfly.

I walked around the macabre display.

The wings sprouted from the man's back just below his shoulders. He had a black stone on a cord around his neck that looked much like the one Erin wore. I felt my chest tighten as I continued to study the body. The wings reminded me of Marissa, the girl who'd been removed from the project because of the growths on her back. Had she been growing wings? It had certainly looked like it. What about Johnathon, the other child with growths? He'd been taken away. Did they kill him, or study him while wings he could never use sprouted from his back?

Did we, the children of the projects, have that same genetic code in us?

"What the hell were they doing in this hellhole?" asked Michael.

Marie knelt next to Erin. "Were you related?"

"What?" Erin stood and whipped tears from her face.

"Were you in a special project together?" I asked.

Erin shook her head. "You've got it all wrong, and I'm not in the mood to explain." She walked out of the room.

"We need to get going," said Michael. "We don't have time for this."

"Just give her a minute, Michael. She's obviously really upset about this. She knew him, no matter what she says."

Michael turned away.

I couldn't believe he wasn't interested in what we'd found. I turned back to the body on the cross. Had Project Wormwood actually been trying to make some sort of bird-human hybrid? No, because that wouldn't work, and the wings weren't actually bird wings. Looking closer, I could see that structurally the wings were more like those of a bat. There was even a protruding thumb on the wing. I couldn't explain the feathers, though.

Michael had said Project Wormwood was about rapid transit. Surely he couldn't mean winged soldiers. That would have been a terrible idea. Wings are fragile structures, and birds can fly only because their bones are hollow.

"I think it might have something to do with that wreckage," said Marie.

"What?"

"You were muttering."

"Oh. You mentioned the wreckage?"

"Well, airplane wreckage goes better with rapid transit, don't you think?"

Michael was watching the door.

Erin still wasn't back.

"I do. We *should* take another look. Michael, we're going to check out the wreckage again."

"Am I the only one worried about that damn monster?" asked Michael.

"You know you aren't the only one worried, but Erin isn't back yet, and I think we need to take another look at the wreckage if we're going to understand all of this."

"Fine," Michael said. "Don't be long."

Marie and I backtracked through the rooms.

I studied the broken equipment. While some parts of it definitely reminded me of airplane wreckage, most of it was of an unknown function. A few parts had manufacturing labels in English. Other than the strange cylinder, I did see anything I could say was all that odd or alien.

The cylinder didn't have any markings.

"Michelle, take a look at this," said Marie.

She pointed at the label on one of the orbs on a stand. I had thought those odd but hadn't noticed the labels. They had *Made in Detroit* stamped on them. Hard to think aliens would make stuff in Detroit. It was hard to think *anyone* would make stuff in Detroit.

"What am I looking at?" I asked.

"Look at the manufacturing date."

It read 2032.

I checked the other labels. Most of the labels read 2032. Two had earlier dates, 2028 and 2031. In one case, the date was actually cast into the metal.

"Are we talking time travel here?" asked Marie.

I shook my head. "I don't think so. Not in the normal sense." The item tags attached to the pieces all had 1967 dates. This wreckage all dated to the storm. "I think this is what was recovered after the storm." I showed her the tags. "From the green meteor."

"So it wasn't a meteor but some kind of time ship?"

"Has Michael told you about Project Brimstone?"

"It has been mentioned."

"Michael told me Brimstone was about using a device from this project to travel to another universe."

"I'm going to kick his ass for not telling me that," said Marie.

"Let's get back."

CHAPTER SIXTY

Erin and Michael were arguing when we returned.

Michael wasn't quite pointing his rifle at Erin, and she had her sword drawn and resting on her shoulder. There was also an improbably large container of gasoline sitting next to the body on the cross. I was pretty sure I knew what the gasoline was for. What I didn't know was why Michael and Erin looked ready to kill each other.

"What's going on here?" I demanded.

"I'm burning the body of my friend Vano," said Erin.

"This is a military operation, and I have been tasked specifically with taking possession of any unusual bodies or technology found on site."

"You knew about this?" I asked.

Michael looked surprised by the edge in my voice; I don't know why. He was being an ass. I've called him out on it enough in the past that he should know it's coming just by the look on my face. I didn't have a lot of tolerance for the government where special projects and genetic experimentation were concerned.

"Not specifically," he said.

"Then no one else does, either," I said. "Have you forgotten about the monster?"

"I haven't," said Michael. "I thought you had, though, wandering off."

"We didn't wander off. We went to look at the wreckage again. We told you that. It was interesting stuff, with manufacturing dates that haven't happened yet. At least not in this universe."

"You're more aware of things than I thought," said Erin.

"What are you trying to say, Michelle?" Michael asked.

"That the government will have plenty of stuff to study with the wreckage. They don't need bodies."

"Michelle –"

"No," I said, cutting him off. "You may not remember what they did to us, but I do. I remember the injections, and the soldiers taking away the children who started to grow fucking *wings*. I'm not about to let them get ahold of this genetic material so they can do that again."

"It went that far, here?" asked Erin.

I was surprised by her question, because the answer was there all along. I just hadn't wanted to see it. Erin wasn't a local. She was an alien, of sorts.

"You're not from this universe, are you?" asked Marie.

Erin sighed. "No, I'm not, and neither was my friend here. You're right, Michelle. We need to make sure your government doesn't get ahold of this again. The old material samples were destroyed. I'm sorry that material led to further torments. I hoped the destruction of the samples and injections in Project Absolution would be the end of it. It wasn't, since they then used you children in the Providence Project."

"Not your fault," I said.

"You sound as if you remember it," said Michael.

"I'm older than I look."

"Michael, back off and let her burn the body."

"Do you have any idea what you're asking of me? I swore an oath, Michelle. I can't just decide not to follow orders."

"You swore an oath to defend the United States from enemies foreign and domestic, didn't you?" I asked. "I'd say this qualifies as both. If we destroy the body, you'll be saving the government from making the same mistakes again."

Michael sighed and lowered his rifle. "Damn it, I hate when you're right."

"No, you don't," I said. "You're too used to following orders. Sometimes you just need someone to remind you to do the right thing."

Michael smiled lopsidedly, making my heart flip-flop. "My old friend Harrison used to help me with my moral compass. I'm going to miss him."

"You're the one who said he isn't dead, just lost."

"True." Michael glanced at Erin, obviously uncomfortable talking about this in front of her.

"Come on," I said.

Erin took the stone from around her friend's neck and then picked up the five-gallon container like it was a soda can to pour and splash gasoline all over the body. The fumes became unbearable, and Michael, Marie, and I moved out of the room into the corridor. I heard Erin murmur something that sounded like a prayer, although I didn't recognize the language. She came out of the room, tossed a flare behind her, and quickly pulled the door shut as the gasoline ignited with a *whump* I could feel in my chest.

"Thank you," Erin said. I noticed her tuck the stone pendant into her jeans pocket.

I nodded. "Let's go find this monster."

"Finally," Michael muttered. He took off up the stairs.

It pained me that this whole situation had caused a strain on our relationship. Michael leaving to rejoin the military was only a part of the problem. He was obviously under a lot of pressure and seemed unwilling to talk about it. At least not in front of Erin.

I love Michael. That doesn't mean I like it when he acts like an ass.

Marie squeezed my shoulder. I'm sure she could feel my pain and turmoil. I hated to burden her with it. Michael and Marie had been estranged for a long time. She didn't need me casting doubt on the decision to reconcile.

"The creature is moving toward the exit," said Erin, "going fast."

"Michael?"

"I heard," he replied. "Chief, blow the outer doors, now!"

The explosion rocked the facility. Dust rained down from the ceiling, and a few chunks of concrete fell near us. The concussion wave was much more powerful. My ears, already traumatized, were ringing again. I spat out dust.

An inhuman scream echoed down the stairwell, sounding more like a cry of rage than of pain. There'd been no way we could have gotten lucky enough kill the thing in the explosion. I've never been that lucky.

"Erin, can you tell us anything about this thing?" I asked.

"Nothing really useful. They're all different, and this one is more erratic than most. I don't know what it can do or how it will fight. I'm not sure why, but I don't think it's the one that killed my friend. This one is younger, I think."

"Is it possible for a person to become something like that?" I asked.

"They are always people," said Erin. "Or were, anyway. Why?"

"I remember, in the project, they injected a boy with something else. It made him change. Not like the other injections. He clawed his face off, and something monstrous was underneath."

Erin hissed like a cat. "It wasn't enough for your government to use Vano's blood, but they had to use the blood of the enemy, as well."

"So it's possible we're fighting someone who was turned into a monster against their will."

"It's complicated," said Erin. "They could be turned with the right injections, during a bout of madness. They wouldn't stay like that unless they embraced the darkness."

"They would turn into something else?" I asked.

"No, they would die. I imagine that would be the fate of most who were injected. The human body wouldn't be able to survive those kinds of changes."

"But you and your friend survived?" asked Michael.

"You still don't understand," Erin said. "We're not the product of some sort of genetic experiment."

" *We?*" Michael asked.

"Surely you've figured out that Hollis and I, and our dead friend, are not the same as you."

Michael shrugged. "You look human enough."

"Did my friend?"

"So you're a different species?" I asked. "You look human."

"I'm not."

"You said you're from different universe," said Marie. "Is everyone there like you?"

"In the entire universe? I doubt it."

"I meant on the Earth you're from."

"I'm not from an Earth," said Erin, "although I suppose my ancestors must have been."

"This *alternate universes* thing is going to take some getting used to," I said. "What year was it, where you're from?"

"The question has no meaning," Erin replied.

"I hate to cut short an interesting conversation," said Michael, "but something is coming."

CHAPTER SIXTY-ONE

I don't know whether or not I believed Erin.

I liked her, but believing she was some super soldier from another universe was a little too much for me. I mean, Michael told me about Project Brimstone, but that wasn't real for me. I hadn't seen anything concrete that could convince me. Even the metal wreckage with the weird labels could have been faked, although I don't know why anyone would bother.

Of course, why did anyone bother with all of this?

The mercs had an industrial incinerator. They could have cut up the bodies and destroyed them. Why go to the trouble of making it look like aliens did it? I think Munson had been holding out on us. Somehow, his story didn't feel true. We didn't find bodies that had been carved up until Munson joined the mercs. I think he must have told them to mutilate the bodies to convince people that aliens were real.

Munson had benefited from the attention. He'd gotten rich from the coverage and from people buying his books. Not to mention that the mercs then had a steady supply of people to feed to their monster.

That bothered me, too. How long had the mercenaries been in possession of this installation? How did they come to control it? What did they want it for? Were they just pawns for someone else?

Munson had also mentioned a Manta. That was a military reconnaissance plane. There'd been one present when I was attacked on the mountain. Was all of this part of something much bigger and far more sinister? Was someone from the military or a private corporation trying to restart the super soldier project?

A scream and a wave of demented exultation interrupted my thoughts.

The creature had found us.

The lights around us began to flicker and dim. Something charged down the corridor toward us. I couldn't get a sense of how many limbs it had before it was on us. As if from far away, I heard the deafening, staccato roar of Michael's rifle on burst fire. I was firing my MP5, and Marie was next to me. I distinctly heard the sound of the pistol slide locking back as she fired her last round.

The thing was roughly man-sized and -shaped. It charged directly into Michael, knocking him from his feet. I emptied my magazine into the monster's bristly back then, to no perceivable effect.

Michael screamed, and I felt a chill as I heard a ghastly sucking noise. The thing had a proboscis, like a mosquito. It jabbed deep into Michael's throat, sucking the blood from him, and all I could do was watch in horror.

Erin moved past me, impossibly fast, and grabbed the thing by the two shriveled stumps of wings on its back. With a grunt of effort, she lifted the thing, at least three times her mass, into the air. The proboscis tore free from Michael's throat, and Erin hurled the monster into the closest wall hard enough for me to hear its bones splinter and crack.

Michael was dazed, lying on the floor in a spreading puddle of blood. I dropped to my knees and clamped my hand over his throat, trying to apply pressure to the deep wound. The warm pulse of blood between my fingers made me feel lightheaded.

I was aware of Erin still trying to fight the thing alone, but I knew if I let up pressure, Michael would bleed out. Marie was next to me, fumbling through the pouches on Michael's harness. I knew she was trying to find bandages or something, anything that would help.

I can't lose you, I thought desperately.

The hallway lit up with a brilliant light. I thought at first that someone had ignited a flare, and then I saw the source: Erin, bathed in white flames so bright I couldn't focus on her. Among the shadows, I could have sworn I saw dark wings for a moment.

Michael was trying to say something. All that came out was a trickle of blood. His eyes, already distant, were starting to lose focus. He was slipping away.

Something hit me hard in the back. I fell over but kept my hand clamped on Michael's throat. I didn't feel as much pressure anymore from his blood against my fingers. I didn't think that was a good thing.

I saw Erin leap over us, slashing with that sword of hers. Another piece of the monster went flying – it had been a severed arm that struck me in the back. It felt like being hit with a baseball bat.

Marie was pulling at my shoulder.

"What?"

"Too much pressure, Michelle. You're choking him. Let up, and let me apply the bandage."

I let go. Blood welled from the wound, but it didn't gush or spray. Marie quickly applied a thick pad and then wrapped his neck. I checked his pulse in his wrist. His heartbeat was slow but steady.

Erin was driving the thing back. A couple of flares burned on the floor. Erin held her sword in her right hand. It must have been the flares that I'd seen before.

The creature was bleeding from dozens of bullet wounds as well as the stump of its right arm. It flailed, trying to slash at Erin. *Snick*, her blade cut cleanly through the thing's left forearm. I don't know whether the blade was just very sharp or it was her tremendous strength that allowed her to cut the thing up like that.

It leapt onto her.

I cried out a warning, but she caught the proboscis and jerked its head back. A flash of her hand, and she'd driven the flare into the small secondary mouth. It rolled off her, unable to scream, burning from the inside out.

I drew my pistol and emptied the magazine into its head, blowing it apart.

The creature immediately began to dissolve into a putrid mass.

Erin was still lying on the floor, panting.

"Are you okay?" I asked. She – impossibly – didn't look injured.

"That really sucked."

"Was that supposed to be a joke?"

"Too soon?"

I helped her up.

"How is Michael?" she asked.

"Stable," Marie replied. "He's lost a lot of blood, but I think he'll be okay. He has to be."

Between us, we were able to carefully drag Michael toward the entrance. The corridor had collapsed from the explosive charges. We weren't getting out that way. I remembered that the soldiers had blown up the other exits, too. We were trapped inside.

"There's always another way," Erin said.

She removed Michael's headset. "Chief, this is Blackbird. Major Delling is down and needs immediate medevac. All enemy combatants have been neutralized."

"Roger, Blackbird. Clear the area near the entrance. We'll blast through."

"Roger, chief. Moving to the northern entrance room."

We dragged Michael into the room and shut the door. The room had been used as equipment storage. I rubbed as much of the blood off my hands as I could and then reloaded the magazines for my weapons while we waited. I didn't want any surprises.

"He'll be okay, right?" asked Marie asked. "When that thing jumped him, I was paralyzed with fear."

"Michael is strong," Erin said. "All three of you are a lot tougher than I ever could have imagined. You all fought an enemy far beyond your capabilities."

"I couldn't do anything," said Marie.

"You stood your ground and emptied your pistol into it," Erin said.

"That's more than most people could have done."

"You know, when you were fighting, I could have sworn I saw wings," I said.

"Really? That's odd." Erin turned to show me her back. "See, no wings," she said.

I noticed she didn't think it an odd thing for me to say. "Unless you're clouding my mind." Her tee-shirt had two long tears where wings would have been. I'm sure she would have said that was from the monster's claws. Funny how there were no marks on her skin, and no blood. If she'd been clawed, there should have been wounds.

"I thought you said I couldn't cloud your mind," Erin replied, smiling.

"I don't think I'd put anything past you, *Blackbird*."

Erin grinned even bigger. "I really do like that nickname."

"Yeah, can't imagine why."

I was thinking of the large, black-feathered wings I'd seen. The feathers had matched her hair. Just like the feathers on her friend, Vano, had matched his. I couldn't help but think of what she'd said about the other projects, and my dream memories of seeing someone with dark wings.

CHAPTER SIXTY-TWO

It took Michael's team about half an hour to blast through to the tunnel. One of the combat medics took over Michael's care then. I was tired, worn down, and I really, *really* wanted to wash the sticky blood from my hands.

Michael's blood.

"Is he going to be okay?" Taylor asked me.

"He's tough. Michael made it this far. He'll be okay." I don't know whether I was trying to convince her or myself.

Michael's second-in-command came over to us. "Which one of you is the FBI lead?" he asked.

"That would be me, Special Agent Taylor."

"I'm the second-in-command," he replied. His face was covered. "We don't want to step on your toes, ma'am, but our orders are to take control of this facility and hold it. A special evaluation team is en route."

"I'm not looking for a jurisdictional pissing match," said Taylor. "We're both federal officers. If you want this mess, you can have it. Less paperwork for me."

"Yes, ma'am. Thank you for understanding."

He didn't look as if he was going to give anyone much choice. After watching Michael's team clear out the installation, I certainly didn't want to mess with them. Special Operations personnel are some seriously badass soldiers. I know I didn't want to tangle with any of them.

I picked my way through the rubble back into the hanger. It was still dark outside, and the lights in the hanger weren't all that bright. Everything on the surface seemed so normal. It made what had happened below ground unreal and distant.

A helicopter came in from the west and settled to the tarmac.

I stood back and watched as Michael was loaded aboard. They were airlifting him to the military hospital at Los Alamos. The same one I'd been at. I wasn't invited along. Not that they had room on a medivac.

"What now?" asked Taylor.

"We drive back to Taos, take showers, and get some sleep," I said. "Maybe we can meet for dinner and try to sort all this out."

"Yeah, sort it out," Taylor said. "This is a grade-a clusterfuck."

"Yeah," I said, watching the helicopter as it flew away. "That, it is."

"Mind if I tag along with you?" asked Erin. "I could really use a shower myself. Dinner sounds good, too."

"Why not?" I said. "Any chance you'll answer some questions?"

Erin grinned. "Well, I don't think I'm up to being interrogated, but I think I could answer a *few* questions."

I was tired. Dead tired. Too tired to drive, really.

I drove back to Taos as the sun rose over the mountains behind us. The clock on the dash said it was only a little after seven in the morning. It didn't seem possible that everything that happened in the installation, and after, had taken place over only a few hours.

I glanced in the mirror at Erin. She was sleeping with her head against the window. She looked vulnerable, but I knew she was as tough as they come. She'd essentially fought that thing in the installation alone.

I decided to believe I was mistaken about her having wings. Not only was it easier on my sanity, but she wouldn't have fit in the back seat if she'd had wings. Clouding my mind wouldn't let her sit on her wings. Right?

She opened an eye, met mine in the mirror, and winked.

Yeah, no wings.

I dropped Marie off at home. Then Taylor by her room. I guess I was stuck with Erin. I was glad there was no one around by my room. We were both covered in drying blood. I could imagine having to explain that to the local police. I'm sure the Taos police department would be happy to see me gone.

"We're here. Come on," I said.

Michael's stuff was packed and sitting by the door, where he'd left it. My breath caught in my chest, but I kept my emotions under wraps. Michael had only done what he needed to, for us to accomplish our goal. He wasn't leaving me. I needed to remind myself of that.

I wished again that I could be there at the hospital with him.

I tossed my keys on the small table by the door. "Who's first?" I asked.

"It's your shower," said Erin.

I washed my hands, then grabbed some clothes out of my bag and took a long, hot shower. It felt weird leaving a stranger in my room while I bathed, but if I didn't trust Erin by this point... Well, anyway. The shower felt great. It was particularly nice to have thoroughly clean hands again. I'd been about to break down from the dried blood on them.

Michael's blood.

"He's going to be fine," Erin said as I stepped out of the bathroom.

She had a small pile of clothes she'd gotten from somewhere. I didn't ask. They weren't mine or Michael's, so if she wanted to be mysterious, more power to her. I was too damn weary to ask.

Erin's sheathed sword was resting against the wall next to the door. The sword radiated a strange aura. I wasn't remotely tempted to touch it. I didn't even want to look at it.

I got a Coke out of the fridge and just sat there on the bed, sipping it. It was nice not to be hunted or scared or covered in blood. I sighed. I just couldn't stop thinking about Michael. He was normally so strong and unflappable. To have seen him lying in his blood, unable to move... The look of vulnerability in his eyes... He'd known he might die, there in those dark corridors under the airport.

Erin came out of the bathroom in black socks and sweatpants, a Massive Attack flame tee-shirt, and a towel around her head. She sat down on the bed next to me and dried her hair. It was an oddly normal activity for her. I could see she still had her necklace on. I somehow knew she never took it off.

"Thanks for the use of your shower."

"Who are you," I asked, "really?"

Erin sighed. "You know who I am, or you wouldn't trust me."

"Who says that I do?"

"Well, you did leave me in your room alone with your guns. Not to mention trusting me to fight the monster today while you saved Michael."

"I figured if anyone had a chance to take that thing out, it was you."

"Yeah. I've run into ones much worse. Last night's was more weird than powerful."

"I believe you."

Since I'd met Erin, I had a million questions I wanted to ask her. Now I couldn't think of more than one. Anything else just didn't seem to matter. I didn't know how to ask it without her thinking I was crazy. Maybe it didn't matter anymore.

"I'm not an angel," Erin said.

"Get asked that a lot?"

"Often enough." Erin sighed. "Could I have one of those?" she asked, pointing at the Coke.

"Absolutely," I said. "Sorry I didn't offer. My brain is frazzled."

"No worries. I'll help myself, if you don't mind." Erin got a bottle of soda out of the fridge and sat back down. "Ah, that's good. It's been a long time since I had a Coke."

"Back at the installation, you said you aren't human," I said.

"Did I?" Erin lay back on the bed.

"Yeah, and what is with the black stone amulet?" I could feel the talismanic power coming from it.

Erin pulled the amulet out of her shirt and looked at it. "It's a promise. I'm sorry, I can't tell you more than that."

"You're a strange one, Erin."

"I hear that a lot, too."

I lay back on the bed. It was odd, sharing my bed with Erin. I hadn't slept in the same bed with someone who wasn't a lover in a very long time. It was actually kind of nice, companionship with any expectations. I finished my Coke and closed my eyes. I just needed a little bit of rest.

Darkness sucked me down.

Sleep took me; it's my enemy and my savior, the bringer of dreams.

INTERLUDE

The moisture in my breath freezes in a little cloud.
There's ice on my face and in my hair.
It is night, and cold. Very cold. Well below freezing.
The ice and snow burn my bare feet.
I hurt, and yet I can't stop moving. Each pounding step is a jolt of pain. I can't stop.
I am running.
I am alone.
I've had this dream before. I don't really wish to dream it all again, not that I have any choice. I know how this dream ends. Drowning in the cold, dark depths of icy waters. Obviously I survived, although I can't remember how I got out of the water.
Tears freeze on my cheeks. I've left Michael behind in the sterile corridors of the place where they hurt us. The tranquilizer dart in his neck had stopped him in his tracks. I left him there. In that place of horror and pain.
I left him.
I had no choice.
Those who hurt us, they know just the right amount of drugs to use to sedate us. It's more than they can survive. I know this from taking syringes away from them and giving them their own medicine. The

ones I did that to all died in convulsions.

The tears are cold tracks on my face, like icy scars.

The tears are for Michael and for myself. I shed no tears for those who hurt us. If we fought back and killed them, that was on them for teaching us how to kill in the first place. The doctors and soldiers made me what I am. I don't regret killing them.

I always give them a better death than they deserve.

My lungs burn from the cold air.

I can't stop running, though.

The hounds are getting closer, but so is the river. I can hear the roaring of the waters. I don't know if I can swim to safety, or if the waters will close over me and seal me in a watery grave. I don't really care either way.

I just don't want to ever go back to that place of torments.

I slide down the steep bank, scraping my legs on sharp rocks and twigs. I'm already scratched and bleeding in dozens of places from the brambles and the wicked thorns of the black locust trees. I know I'm leaving an easy trail for the hounds. I must cross the river like Eliza in the story from school.

The water is high and shockingly cold on my bare feet.

There is a small waterfall here. I try to cross, but the stones are slippery, and I fall. The dark water takes me and sweeps over me. I'm falling, tumbling in the water. Out of control. I could die here. I'm not sure if that wouldn't be for the best.

I plunge into a deep pool. The current has me in its chill embrace. I struggle to rise up to the light. The water is swift and powerful. I've been dragged miles under the water, and my chest aches from holding my breath.

I am so cold.

I can feel my chilled, overworked muscles beginning to knot, my lungs longing for the air so close above me. The silvery surface of the water mocks me. My vision is beginning to dim.

I wondered at the time if I was going to die.

It's strange to be having a memory-dream in which I'm uncertain about a future that I've now lived through. I know that there, in that dark water, I wasn't sure I wanted to live. The things that had been done to me, the things I had seen, those I had left behind.

What I'd done to survive.

I never wanted to be a killer.

They had made me into that.

Perhaps this was for the best. The pain was fading, as was my sight. Maybe death wasn't so bad, after all, if I could face it on my own terms. I would fight until the end to keep from dying the way they wanted to hurt me.

This, though, this could be peaceful.

It could all be over here, now. It wasn't as if I had much choice. My strength was gone. The icy waters had me. I didn't think the water was just going to deposit me someplace safe. Even if I didn't drown, I'd probably die from exposure.

If the guards with the hounds didn't find me first.

I stopped struggling. I would accept my death. It was better than living.

A splash and a rushing sound of water, as if someone had jumped into the river near me.

Warm hands on my arms, pulling me up to the air.

Breath. Breathe. Gasp and cough out the water in my lungs.

The crunch of snow, a moss-covered bank under me.

Warmth from a tight embrace.

Not the guards or the dogs.

Rocking.

Too weak and cold to move.

Someone sobbing. Not me.

Water dripping from dark feathers.

CHAPTER SIXTY-THREE

Michael called that evening as I was getting ready for dinner with Erin.

"How are you doing?" I asked, lamely.

"About how you'd imagine, but getting better," Michael said. His voice sounded rough. "How did you manage to take that thing down? I kind of missed that part."

I smiled grimly at the memory. "Erin cut the monster into pieces, and then I shot it in the head. A lot."

"That'll do it. Michelle..."

"I'll probably be here in Taos for a few more days," I said, "helping Taylor wrap things up. We're supposed to meet for dinner tonight. Dr. Munson will probably take the blame, even though he's dead."

"Well, he did have a big hand in what happened."

"He facilitated it, certainly. Marie and I are fine. After I help Taylor, I'll be heading back home." I knew I sounded clipped and angry.

I was holding back a lot of pain. It wasn't his fault. I understood why Michael had rejoined the military. We'd really needed that assistance, more than we'd realized. That didn't make it hurt any less.

"I'll be heading to my new assignment in a few days. I don't think the doctor here wants to let me go. She doesn't quite realize how quickly I heal."

"Yeah, doctors don't seem to like that about us, do they?" I asked. "I think they're worried about their jobs."

"Michelle… Are we still good?"

"You're not getting away from me that easily. I'll expect you to call regularly, at least once a week when you can. We'll meet up when we can. We won't be that far apart. We'll get through this. It's only a couple of years."

"A couple of potentially very dangerous years," said Michael.

"Well, it isn't as if I'm likely to be taking it easy," I said, "given what the last year has been like."

"I hadn't mean dangerous for me. I'm worried about you."

"I'll be fine, Michael. Honestly, after this job, I'm going to call it quits for a while. I've got enough money."

"I know you do. I was going to suggest that. Ugh. The doctor is giving me that look. I need to go. I love you, Michelle."

"I love you, too."

I disconnected and sat looking forlornly at my phone.

"Is Michael doing okay?" asked Erin.

"Yeah," I said, looking up.

I had to do a double take. Erin was dressing in boots, jeans, a faded Pink Floyd *Wish You Were Here* tee-shirt, and a leather jacket. She hadn't taken any of those clothes into the bathroom with her. I had no idea where she'd gotten them.

"I borrowed a hair elastic," she said. "I hope you don't mind."

"You can conjure clothes out of thin air, but not a hair elastic?"

She smiled and shrugged.

"Fine. Keep your secrets, then."

I grabbed my keys, and we left the hotel room. I dreaded facing the dried blood in the Jeep, but when I opened the door, I was greeted with a spotless interior. The Jeep smelled faintly of oranges. I almost cried from relief.

"I hope you don't mind. I snuck out and cleaned it while you were asleep," said Erin.

"Thank you," I said, wiping the dampness from my eyes. "Really."

I drove around to Taylor's room. She was waiting for us. I'd talked to her just before Michael called.

"You take the scenic route?" Taylor asked as she climbed into the back seat.

"Michael called, and before you ask, he's fine."

"You people and your super healing," Taylor said. "I'm glad he's okay."

Marie was riding to the restaurant with Lawrence and Jean. I was glad to see they'd become friends. I also felt a little jealous. I hadn't gotten to spend as much time with all of them as I wanted to. Of course, that was my fault. I was the one who'd taken a job out here, although I felt as if the word *job* was inadequate for what I'd had to do.

What we'd all had to do.

There were lots of hugs when we reached the restaurant. It was an activity that Erin joyously and confusingly took part in. Everyone got hugs from her, even Taylor.

"Who are you?" Lawrence asked, rubbing his arm after a second vigorous hug from Erin.

"I'm Erin."

"Oh, *that* Erin?" he asked.

"The one and only." She did a little comic dance. "Hmm. Are you single?"

"What?" Lawrence looked confused. "I'm gay."

She pouted. "Well, I'll just have to settle for your sister, then."

"What?" Jean looked *even more* confused and alarmed.

"Erin, stop messing with them. Don't worry about her, Jean. She's a harmless flirt."

"Harmless?" Erin grinned. "A flirt? I'm serious, she's damned cute."

"Erin," I said warningly.

"Fine. It's just that this place smells good, and I'm trying to get someone to buy me dinner. I'm somewhat cashless at the moment."

"Leave your wallet in another universe?" I asked.

"Ouch."

"I've got you covered," I said. "No jokes about that, either. Come on."

Dinner was relaxing. And cathartic. Nothing like fluffy garlic breadsticks to ease the burdens of the soul. We all talked and made plans. We talked about Michael. Erin was a stranger to most of them, but her good humor and infectious positive mood helped lift everyone's spirits.

One by one, the others left, until it was just Erin and me finishing off the bottle of wine.

"I didn't get a chance to say so earlier," Erin said, "but thank you for helping out with this late unpleasantness."

"Hey, if you can't count on your friends to help you hunt monsters, who can you count on?"

"Well, it means a lot to me. If you ever need my help with anything, let me know."

"Am supposed to call you?" I asked.

"We're bound together by blood and shared sacrifice," Erin said softly. "I'll hear you, if you have a need for me."

I nodded and knocked back the last of the wine. "Need a lift anywhere?" I asked.

"I'll be fine. Are you sure you should be driving?"

"Are you sure you should be flying?"

"Ha-ha."

"I'll be fine. I only had two glasses of wine, with food."

"Okay. It was more like four, but okay. I'll see you around, Dr. Fredericks."

"Likewise, Blackbird."

She gave me a hug and then turned away. I unlocked the Jeep and had started to get in when I heard a *whoosh* behind me. I turned to look, but she was gone. Wings? Maybe. Maybe not. Who am I to doubt?

In the distance, I could see suspicious lights moving around the slopes of the mountains. Aliens? Or the military looking for escaped things? Nothing at all? Who knows?

This had been a very strange vacation for me. Stranger than just about anything I'd ever experienced. I decided it really didn't matter. Every day of my life had been weird.

Why should I expect anything different at this point?

My whole life has been angels, aliens, demons, monsters, psychopaths, secret government projects, and conspiracies to cover up the truth. Whatever the truth actually is. I don't know if I'll ever discover everything about what was done to us as children. I'm not sure, after what I *have* learned, that I really want to know more about it.

I have a feeling, though, that what I've learned so far is just the tip of the iceberg. The ship of my life is still afloat, but I don't know for how long. I wish I knew what the destination is. If there is one.

I'll need to keep my wits about me if I don't want to drown in the icy waters of the past.

About the Author

Paul B. Spence is a practicing archaeologist who hopes to one day get it right. He currently lives in New Mexico, where all the cool kids hang out, with too many cats.

Like most authors, he had an eclectic career path. He's worked as a retail gofer, a food service monkey, brute laborer, a rennie, a writer for the RPG industry, and many other rewarding jobs that didn't pay enough to feed him or his cats.